The ECLIPSED

WICKED Press WIXX

AVA WIXX

The Eclipsed

First Edition: May 2023
Published in the United States of America by
Wicked Wixx Press.
The Wicked Wixx Press Logo is a trademark of
Wicked Wixx Press.

Cover Art, Ava Wixx Logo, Wicked Wixx Logo, & Interior Book Graphics by Lindsay Tiry of LT Arts
Edited by Melissa Ringsted of There For You Editing

Print ISBN: 978-1-955950-15-2
Kindle ISBN: 978-1-955950-16-9
EPUB ISBN: 978-1-955950-17-6

For more information visit: avawixx.com

For

A.J.H.

1979-2018

It's so hard to say goodbye to yesterday.

To the light I fly, to watch you all die.

Chapter 1

I'm a nocturnal creature, a beast who thrives in the dark. And yet, I crave the warm embrace of the light ... the flames of humanity. The yearning never fades, only heightened by the knowledge that I can look, but never truly touch.

I suppose my kind was created with this unquenchable appetite for a reason, to make our life's purpose more than a job, to make it an unavoidable compulsion ... an obsession.

"Lord, have mercy! Are those bodies?"

Lifting my chin, I watched as people hurled themselves from the skyscraper in an attempt to escape being burnt alive. As others ran in horror, I took deliberate strides toward the building, my gaze never wavering.

Nothing is brighter than life just before it's snuffed out, and I couldn't look away. Not that I had the option. I was there to record this calamity, this massive extinguishment of human life.

In my peripheral vision, a reaper appeared, recognizable by its dark garb and familiar power signature. At all such events in human history, there was always at least one reaper, and of course, one of my kind. We never interfered with each other, and merely went about our separate business, both cogs in the machinations of the universe.

As I inched closer, my wings appeared, snapping wide in an arc. My body hummed with something akin to delight, not relishing in the disaster before me, but appreciating the warmth I could only feel in times like these.

"Careful, lest someone see you." The reaper's warning cut through the smoke and screams, giving me pause.

I inclined my head. "And what difference would it make if someone did? Either they will be dead soon, or no one will believe them."

"Smartphones available to any who desire them has changed the game for many," he replied.

Ah, so we must be in a relatively current time frame. I often forgot to check minor details since my clothing automatically morphed to my current needs. Admittedly, it was a bit sloppy to not pay attention to such things though. Even still, I couldn't withhold my chuckle. "No one ever notices me."

Like all lunas, I blended in. Human eyes passed over me with disinterest, everything about me ... neutral. They saw: Not quite cute, neither pretty nor ugly. Thin, not skinny or curvy. Average height for a female, not short or tall. Neutral, beige skin tone. Brown hair, not strikingly dark or mousy. Even when my wings appeared, they were drab tones of brown, resembling that of the insect called moth. I was the real-life equivalent to background noise. You know it's there, but you don't pay it any mind, and can't recall it later if asked to.

The reaper shifted under his hood, his gaze tangible even though I couldn't see his face. "Your wings, as boring as you think them, are something that holds amazement to humans."

Silence fell over us, the rare conversation between a reaper and me coming to a close. However, I did consider his words.

Even my brown-toned, moth-like wings were still wings. And yet all the years I'd been cataloguing human catastrophes, and ensuring that fixed points in time stayed just that … fixed, no one had ever noticed them or me.

Sure, a few lunas had been the source of urban legends over the years, such as with The Mothman Prophecies, but that incident was tricky. The need for my brother's interference was impossible to avoid. Those people in West Virginia needed to die in order to preserve the fabric of time and reality, which is why it was a fixed point in time. But my brother also got carried away, the need to complete his job overriding all else, his carelessness exposing his existence. Luckily, those who witnessed his work were dismissed as crazy, even if the story lived on.

Although ... the reaper speaks the truth. Smartphones did change things. What would have happened if those existed years ago? My brother's mishap might have turned into a disaster for our kind, instead of the embarrassing memory he was still mocked about to this day. It could have ruined everything, the precarious balance of what we do destroyed by future human interference. *And if we fail, reality itself will eventually crumble.* Shuddering, I dispelled that thought. I needed to focus on the present, and not a bunch of what-ifs.

Creeping closer, I willed my wings to slacken. I would release them again only when they were needed—when the last moments of human life burned through me. During that time, when I recorded the souls and events surrounding their deaths, I would be invisible as I shifted between worlds. Until then I'd simply have to remain an inconspicuous bystander.

"You seem to have a problem," the reaper said, his tone bored.

I snorted. "Right. *My* problem, because you don't have a horse in this race, too." Would a reaper actually bother to help me if I needed it? Did they even care if reality as we all knew it ceased to exist? *Hopefully, I'll never need to find out.*

My gaze zeroed in on the *problem* the reaper spoke of. One of the tagged humans—as I liked to call them because of the bright orange aura surrounding their bodies—wasn't doing what he was supposed to be doing, which was dying. I wasn't sure how it happened, but once in awhile a human was able to break away from the planned pattern to throw things out of whack. These were the times when I had to do more than watch and record. It's when I needed to get my hands dirty.

And my day was going so well.

The human male in question had to die, and yet he was not only alive and kicking, but attempting to help others survive when they were scheduled to exit this mortal coil at this time and date. Any variation of the final deceased tally … would fuck shit up.

"You're going to be fine, ma'am, just fine." The problem mortal—my current pain in the ass—set an elderly woman in a business suit down on the sidewalk, before rushing back into the ablaze building.

The wail of emergency vehicles racing to the scene grew louder, and I knew I had to act fast. Sprinting after the would-be hero, I spared a glance at the woman he saved as I passed her, relief washing over me when she collapsed, gasping for breath. She would die soon, and therefore I didn't need to bother with her.

As I entered the building, smoke clouded my vision and burned my throat.

"What are you doing?" The problem man shoved at me as if I was a confused horse heading in the wrong direction. "Get out of here, now!" A coughing fit doubled him over for a moment before he managed to overcome his body's need for oxygen by what seemed to be sheer willpower alone.

Interesting.

What is it about certain humans that make them different? How and why is he able to act outside of the pattern the universe has planned for him when so many can't? Free will is a thing to a certain degree, but there are still parameters.

My gaze swept over him with curiosity. He was average height for a human male, although slightly taller than me. His complexion was pale, his hair a contrasting dark brown, framing an attractive face of sorts, although his nose was slightly too large. There was a deep scar through his left eyebrow, and his eyes were a dark blue. Nothing in particular stood out about him. He was just a human like any other as far as I could tell.

With preternatural reflexes, I rushed the guy, causing him to stumble backward in confusion. "Hey, what … How'd you—"

Grabbing the nape of his neck, I forced him to look me in the eyes. They glowed red, the eerie cast highlighting the man's stark expression. "I'm sorry," I murmured, "but you and all of these people must die today. It can't be helped."

"No," he croaked, his voice hoarse, "I have to save them."

"Those who perish here will preserve the fabric of the universe. The tragedy of today serves a greater purpose, one that you can't begin to fathom. You must not interfere anymore." *This is the point where the human will accept my truths and let go.* Something inside of them when faced with my 'otherness' sensed it was the only way, giving up the struggle easily.

"No. I can't accept that."

Huh. The strength of his resolve intrigued me. Never

before had a human resisted my brand of coercion. It was a shame I didn't have more time to study him.

"I'm sorry," I murmured, tightening my grip on his nape, and dragging a strangled cry from him, "but it has to happen this way."

I didn't regret or grieve what needed to be done, but I was sorry that any lives had to be lost. I felt empathy for humans. Although I knew I would never fully understand them, I'd garnered much from books and movies. I especially loved their fiction … so much imagination for a species with such little control over their own lives.

I snapped the mortal's neck with ease, stepping back to watch his body slump to the ground, his eyes seemingly still fixated on me in surprise.

I bowed my head. "May you find peace in the ever after or your next life."

A surge of energy danced along my skin, goose bumps erupting in its wake. *It's time.*

My wings flared out behind me, and I threw my head back as I rose into the air. Hovering between worlds, the recently dead souls passed through me one after another in lightning fast succession. I recorded their essences, making sure all that should be was.

As the numbers of dead added up, the warmth their souls offered seeped into my bones. My body hummed with delight, the energy of the deceased an addictive force, for it was in these few moments I felt satiated, content, full … like I actually belonged there … or anywhere. I was whole. It's what drew my kind to these types of scenes unwaveringly, even if we grew to despise them on some level.

A moment of true peace in our nearly endless existences.

And then it was over practically before it began. Or at least it always seemed that way.

The vast emptiness gaped in my chest once more, threatening to consume me.

So cold. Need to get home.

Wrapping my arms around my middle, I stumbled from the building, my teeth chattering. I paused on the sidewalk, surveying the scene. First responders worked in a controlled chaos; bustling around, trying to save lives I already knew were gone. News crews unloaded equipment, preparing to film. Bystanders live-streamed and recorded on their phones.

Not a single person noticed me.

I wasn't invisible anymore, and yet ... *I might as well be.*

Chapter 2

I resided in the lunas' hold, like all others of my kind. The massive castle, and the land it was perched on, existed in a pocket dimension accessible only by us, and a few other supernatural creatures. For me to travel to my home, I merely had to will myself there, and boom, there I was staring up at the large, wooden front door.

I pushed at the bright red lacquer, exhaustion making the simple task of moving it difficult. With a groan, the door finally swung open, and I lurched forward, barely avoiding a face plant.

"Eighty-nine!" Six scurried to my side, lending his strong body for support as he wrapped his arm around my middle. "You look even worse than usual. Let's get you to Archives, and then to bed."

I gave him a shaky smile. "Were you waiting for me to get back?"

"Of course. You know Six will always watch your six."

I snorted. No matter how many times Six used that lame expression just because of his name, it still managed to draw a bit of amusement from me, which was probably why he continued to say it.

"If only you would have come to our eclipse at a different time so I could be saved from your Six on six commentary."

There were one hundred lunas in existence at all times, the grand total of us called an eclipse. When one of us burnt up, however rare, leaving this plane behind, another luna would appear, fully-grown and filled to the brim with knowledge of its life purpose. And since we were not born, we had no parents and no human names. We simply went by the number that was left open for us. I was one of the original hundred, and no other had ever had the number Eighty-nine for a name, but Six was the second to grace his slot. Truth be told, I liked him much better than the old Six, since my Six had become my closest and only friend in a world where true friendships were even rarer than unicorns.

I staggered, and Six's grip on me tightened as I leaned on him more, and he struggled to keep me moving. "Please, you were bored before I showed up with all my awesomeness."

I snorted again. "Alas, he speaks the truth."

He chuckled. "Alas. Nobody uses that word anymore."

I quirked an eyebrow but remained silent. Six thought it funny how I mixed modern slang with what he referred to as old school words. But I didn't do it on purpose, nor did I think words like alas were outdated. I'd simply existed for so long that I … had a different knowledge base to draw on. Six was too young to understand. *Give him a few hundred more years, and we'll see if he's singing a different tune. He'll still be saying YOLO and the human world will have moved on.*

Another wave of exhaustion washed over me, and I stifled a yawn. Slumping more into Six's side, my eyelids fluttered shut, and my feet dragged behind me.

"Ugh. Seriously, I might as well be carrying you," Six muttered. "What happened out there today?"

"Nothing out of the ordinary."

"You're colder than normal, and—"

"Really, nothing out of the ordinary happened. I guess I just haven't been sleeping much lately."

Six swung me up into his arms, a grunt of exertion escaping his lips. "I don't think that'll be a problem now."

On the edge of consciousness, I listened to the steady cadence of Six's heart beneath my ear, my thoughts wandering back to the human male I killed with my bare hands today. When his soul passed through me, even though it was along with all the other souls from the scene, there was something exceptional about him even in death. He'd burned brighter, and hotter—scalding almost. Was he the reason for my heightened state of exhaustion? But it didn't make sense. He wasn't the first human I'd ever encountered who'd broken out of the pattern. He wasn't—

"Here we are, Archives." Six set me on my feet

abruptly, and my eyes snapped open. "Do you want me to go in with you?"

Stepping away from him, I only swayed for a moment before drawing on every ounce of reserves I had. "No, but I may need your help to get to my room."

He propped himself against the wall, crossing his arms over his chest, and legs at the ankles. "All right, I'll wait for you here. But if you take too long, I'm going to come looking for you."

I nodded, shoving on the huge, black door with gold inlay. Staggering over the threshold, I leaned on the heavy mahogany from the other side to shut it behind me.

Unnatural silence saturated me; even the sound of my own heartbeat quieted to nothing. I inhaled a deep breath, the scent of ancient books swirling up my nostrils. It was here in Archives where the history of every fixed point in time, and the imprints of the souls that had been sacrificed to maintain them, were held.

To the casual observer, it might appear to be a library of sorts, and in many ways it was. Books lined endless shelves from floor to ceiling as far as the eye could see. And yet no numbers or letters adorned the immaculate leather spines of these books. For if anyone were to search for something here, they already knew where to find it. Of course, the architects of the universe were the only ones who made use of the Archives, even myself never having revisited any of the many, many books I had placed on the shelves personally. What we did was just a tiny piece of a much bigger puzzle—a puzzle in which I was only familiar with my own misshapen part.

Sighing heavily, I shuffled past another luna, both of us ignoring each other, which was easy to do in the forced silence. What were we going to do, mime at each other? No, any in the Archives were there to do a job, and didn't relish being interrupted for any reason, let alone etiquette encouraged pleasantries.

Rounding the first aisle, I found myself alone in the shadows, which is where I preferred to do my transfers. I dropped to the ground and crossed my legs, resting my hands against my knees, palms up. Inhaling a few times, I let my eyes slide shut. A moment later the weight of an empty book settled across my lap. I let go of the breath I was holding, my lips tingling as I exhaled the information I gathered from today's event into the waiting pages.

I peeked through my lashes, the pages fluttering by, words and symbols forming on the mystical paper. I ran out of breath, and my eyes snapped open, just as the end of the book was reached. *It's done.* Smoothing my palms over the delicate leather, I closed the book gently, placing it within the empty slot on the shelf that appeared in front of me.

It always seemed anticlimactic somehow, all the buildup boiling down to a single book sitting silently on a shelf. And yet the very fabric of reality rested on the events that had happened to fill those pages.

I yawned. *Glad I'm not the one who has to make sense of the universe.*

I AWOKE IN MY ROOM, the warm breeze from the open skylight rustling my hair. I had no recollection of how I got there, my exhaustion surely causing me to be propelled by autopilot. I was alone, Six having left me to sleep on my bed piled under no less than a half dozen blankets. I yawned, and stretched, feeling refreshed.

My bare feet touched the cool hardwood, as my gaze snagged on the moon, hanging large, bright, and full in the sky. It was an ever-present fixture in our realm, a constant maintained by whatever power that had created us in the beginning.

The night called to me, the urge to fly beyond my will to resist. Letting my wings snap free, I hopped into the air and headed out the skylight. The moonlight bathed my skin as I kept my face upturned toward its origins. Higher and higher I flew, until the air was impossibly thin, and my lungs burned with effort.

All around me, other lunas filled the night sky, eager to reach an unattainable destination. If only we could somehow grasp the softly glowing orb in the sky, maybe we wouldn't feel compelled to return to the human realm, perhaps we could be content to exist where we truly thrived … in the dark. But our lives were the way they were for a reason, one that I would never understand. I simply did what I had to in order to keep the emptiness at bay. We all did.

Stretching my arms wide, my wings fluttered as I fell

through the air. I stared at the moon, several silhouettes of my brothers and sisters passing through my view. I began my ascent again, my mind wandering to useless things.

Why do we even have wings? Is it so that we have one thing to keep us almost content between jobs? Why make us yearn for something when we can never actually have it? Are any of my brothers and sisters content on any level? Am I the only one who wishes for more? Why is there so much about lunas that makes us a contradiction of sorts? Is there any—

"Hey, watch where you're going!" Thirty-two shouted, his shoulder skimming my foot.

"Sorry," I muttered, moving to dodge Ten as well, her eyes narrowed with annoyance. Shaking my head, I descended to the ground, settling myself on my back. It was possible I needed to rest a bit more before taking to the sky again. But I wasn't ready to abandon the warm night air or the soft glow of the moon.

What if I could break out of my planned pattern the way the humans sometimes do? What if I could live a life I enjoyed, one that was more than ... just more. Or maybe it's wrong for one such as me to crave those things. I have no idea why I am what I am. There's a chance I'm not capable of true happiness. Or possibly don't deserve it.

"Hey." Six settled down beside me, his hand brushing mine. "You're looking a lot better. Wanna go to the human realm for some food?"

Shadows danced over me as my brothers and sisters flitted through the sky above us. "I don't know. Maybe." My mood was sullen, even more so than usual after a job.

I couldn't decide if I wanted to dwell or let Six cheer me up.

Dwelling probably isn't a good idea. I heaved a huge sigh. "I guess we can go."

Six jumped into the air, his wings flapping hard, a huge grin adorning his face. "Great! Meet you out front after I change real quick." He zoomed into the air, calling over his shoulder, "You might want to change, too. Or at least put some shoes on."

I glanced down at my attire. When not working, my clothing was a choice I actually got to make, and even though a job could be anywhere in time, my outfit morphing to reflect that, the luna pocket dimension progressed forward in a linear manner in line with the human world. Lately, my standard fare was jeans and a T-shirt. The one I currently had on was a faded *Doctor Who* shirt. I shrugged. Who knew how long human styles would allow me such comfort? My body practically broke out in hives at the mere thought of corsets. Besides, who was I trying to impress? I was comfortable, and I would blend in like we were supposed to.

I wiggled my toes in the grass. Although Six did have a point about shoes.

As if on cue, Six's voice bellowed from inside, "Let's go, Eighty-nine! Chop, chop!"

I heaved another sigh. *Is it too late to change my mind?*

Chapter 3

Lunas didn't require traditional food of any kind to survive, our bodies sustained by the energy from the souls that passed through us, but the majority of us did delight in human morsels. For me personally, I quite enjoyed what was considered junk food, especially chocolate, and ice cream. Put the two together, and, well … I could quite possibly eat my weight in the stuff.

"You all right, Eighty-nine?" Six squeezed my shoulder, chuckling under his breath.

Glowering, I squinted at him, the bright day practically blinding. "We need to stop to get me some sunglasses somewhere."

He shook his head slowly, fingering the pair on his face. "I'm not sure why you didn't think to bring any."

"I don't know, my mind was elsewhere, obviously." I swiped at the tears forming in the corners of my eyes. It wasn't like lunas had an aversion to daylight, not like vampires or other fictitious creatures of that ilk, we simply preferred the night, and to stalk in the shadows. Plus, being out in the day made me tired and cranky. But when moving around in the human world during times of leisure, I couldn't force them to function on my nocturnal schedule ... unfortunately. It was only the promise of my favorite foods that kept me from going home.

"It's not that much farther, and you'll be fine once we get inside," Six said, fiddling with the zipper on his jacket. He'd chosen to wear clothes out of the norm for him. He swapped out his green, military-style jacket for a crisp leather one, and his faded jeans for dark denim. Ratty sneakers no longer adorned his feet, but rather black leather motorcycle boots. If not for his neutral skin tone and hair, like all lunas, he would almost stand out.

I narrowed my eyes while motioning to his suspicious attire. "What's up with the style change? Something you want to tell me?"

His shoulders wiggled as if he was rustling his wings that weren't there at the moment. "Just felt like something different."

"Uh-huh." If he didn't want to tell me I wasn't in the mood to pry it out of him. "Can I borrow your sunglasses for a while? My eyes are watering, and my nose is itching. I'm a few seconds away from a sneezing fit, I can feel it. You could have at least brought me somewhere overcast. You know, like Seattle or London, or I don't know, anywhere where I'm not like an ant under a magnifying glass."

Grabbing my forearm roughly, Six hauled me down the street, and into what appeared to be a small, bustling diner. "See, told you we were almost there. No need to be a drama queen about it."

"Fine. I'm sorry I'm being a brat. The copious amounts of junk food I'm about to inhale will surely put me in a better mood though. So, you won't have to tolerate it for much longer."

"Yeah, sure." Six was no longer paying attention to me, his gaze riveted to something or someone inside of the diner.

Peering around him, I attempted to trace his line of sight with my own, but it was too crowded for me to get a lock on what was drawing his undivided attention. "Maybe we should go somewhere else because it looks like we're in for a bit of a wait here."

"No. I want to eat here."

Nibbling my bottom lip, I surveyed the scene again. There were already a handful of humans waiting to be seated ahead of us. "You positive you don't want to go somewhere else?"

"Yup."

Crossing my arms over my chest, I leaned against the bit of wall space near me. "Fine." Although it wasn't completely fine since I was in a bad mood, and most certainly didn't want to wait to be fed.

A hostess waved Six over, taking down whatever

human name he chose to give her. I scowled at the back of his head, not that it would make a difference. Even though lunas came into existence as adults, a creation of some higher power, we still all had very distinct personalities, and Six was someone who wouldn't budge once his mind was made up. It wasn't worth my time or energy to fight him on something unless it was extremely important. Now was not one of those times.

"It's only about a twenty-minute wait. The people ahead of us are all in the same party and are going to be seated at the big booth in the back." Six stood on his tiptoes, his gaze intent, and this time the recipient of his attention was crystal clear, and definitely a some*one*.

She was petite, somewhere between five foot and five foot one, I guessed, with a bright red, close-cropped pixie cut. Freckles dotted her tiny, upturned nose, as if underscoring her bright green almost cat-like eyes. There was a vibrancy about her, a certain *je ne sais quoi*. Whatever it was that made her stand out had definitely intrigued Six.

I cleared my throat. "This isn't your first time here."

Without taking his eyes off the redheaded waitress, Six said, "I've been here a few times."

"Is this what the style change is about? Do you like her?"

It wasn't abnormal for a luna to develop a crush or infatuation on an especially dynamic human. After all, it was part of our nature to be drawn to bright souls, even if usually those souls only revealed their essence at the end of a life. But what concerned me was Six attempting to draw attention to himself. He could not have a relationship of any type with a human beyond casual sex.

I shook my head, and muttered to myself, "It doesn't matter." For a millisecond, a mere moment in time, I forgot that it didn't make a difference how much Six tried to get a human's undivided attention, lunas were all just background noise in the end.

My stomach twisted, and nausea roiled through my gut. *So why is this whole thing making me want to puke with worry?*

I considered Six's behavior and my reaction. My stomach twisted again. *I think ... I think I'm jealous.* But not of the girl in the way one might automatically assume. All lunas were like my brothers and sisters. Relationships beyond friendship never developed between any of us, and Six and I weren't to be the exception since my love for him was completely platonic.

No, it was something else entirely. There was some deep-seated fear that Six would abandon me, leaving me completely alone. Until he appeared, replacing the previous Six, I'd never realized how lonely I was. Six's friendship was a balm to my soul, and some days, it was as if it was the only thing that kept me from disappearing completely. I liked being the focus of his attention, even if I didn't desire any kind of romantic attention. Six made me feel important, like I mattered to someone. He knew things about me—details—that no one else did or cared to find out. Like what kind of books I enjoyed, and which

TV shows I obsessed about. If I ever ceased to exist, I didn't want it to be as if I was never there, like my life had meant nothing. As selfish as it was, I wanted to be missed —to be mourned.

I bit the inside of my cheek, tasting a metallic tang. *Stop it. You* are *being a drama queen today. Since when do you fear death? If you ever burn up, then it doesn't matter what's left behind because you won't be here to know.*

Forcing a smile, I nudged Six with my shoulder. "You didn't answer. Do you like that waitress?"

Color bloomed across the tips of his ears. "Sure, I guess ... I mean, she seems nice."

"That's not the kind of like I meant." Snagging a menu off the hostess' podium, I scanned the food offerings.

What the hell? Clenching my jaw, I spoke between gritted teeth. "There aren't any chocolate items on this menu, Six. Why aren't there chocolate items on this menu?" I waved it in his face.

Six stabbed his finger on the back of the plastic. "Right there. Ice cream sundae."

I yanked the menu away, staring aghast at what he was attempting to placate me with. "It's vanilla ice cream with a little bit of chocolate sauce on top. Not what I had in mind and you know it."

"Everything isn't all about you," Six grated. "How about compromising just a little—"

"Everything isn't all about me, but this little excursion was supposed to be. At least you led me to believe it was. Clearly, I misread the situation." I slapped the menu against his chest, pivoting on my heel. "I'll be at the closest Dairy Queen or Baskin Robbins or any place that actually has what I want to eat."

Kicking the door open, it clanked against the wall, causing heads to whip in my direction. *Oh, now you all notice me. But don't worry, you'll forget soon enough.*

I made it no more than twenty feet outside of the diner when Six caught up. "Eighty-nine, seriously, what is your deal today?" He grabbed my shoulder and shoved his sunglasses on my face.

All my anger drained as suddenly as it had appeared, and I sagged with exhaustion. "I just want my chocolate ice cream, and then to go back to bed, okay?" There was no need to share my feelings of insecurity and neediness; they would pass on their own soon enough.

Six's head tilted to the side, his eyes glazing over. "I'm going to have to take a rain check. Duty calls."

I waved him off. "Don't worry about me. I'll be fine by the time you get back, and then it'll be my turn to take care of you."

He smiled with affection, kissed the top of my head, and sprinted to the nearby alleyway so he could disappear into thin air without raising suspicions.

And that's how it was with lunas—we went about our lives, minding our own business until we felt the pull. There was no way to predict it since we always craved the fire of human souls, only satiated for a moment in time, forever waiting until we could experience a millisecond of peace again.

I envied Six, wishing it had been me being drawn to the event. But it would be soon enough, something I both loved and hated.

My stomach fluttered, and an invisible thread attached to my sternum was yanked, drawing my undivided attention. The location of my pending job appeared in my mind's eye, along with every other detail I would need. Dread and anticipation warred.

Well, well, well, looks like I didn't have long to wait after all. Milwaukee, here I come.

Chapter 4

Smoke billowed from the first few floors of the apartment complex, screams for help saturating the air. The old building, despite its age, should have been equipped with a working fire escape, but it was clear something had gone wrong.

Sirens blared in the distance, and concerned citizens gathered on the sidewalk, not a smartphone in sight. *Simpler times mean an easier job for me. All the pay off with none of the extra hassles of worrying about going viral.* I skulked into the shadows, a reaper appearing a few feet away.

"Aren't you concerned one of these pedestrians will help one of the marked escape their fate?"

Surprise surged through me. It was a rare thing for a reaper to speak, and it had happened at two events in a row. I narrowed my eyes. "Are you the same reaper from before?" His features were hidden under his hood, like all reapers seemed to prefer, which was exactly why I had no real way of identifying him beyond his voice. And that method was spotty at best.

The reaper cocked his head. “Before? Before what? If you are referring to the last incident where you had to intervene, then yes, that was me there as well.”

Two conversations in all my years and I was already learning how strange reapers truly were. “Well, aren’t you a Chatty Cathy then?” I turned my gaze back to the building. “And to answer your question, no, I’m not worried, humans don’t like to risk their own necks when someone else can take the risk. All these people can hear the sirens as well as we can, so they know help is on the way. They won’t feel the urge to intervene.”

“Are you sure about that?”

A man darted past me, heading around the side of the building. I glared at the reaper. “You saw him coming, didn’t you?”

He shrugged, and even though I couldn’t see it, I could feel his smirk, I swear.

Two times in a row with this crap, too? What is going on?

I sprinted after the guy, growling under my breath.

“Hey! A little help here!” I found my current pain in the ass attempting to shove a dumpster up below the broken fire escape. I wasn’t sure what his plan was exactly, but he wouldn’t be getting any help from me, at least not the kind he was hoping for.

My gaze swept over him with interest, despite the current predicament. His aura flared a bright orange, letting me know he was among my number of souls to archive, but it hadn't been so a moment ago.

No, not possible. This is a fixed point in time. Fixed means things don't change without monumental interference. But they had.

My feet carried me closer to the human male without conscious thought. What was it about him that made him so special? The first I'd ever encountered like him.

He was tall, probably a good foot taller than my average height. His skin and hair were nearly the same dark brown shade, his eyes almost black. His high cheekbones and full lips made him quite attractive by my estimations, and yet … yet, he was just a human male like any other as far as I could tell. Exactly like the last one I encountered who broke the pattern. If there was something intrinsically special or unique about him, it wasn't anything I could easily detect.

With preternatural reflexes I rushed the guy, causing him to stumble backward in confusion. "Hey, what … how'd you—" He grabbed my wrist. "I know you. We've done this before." He shook his head. "Or I dreamed about it."

Eyes widening, I recoiled. *He knows me? But how? None of this is possible. None of it.*

He took a hesitant step toward me, his gaze locked with mine. "Yes, I-I-I don't know. I'll figure it out later." He spun to face the building again. "We don't have time for this. I need to get up there … all those people." He visibly shuddered. "I need to save them."

He was right. It wasn't the time to decipher the clues of his existence or link to me; I would have to figure it all out later. I needed to do my job before it was too late.

Gliding up behind him, I leaned forward to whisper in his ear, "I'm sorry." I snapped his neck, not giving him time to react.

His body fell forward and then slid down the dumpster, landing in a heap on the ground. My stomach twisted at the sight. It didn't seem right to leave his body there like a piece of discarded trash.

Stop. He's dead. It's just a body, and you have a job to do.

I bowed my head. "May you find peace in the ever after or your next life."

Glass exploded, and flames climbed higher, engulfing the building. Screams from inside were cut off, triggering cries of dismay from the people watching from a safe distance.

My gaze strayed back to the human I just killed. *Out of all of them, you were the only one who tried to help. And the thanks you get is somehow changing your fate to be one of the fallen.*

A surge of energy danced along my skin, goose bumps erupting in its wake. *It's time.*

My wings flared out behind me, and I threw my head back as I rose into the air. Hovering between worlds, the recently dead souls passed through me one after another in lightning fast succession. I recorded their essences, making sure all that should be was.

As the numbers of dead added up, the warmth their

souls offered seeped into my bones. My body hummed with delight, the energy of the deceased an addictive force, for it was in these few moments I felt satiated, content, full ... like I actually belonged there ... or anywhere. I would be whole.

But wait.

One of the souls burned brighter, hotter, and its essence was familiar, one I was positive I'd tasted before. Focusing on it, I realized it was the soul of the man I just killed ... but it was also the soul of the man I killed at my last job.

Confusion zinged through me, even as I continued to record the rest of the souls.

Since our jobs weren't linear in time, we could be in 2025 one day, and 1902 the next. This particular soul was not the first I'd encountered that had been a reincarnation. But it was the first repeat offender to try to break out of the universe's pattern. Just its existence triggered endless questions.

I held it there within me, studying it, the task fully consuming my attention.

It's so bright. Why is it so much brighter? And hotter? It was staggeringly so. More than I realized before. I wanted to hold it within me forever, to make it a part of me. To luxuriate in the heat it offered, to—

Some unseen force snatched the soul from my grasp. Crying out in anguish, I dropped to my knees. *No! Come back! Please, come back! I want to feel your heat for just a little bit longer. I want to understand.*

I tore at my hair and gnashed my teeth. The vast emptiness that was always a part of me yawned wider, threatening to swallow me whole.

A large hand palmed the top of my head. "You need to leave here before you draw unwanted attention to yourself."

Shivering, I stared at the ground, my pulse thundering in my ears. "I don't understand."

"And maybe you never will. But it is time for you to leave." The reaper's even tone combined with the steel in his voice forced me to acknowledge him.

I nodded, my body numb, and willed myself home.

Chapter 5

Minutes, hours, days, I wasn't sure how long I laid under the mountain of blankets in my bed, gaze riveted on the moon, and yet my attention fully elsewhere. It was as if my entire world had spun off its axis, hurtling me into oblivion.

All because of one soul. One utterly, and completely unique soul.

How had the human broken out of the pattern it was supposed to adhere to the first time I encountered it, and completely changed his fate the next? Fixed points in time were supposed to be just that … fixed. By the rules of the game I'd always played by, if anyone didn't die when they were supposed to then reality itself could dissolve. So, wouldn't the opposite be true as well? And yet the human had gone from not tagged to tagged by his own accord essentially. *How is any of it possible?*

Six's hand squeezed mine, reminding me that he was nestled under the blankets beside me. Fresh off his own job, he sought the same recuperating time as I did, and since neither of us were in the position to take care of the other, we were wallowing together.

I turned toward him, one of the wool blankets scratching at my cheek. "Did you ever wonder why we're always sent to the fixed points in time where people die? Why do we never get sent to record and ensure other types of fixed points?"

He blinked at me several times, his gaze darting over my face with amusement. "Two jobs so close together must have fried your brain a bit. Because duh … those are the scenes we're pulled to because we crave the heat of the deceased souls when they pass through us on their way to the reapers. We wouldn't get any of that without the, I don't know, deaths. Who knows if we're sent or pulled there? I've never been able to even figure out why one of us is pulled to a scene over another luna, especially when we're in the same place together. And why do we jump around in time? If it's a fixed point, wouldn't that point already need to be set to move reality forward? But apparently, that's not what happens at all."

I shifted again, returning my gaze to the moon. "There's so much we don't know. All lunas are created with the knowledge of what we need to do, but not why. Never why."

"Maybe if we knew why then we wouldn't want to be

us anymore?" Six shrugged, the blankets moving up and down with his motion. "Or it could be that we're being punished for something we did before we became lunas."

"What do you mean before we became lunas?"

"Maybe our souls weren't created for this job, but brought here, our memories wiped clean, and this is our punishment for something we can't even remember."

Silhouettes of our brothers and sisters danced in the light of the moon above us, the sight normally comforting, until now. "I … I never considered that." What if Six was right? What if my entire existence as a luna was some kind of punishment, a purgatory of sorts?

Six patted my head. "But don't hurt your brain thinking about it. Whatever reason we're here, it doesn't change the fact that we are here."

"Who or what enforces other fixed points in time? Do you know?" Because I didn't. The reality was that there was so much I didn't know.

"Huh-uh, but I'm sure it's a more responsible race than us. Because like I said, without the pull of the souls for us, why bother going? Why not have a more fulfilling life? One where we actually have choices."

I scrubbed a hand over my face. I needed to think about something else. Me questioning lunas' existence wasn't going to change anything about it. We were what we were, for better or worse. *Could ignorance be bliss in this situation? What would I do if I found out I was being punished? It would make everything worse, wouldn't it?*

Or maybe it would change nothing at all.

"Why do you read this stuff?" Six had rolled over toward my tiny nightstand, the one piled high with romance novels.

Grabbing him by the scruff of his neck, I yanked him back before his exploring fingers could make contact with any of my books. "Hands off, Six. I mean it. I'm not in the mood for you to mock my choice in literature today."

"But why read that kind of stuff when we can never experience it?"

"We can experience sex with humans if we want, as long as we don't reveal ourselves. We can also—"

"Sex is sex. We can't experience the kind of relationships that exist in your romance novels. We can never have true love. So why torture yourself with reading about something you can't have?"

I quirked an eyebrow. "Either you've been secretly reading my books or you watched *The Princess Bride* again."

"It just seems to me that our lives can't be fulfilled without that kind of love, and we can never experience it. Maybe it isn't the warmth of the dead souls that temporarily satiates us, maybe it's the love those souls felt when they were alive, and even getting it secondhand is addicting."

I nibbled on my thumbnail. "No, because even souls nobody loved, or cruel souls, warm us, and you know it. You're just feeling the post job let down."

Six sighed heavily. "Am I? Or am I simply wanting more out of this dull existence of ours?"

I didn't know what to say to him. After all, hadn't I been in a morose mood of my own lately? Our lives as lunas were limited, and yes, we missed out on the human experience because we weren't human. I would be lying if I said I'd never yearned for the kinds of relationships I read about in my favorite books. Even to have loved and lost seemed a great deal better than never knowing what true love was all about from firsthand experience. But for me, it wasn't just romantic love, it was the love and bond between parent and child, something else we as lunas could never experience.

Although who was to say any of it was true? Maybe humans created such things from their imaginations because they coveted it as well. They certainly didn't get paranormal creatures right. They almost always made it seem as if being some kind of supernatural was more desirable than human, and that was a bunch of crap. To me, being human would be the goal to strive for, the fragile beauty of humanity better than any other kind of life I'd ever heard of.

I cleared my throat. "Have you ever seen true love outside of fiction? How do we know it even exists?"

Six grinned. "I love you, but I'm guessing you mean romantic love, right?"

"Yes, of course, that's what I mean. In all the jobs I've worked over the years, I've never seen anything even hinting at true romantic love, but I have seen the love of parents, of friends, stuff like that." I squeezed his hand. "And I hope you know, I love you, too. You're my best friend and I don't know how I got by before you became Six."

He shifted, staring straight ahead as if he was suddenly somewhere else. "I've seen it. I've seen true love, and it changed me. It changed everything."

My mouth opened and closed a few times before I could form words. "You've seen it? When? What do you mean it changed everything?"

Sitting up, he threw the blankets off of us. "You know what, I don't want to talk about such things anymore. Let's go flying. It'll make us both feel better."

Yanking the covers back over me, I tucked them under my chin. "I'm still too cold. Go ahead without me, and I'll be here when you get back."

Without another word, Six zoomed out of the skylight to become another silhouette in the illuminated night.

My eyes drifted shut as my thoughts returned to the anomaly of a human I killed twice, and his dazzling soul.

"WAKE UP, EIGHTY-NINE."

Flopping over, I burrowed deeper under the mountain of blankets. I didn't remember actually drifting off, or if I'd had any dreams, but I knew I didn't get enough rest yet.

"You need to wake up."

Wait. That isn't Six. The voice was masculine and somewhat familiar, but not someone I could place half awake. *Who else would come into my room to wake me up?* Besides Six, another luna had never breached my personal space. *What the hell?*

Blinking open blurry eyes, I peered from under my lashes at a dark form. "Why are you here?" The "who are you" business suddenly took a distinct second place to figuring out the point to this little wake-up call. "And where's Six?" Because my best friend wouldn't take lightly to someone disturbing me if he was around to see it, which meant he wasn't nearby.

"You are not listening. You need to wake up. When you do, the answers you seek will become clear."

"What?"

Sitting up, I tried to focus on the intruder, but it was if he was masked by shadows. Even the outline of his body wavered. In fact, the harder I looked, the more difficult he was to see. *What in the—*

"Oh," I muttered to myself. "This is a dream. I didn't actually wake up."

Collapsing back onto the bed, I released a long breath. I didn't dream often, or at least I didn't remember my dreams often, but when I did they were usually weird ones that made zero sense. They definitely weren't like what humans had where their subconscious' were communicating with them.

"For such an intelligent creature, you are being

incredibly obtuse. Your body is currently in an awakened state, but I'm telling you to wake up your mind. You need to pay attention to the things that are soon to come in order for you to receive the answers you seek."

Fine, I'd play along since this stupid dream was dragging on. "What answers am I supposedly seeking?"

"Why the human soul is different. And why you're here."

My heart quadrupled in time, thrashing against my ribcage, adrenaline surging through my veins. My vision cleared, and I sucked in a sharp breath. No longer engulfed in shadows, my dark visitor became recognizable in an instant. "Reaper? You're a reaper. In my room, in the luna realm. Wh-What—"

"Heed my words, little luna. There is hope for you yet." He disappeared as if he was never there.

My mouth fell open, and I sputtered. Clutching the blankets to my chest, my gaze darted wildly around my room. *What the hell just happened?* I gulped repeatedly, mind reeling. *I need to find Six.*

Stumbling from bed, I knocked into my nightstand, sending my books across the floor. Kicking them out of the way, a disrespect I would normally cringe at, I scrambled for my boots and dashed for the door as soon as I managed to pull them on.

No. Wait. Six is probably still flying.

Spinning on my heel, I leapt for the skylight, taking flight.

"Hey, watch it. Do you ever fly in a straight line?" Thirteen hissed at me, as I grazed his wings with mine.

Ignoring him, I fixated on my mission to find Six. *He's the only one who can help me figure this out—the only one who would even care.*

Chapter 6

"He knew my name. How did the reaper know my name?" And why was he encouraging me to delve further into the mystery of the soul that intrigued me? Plus, what had he meant by there was hope for me yet? It wasn't like a reaper to get involved in … anything as far as I'd ever heard. What was his endgame in this little scenario? What could—

"I'm beginning to think you're half-blind." Thirteen glared down at me, my face scant inches from his chest. "You were about to collide with me again, and we're not even in the air this time."

Shuffling back a few feet, I realized I'd somehow ended up in one of the long corridors leading to Archives. I gave Thirteen a half-hearted smile. "Sorry, my mind was elsewhere, so I guess you could say I was kind of blind there for a second and didn't see where I was going."

"You need to pay attention, Eighty-nine. You and Six both."

"Umm … speaking of Six," I nibbled on my bottom lip, "you wouldn't happen to know where he is, would you?"

Thirteen snorted. "He must be lost if you don't know since the two of you are practically attached at the hip." He pushed past me without another word.

Some lunas are crotchety old assholes. Of course without my friendship with Six, who knew what kind of attitude I would have developed by now. Especially since I was one of the original hundred. Although I was pretty sure general temperament had a lot to do with a luna's overall attitude.

Are any of the other lunas friends the way Six and I are? It saddened me to think that maybe none of them even had that kind of intimacy. Not that any of them had ever accepted Six's invitations to hang out when he first arrived. I was the only one who gave him a chance. Something I was thankful for every single day.

I paused in front of the massive door to Archives; the black paint shiny enough that I could see my distorted reflection in the carved wood. *Am I losing my mind? Is that even possible for a luna?* Could one soul—a dazzlingly bright soul—have been so different that it caused me to snap? Lunas were creatures of habit in so many ways … was something a bit out of the ordinary enough to short circuit my system? What if the reaper in my room hadn't been real?

I took a step closer to the door, running my fingertips

along the gold inlay. Why were the architects the only ones who used the information we collected on our jobs? What did they do with it? Did lunas jump around in time for jobs because we were patching up plot holes in the universe like some complicated novel of sorts? And the architects were revising what was already written? Could fixed points in time not be what I perceived them to be? *Maybe nothing is.*

I clutched my head, a headache blooming. *Shit. I need to stop. If my brain isn't already broken it's going to be soon at this rate. Six. I need to find Six.*

My stomach fluttered, and an invisible thread attached to my sternum was yanked, drawing my undivided attention. The location of my pending job appeared in my mind's eye, along with every other detail I would need. Dread and anticipation warred, the internal battle more than normal.

So soon? I just had two jobs back-to-back already. Having a third packed in so close is nearly unheard of. What is going on?

I gave myself an internal shake. *I don't have time to think about any of that. The warmth and comfort of humanity calls. You need this right now.*

London, here I come.

LURKING in the back of the crowd on a train platform, I pretended to ready myself for boarding like all the other tagged humans. Amongst animated chatter, the passengers slowly began filling the empty cars. In the distance, the clickity-clack of another train hastened our way.

My nostrils flared, and I dug my nails into my palms, anticipation coiling through my muscles. But I wasn't on high alert because of the impending disaster like normal, no. Instead, I vibrated with tension as I awaited the arrival of a reaper. Hopefully, the same reaper who'd appeared at both of my most recent jobs.

Amid my doubts of sanity bloomed the seedling thought that the reaper actually had paid me a visit in my room to dispense cryptic lines about answers, which of course only raised more questions. Therefore, the best course of action was to go straight to the source of my existential crisis of sorts. I had to talk to the reaper again, and then, and only then, could I make an educated decision about what to do next.

A tall, lanky man with a shock of red hair pushed past me, his face flushed and sweaty. "Get back! Please! You must all get off of this platform!" The man waved his arms around in a desperate plea to garner everyone's attention.

My spine went ramrod straight, and my gaze locked onto the man. Was this human's soul—the same soul—here again, attempting to break the pattern for a third time? The chances of that were nearly impossible, and yet …

I shoved around several well-dressed women in what appeared to be 1950s-ish garb, snatching at the man-in-question's forearm. "What are you doing?" I hissed.

His green eyes widened, and he lurched to the side slightly. "You. I know you."

Well, I guess that answers that question. It was indeed the same soul trying to throw a wrench in the universe's engine for the third time in a row. Only this round he wasn't merely saving people who were meant to die, or at least attempting to, he was actually trying to prevent the entire disaster. *How does he know what's coming? How can he possibly know anything about it?*

Scanning him from top to bottom, I didn't notice his physical appearance beyond my initial observations: he was a tall ginger. I was looking for something else—anything else that might give me a clue to what made him different from other humans. Whatever it was had been undetectable in his body the first two encounters, so obviously it was his soul. But what about it, beyond the heat, the taste, was so unusual?

"Please, miss, we must get these people away from here. There is going to be an accident. The train," he waved his free arm, "the other train is going to crash into this one."

I gritted my teeth. "Don't be ridiculous, such things don't happen." No tag. This man didn't have the bright orange aura, so, therefore, it wasn't his time. Dragging him away would be simple, but doing it in time to complete my job was another thing. "Now, get out of here before you cause a panic."

He squirmed within my grip, his expression stricken. "I know what I'm saying sounds quite loony, but I speak the truth. I know what is coming, and I must save these people."

Yanking him hard, he stumbled after me into the corner. The red glow of my eyes met his terrified gaze. "You need to let this happen. It has to happen. The reasons are beyond your comprehension, so leave here because it's not your time to die today."

"Are you the Grim Reaper or a demon from the depths of hell itself?"

"Neither. I'm a creature here to protect the fabric of reality."

He clenched his jaw, the tendons rippling. "No. I do not accept any of that. I will save those people."

I shook him, frustration getting the better of me. "Just leave. There's nothing you can do to save these people. And even if there was, you'd doom the rest of humanity ... the very fabric of reality itself, so you wouldn't be saving them at all in the end. A few die here today to save the many. It's that simple."

He swallowed hard, his Adam's apple dancing up and down in his throat. "It is never that simple."

"Fine, it's not. But you have to trust me on this."

He lifted his chin, peering down his nose at me. "No. I must remain constant in my morality. I will not leave these people to die." His aura flickered, flaring to the bright orange of a tagged human.

I stared, having witnessed this soul change its own fate before my very eyes twice now. He was willing to die for his convictions, which made me question again what fixed points in time really were if they were not, in fact, fixed.

I released his arm and stepped back. "I guess I was wrong. You convinced me. Go ahead." I waved at the people still boarding the train. "Do what you can."

He glanced down at his jacket where I'd been touching him, before shaking his head, and dashing off in a flurry of panic. "Please, get off the train! All of you must get off this train!"

"It's almost a shame he has to die, isn't it?" The reaper appeared directly beside me, his voice low. "It's so rare for a human to question reality like he does. I'd wager that's the reason he sees so much, because he doesn't walk around in a stupor like others of his kind. It doesn't take much to see the truth, if one actually takes the time to look for it."

"You!" I stabbed my index finger in his direction. "Were you in my bedroom before? Or did I imagine all of it?"

A low chuckle was his only response.

"Hey, you don't get to go silent on me now. I need answers, damnit!"

His hood shifted, and I caught the barest hint of his jaw. "Find them then. If a human can, I'm certain you have the ability as well."

"If a human can what? Find answers?" I tugged at my hair. "I don't have time for more cryptic bullshit!" The truth was, I'd been so flustered since my possible wake-up visitation from the reaper that I wasn't entirely sure my brain was properly functioning at all, sanity notwithstanding. How was I supposed to figure anything out when I was in such a state?

Brakes screeched, metal on metal sounding more like a high-pitched whine … and then impact. Screams rang out abruptly, the majority of them cut short almost instantly. I stared at the wreckage, knowing there would be more to come at any moment.

The boom of a second impact from the opposite direction shook the platform, and I swayed on my feet. An eerie silence blanketed everything, the people not on the trains that had survived stunned beyond belief.

My wings flared out behind me, and I threw my head back as I rose into the air. Hovering between worlds, the recently dead souls passed through me one after another in lightning fast succession. I recorded their essences, making sure all that should be was.

As the numbers of dead added up, the warmth their souls offered seeped into my bones.

But … but, it's different this time.

My body still hummed with delight, the energy of the deceased an addictive force. However, there was no satisfaction, no contentedness …

All of my focus narrowed down to the soul that burned the brightest, the heat from it scorching every fiber of my being. I yearned to hold it inside of me for all of eternity, to wrap myself around it, and never let go. If I could just manage to keep it, to have it for my own, then

I'd no longer be drawn to scenes filled with death and destruction. I would be whole … and free.

I need it.

The reaper glided up beside me, his hand latching onto my shoulder, digging into it painfully. "It is not yours. Your salvation lies elsewhere."

What? My salvation, whatever that means, is here and now. With this soul. I need it, and then I'll be free—free from all of this. "You can't have it," I snarled.

"It is not mine either. But I will shepherd it on from here. It must be this way."

"No."

A pulse of energy swept through me, emanating from the reaper's palm, tearing the soul from my grasp.

I wailed incoherent words, scrambling to find the soul again. To touch it for even one more moment …

But it was gone. Beyond my reach.

Black spots danced before my eyes, the ground tilting up to meet me.

Chapter 7

I squeezed my eyes shut, the staccato beat of my heart pounding against my eardrums. I wasn't exactly sure what had happened, and I didn't know if I was ready to find out. If I thought I felt off-balance within my world before … I'd been sadly mistaken.

I didn't understand what I was fighting to protect anymore. Because that's exactly what I did, to wage battles against anything or anyone who dared attempt to break the pattern the universe had laid out … to save reality itself. But when I stopped to contemplate the concept of reality, I had to admit, even a being such as myself who had been around since nearly the beginning of time, had no idea what reality actually was. Would it be such a bad thing if it did collapse or dissolve? Did the absence of reality translate to a catastrophe or merely something else, something new? And new wasn't necessarily a bad thing. It was simply something not yet comprehended, and quite possibly better. What if reality was merely my prison, and its destruction meant my freedom? What if all creatures had been tricked into being their own prison wards?

I need answers. And I don't have the faintest clue where to start looking for them.

My eyelids fluttered open to reveal the glittering sky of my home, the silhouettes of my brothers and sisters dancing through beams of moonlight. Not one of them paid any mind to me lying on the cold ground. I'd obviously willed myself there at some point, even though my recollection of anything after my latest job was completely blank. The energy from the events I recorded was no longer with me either. How I'd possibly made a deposit in Archives was beyond my comprehension at the moment, but clearly I had, there was no other explanation.

Six. I need to talk to Six. He was the only one I could talk to that could begin to help me unravel my current state of confusion. He would tell me honestly if I'd lost my marbles.

Blindly making my way inside, my thoughts consumed, I headed straight for Six's room. *Please be back. Please be back.* Not bothering to knock, I threw his door open, the heavy wood thumping against the wall.

I stopped short, blinking rapidly. A completely unfamiliar luna stood in the middle of Six's room, his mouth pursed in surprise.

Someone new. Okay. Obviously, he was in the wrong

place. "You're clearly lost. This is Six's room. Who are you?"

"Six."

This luna must be defective if he doesn't know where his space is. We're all supposed to know as soon as we're created. I don't have time for this right now. "Yes, this is Six's room. I'm Eighty-nine, and who are you?"

"Six."

"No, not who's room is this, but who are you?"

His mouth pressed down into a thin line, and he approached me slowly. "This is my room because I am Six."

The words filtered into my brain slowly, as if my mind was resisting the knowledge they brought with them. Then they swept through my body like a poison, numbing my insides even as I felt my face scrunch up in horror. "You are Six." My lips moved on their own accord. "You are Six."

"Yes, that's what I said. I am Six."

My gaze swung wildly around the room, only then noticing that all of Six's, *my* Six's, things had disappeared.

No. This isn't happening. It's not true. There's been a mistake. It can't be real. It's not real.

My legs buckled, and I dropped to the floor, a sob stuck in my throat. *He's not gone. He can't be ... just gone. It's not possible.* I swiped at my face, my fingertips damp from tears I didn't realize I was shedding.

Bringing my knees up to my chest, I began to rock back and forth. *No, he wouldn't leave me. He wouldn't just abandon me like that. He wouldn't. This is all a lie. He would fight to stay. No matter what, he wouldn't just leave me here like this.*

Six—the imposter Six—said something to me, but I didn't register the words. Instead, I stared down at the grains in the hardwood floor, unable to look anywhere but there.

A hand touched my shoulder, and I spun, rage erupting. "How dare you?" I was suddenly on my feet. "How dare you think you can just move in here and replace him!?" My fists balled up, and I pummeled his chest, screeching, "How dare you think you can be Six?" over and over, before I had no concept or control over my words or actions, or even my body itself.

I was there, and yet I wasn't, my entire focus narrowing down to one train of thought: *There has to be a way. There has to be a way to bring him back. I have to bring him back. I will bring him back. Six, my Six, will come back. There is a way, and I will find it. Somehow, some way, I will bring him back ...*

AN AVALANCHE of numbness had crashed over me, and I had no hope of digging my way out. I couldn't even begin to wrap my mind around the fact that Six was gone. It was a nightmare brought to life. I'd always thought that out of the two of us, I would be the one to burn out first, if it were to happen at all. Sometimes when I contemplated letting go, I'd held on for Six, knowing he would be alone without me. Had he put up any kind of fight at all? Or had he welcomed the bliss of oblivion with open arms?

Maybe he'd been right, and our existence was some kind of punishment. He could have been taken away from me because of my attempt to hold onto the soul at the train depot. Although it could also be that I was connecting dots that didn't exist. Six could have merely let go because I wasn't a good enough friend to him. I always helped him with his problems as best I could, but we both had our issues. After all, we were lunas. Maybe I simply hadn't done all I could or should have. Had I missed something? I had to have, there was no other explanation.

In some way I had completely failed Six.

I have to know why. If I can figure out why he burned out, then maybe, just maybe, I can ... I don't fucking know. Nothing will change. He'll still be gone. But I have to—I simply have to know why. For my own sanity's sake.

An abrupt laugh escaped my throat. *Yeah, my sanity. I'm pretty sure that boat has sailed. Or rather, my spot in a padded cell is reserved.*

I had arrived at Archives at some point, my feet carrying me there without conscious thought. The black lacquered door with its gold intricate inlay loomed in front of me, seemingly larger than normal, possessing an ominous presence it usually lacked. I hadn't yet admitted to myself what I was considering, the option just as insane as I was pretty sure I'd become.

If I can find his books ... yes, if I can find his books, then maybe I can go back to those dates. And if I can go back, then maybe I can bring him forward with me again. I can fix this. I can fix whatever I fucked up. However I let him down ... I can fix it if I can just go back.

I shook my head, my gaze never wavering from the door. I knew what was happening. I was grieving. I saw humans experience it, and I read about it, but I myself had never grieved before. It all bubbled down to a list, or stages: denial, anger, bargaining, depression, and acceptance. I was pretty sure I'd gone straight from denial to bargaining. Or possibly I was still in denial that Six was truly gone? Of course, there was the fact that I wasn't human, and even though lunas seemed to share a similar emotional palette as humans, we were completely different. So, it would make sense if the stages in a luna weren't the same or happened out of order.

I tugged at my hair, a distant part of myself welcoming the pain, or really the ability to still feel anything at all. *There's no point in worrying about defining my emotions in any way, my anguish over losing Six simply can't be measured by a human scale of any kind because I'm a luna.*

Letting loose a battle cry, I hurtled myself at the Archive's entrance, my shoulder slamming into the heavy wood. With a groan, I scurried over the threshold, the artificial silence swallowing me whole in an instant.

I let the complete isolation from noise center me on my purpose. *I can do this. I will do this. And the first step is to find one of Six's books.*

Marching forward, I clenched my jaw as my gaze

darted over the seemingly endless shelves of books. I'd never come to Archives for anything but to create a book of my own, and I wondered if anyone would suspect what I was doing—or care?

Squeezing my eyes shut, I imagined Six's face and the way his brown eyes crinkled at the corners when he smiled. I heard his braying laugh, the one he used when he thought something was extremely funny, as I spun in a circle, searching … searching, searching.

Warmth, subtle and comforting, washed over me, and then ...

A tug, the smallest of pulls fluttered in my sternum, causing me to stumble forward, hands outstretched. My fingers curled around the supple leather spine of a book, and I lifted it to my nose, inhaling deeply.

Six, it smells like Six. Like home.

My eyes still tightly squeezed shut, I opened the book, placing my palms on the smooth pages.

Take me here. Take me to this time and place. To Six.

A hand squeezed my shoulder, and I whirled around, dropping the book.

A reaper stood before me, only the barest hint of a smirk visible from within the shadows of his hood. He swept me up into his arms, and my world blurred to nothing.

Chapter 8

"*Don't worry, Eighty-nine, Six will always watch your six."*

I stifled a laugh. "Not with that again."

"Always with that. Always."

A snippet of a long-ago conversation rose up inside of my head, the memory tearing a sob from my chest.

Screams saturated the air, stealing my attention. I swung my head around, taking in chaos, buildings burning all around me. Confusion kept me rooted in place, my breath stuck in my throat.

And then my gaze zeroed in on him ... *Six*.

Lurking in the shadows, where lunas preferred to stay, my friend watched the disaster unfold before him, his expression much like I imagined mine was at every one of my jobs—twisted between anguish and anticipation. I'd never witnessed another luna at work, and seeing Six before me, I realized we were every bit the outsiders I'd come to think of us as.

How does no one ever notice us when we're so out of place? It should be clear to any and all who glance in our direction that we don't belong in the human realm.

His eyes sparked red as he moved a few paces closer to the building directly in front of him. I moved in tandem, shrinking the distance between us.

A hand clamped down onto my shoulder, pinching painfully. "Be careful what you do next, for you are complicating things more than you can possibly fathom as is." The reaper stared down at me, his gaze burning intently from the depths of his hood.

"Why did you bring me here? Why are you helping me?"

He tilted his head, a low chuckle rumbling in his chest. "Am I helping you? Are you so sure of that?"

He was right. I had no idea if he was actually helping me or not. In fact, being that his kind usually never got involved in anything beyond escorting souls to the next realm, I was guessing he had an ulterior motive, one that had absolutely nothing to do with me, or my end game.

I crossed my arms over my chest. "Different question then. Do your end goals align with mine?"

"Quite possibly. Hard to tell at this point."

"Whatever. I don't have time for your cryptic bullshit right now." Pivoting back in the direction of Six, I sprinted toward him.

"Six! Six, I have to talk to you!" I had no idea when or

where we were, or how long ago in his timeline Six had done this particular job, but I knew I had to take him with me. I had to save him from whatever had stolen him from me.

He froze, every muscle in his body tensing, and just when I thought he was going to turn around, demanding how and why I was there, he ran across the street, and straight into the burning building.

What the fuck? How the hell didn't he hear me? It might be utter chaos around here, but I was just yelling his name less than two feet from him.

Dashing into the building after Six, the thick smoke ripped at my throat and welled up my eyes. I caught a flash of movement off to my left, and staggered that way, pulling my shirt up to cover my nose and mouth. Inhaling the smoke wouldn't kill one such as me, but it certainly could make things uncomfortable.

"Tina! Tina, where are you?" Six's familiar voice was strung tight with anxiety bordering on panic. "Tina! Please, answer me!"

I froze, fear spiking through my veins, and my heart thrashing painfully against my ribcage. *Why is Six searching for someone in here? It couldn't possibly mean what I think it does.*

A moment later, Six pushed past me with a girl his arms, completely oblivious to my presence. I trailed after them, my stomach twisting into knots. The girl was tagged, the bright orange aura of those marked for death visible even through the dense smoke.

No. He can't. It can't be what it looks like.

"Shh ... Tina, I've got you. You're going to be fine." Six planted a tender kiss on her forehead before depositing her gently on the sidewalk.

Tina—the girl from the diner that Six had been so fixated on—squinted up at him, her bright green eyes brimming with tears. "Simon, I was so scared. How did you know? How did you get here?"

"It's going to be just fine, my tiny Tina." Six smiled, but the emotion didn't reach his eyes.

She doubled over as a coughing fit wracked her body, her lungs gasping for enough air to keep her breathing. Shuffling forward, I studied her, realizing that despite Six's efforts she would die without immediate medical attention. Not only had she inhaled too much smoke, but her shirt and hair were saturated in crimson, evidence of her severe injuries.

Tina will die this day as she's supposed to.

Six palmed Tina's face between his hands just as her eyes slid shut. Her chest rattled out one last shaky breath before remaining still.

Dodging behind a car, I peered at Six over the hood, not wanting to interfere until he was ready for me to comfort him. I smiled to myself. *This is what happened. It has to be. He burned up from grief because I wasn't there in time to help him, but I am now. I can save him ... and change everything. It's all easier than I thought it would turn out to be.*

Six's wings flared out behind him, and his feet rose off the ground as he disappeared from sight. He was recording the calamity and the souls who died because of the disaster, invisible even to me until he was done.

My gaze dropped to Tina's body as I waited. Blood haloed her small form, the macabre scene oddly mesmerizing. When had Six met her, and why hadn't he given me any kind of clue about her? Sure, we both had occasional dalliances with humans, but it was clear that Tina was more to him than sex. There had been a moment when I'd actually thought Six was going to risk reality itself for her.

Six has a lot of explaining to do when we get home. But I couldn't even manage an ounce of anger with the jubilation rising up within me. I'd come so close to losing my best friend forever … so close.

Six reappeared in front of me, dropping down to his knees beside Tina. A high-pitched keening sound filled the air, his glowing eyes casting shadows across her motionless features. He yanked her body into his chest, cradling her while swaying back and forth. A few minutes later he stilled, and then gently laid Tina back on the ground. His fingers danced along her hairline, smoothing a few wisps away from her forehead. Rocking back on his heels, he sucked in a sharp breath.

Move, move, move, this is the time. I have to talk to him now. Comfort him. Stop him from burning up. Stop hovering behind him like an idiot and save your best friend before it's too late ... again.

With lightning speed, Six exposed his wings and arched them forward. He bared his teeth in a grimace, ripping the delicate forms from his back. Blood spurted from the gaping holes in his flesh, his torn shirt billowing like a cape.

My mouth fell open, a scream bubbling up from my throat.

Six's head whipped around, our gazes clashing, his filled with determination, and mine with horror.

Golden energy blobs streaked out from Six's wings where they lay discarded on the ground. His attention shifted as he deftly plucked a blob out of the air, shoving it into Tina's chest before it raced away.

Tina jolted up, sputtering, her wounds fully healed.

My vision wavered. *What have you done?*

In a burst of flame, Six and his wings were gone.

Just like that, there one instant, gone the next.

"Simon?" Tina's hands passed through the empty space where Six had been. With a whimper, she fainted dead away.

Reeling back, I attempted to wrap my brain around what I'd just witnessed. Six sacrificed his life to bring back Tina, and in the process, not only broke the rules, but released the other fixed-point souls before a reaper could collect them. I wasn't sure what would happen to those souls, but I did know that Tina was alive when she wasn't supposed to be. That was a threat to reality itself.

My instincts as a luna drove me forward, my intent to put to rights the fixed point in time.

I halted mid-stride, several humans rushing to Tina as

if conjured from nowhere. A flurry of questions ensued, all directed at her:

"Are you all right?"

"How did you get out of the building?"

"Was anyone else with you inside?"

"Did anyone else make it out with you?"

A paramedic with an oxygen tank and mask scurried to her side. "Here, ma'am, put this on while I check your vitals."

Backing away, realization settled in. Despite my and Six's paranormal display of otherness, no one had noticed us. Not one single person. It was how lunas were designed, but until that moment I'd nearly forgotten.

How exactly had Tina seen Six to begin with? I mean really *seen* him? How had their relationship been forged? One-night stands were usually the extent of connection between my species and humans. We couldn't hold their attention beyond something meaningless, something forgettable, just like us. It wasn't merely that we weren't permitted to reveal what we were, it was also the not so minor detail that no one cared enough to get to know us. Or at least no one ever had before Tina.

"You did an astounding job of fixing things, I see," the reaper murmured from scant inches away.

My blood heated, and my skin flushed. "You were no help at all."

"Not true. I brought you here."

My fists balled up at my sides. Anger hot and bright boiled within me, difficult to contain. The reaper had brought me here, but he hadn't done a damn thing to help with anything after that. Not only had Six burnt up again, but reality itself was in danger because of what my dearly departed best friend had done.

My stomach fluttered, and an invisible thread attached to my sternum was yanked, drawing my undivided attention.

Fuck! Not now! Not fucking now!

But there it was … the location of my pending job in my mind's eye, along with every other detail I would need.

For the first time in my long existence, I pondered the possibility of resisting the pull, to actually not go to a job.

Uncertainty warred.

In the end, I let myself do what I was born to do: I flew through time and space, to a place where humans would die so I could protect reality. A reality I wasn't so sure was safe to begin with anymore.

Chapter 9

W*hat is reality?* It wasn't the first time I'd asked that question, but it was the first I'd done it with an actual purpose of sorts.

Huddling in the shade provided by a tall sculpture, my face was upturned to take in a group of humans a few levels up inside of a glass office building. They appeared to be in a meeting, one that's abrupt ending was imminent according to what I knew.

A mother and child strolled past me, heading for the entrance of the building. Bright orange auras blazed around both of them. I swore under my breath. No matter how jaded I'd become in so many ways, I still couldn't stomach the deaths of children. There was just something about their innocence that got me every single time.

So why not save them? Tina lives, and reality still remains seemingly intact. Maybe nothing is what you thought it was. Your life, your purpose—everything has been filled with lies.

Indecisiveness, something I was becoming all too familiar with lately, kept me rooted in place. *If I save them, who's to say another luna won't get the same job after I do, and then they'll die anyways? Isn't that what a fixed point in time is —fixed? Or maybe the fixed part doesn't mean that it's unchanging, but that it constantly needs fixed? What if lunas are moving through time to the same group of core jobs over and over again? What if—*

Clutching at my head, I groaned. Moving through time in a non-linear manner the way lunas did was complicated, and confusing. This is why I'd never bothered to seek answers before. I did my job and lived my life as I was born to do, but now … now everything had changed. Now I had more questions than answers, and I was no longer satisfied with the status quo.

A reaper appeared beside me, too close inside my personal bubble for any doubt that it was the same reaper who'd become my second shadow.

"I can practically see the wheels turning. Should I expect smoke soon?" His low chuckle accompanied a pat to the top of my head.

I slapped at his arm, catching my fingers on his robe. "What? Why … you aren't like any reaper I've ever encountered before. Reapers barely talk, let alone get involved. What is your deal, seriously?"

"Oh, reapers talk. In fact, we do many things that would surprise you. Lunas wouldn't know this because we don't normally care to speak to your species in particular. We find you boring."

"B-Boring?" I sputtered. "Says the normally mute guy in a black robe that hides … well, everything." Were reapers hideous? Humanoid at all? Maybe they had three eyes or no nose? The possibilities of what could lurk under the dark folds of their signature look were nearly endless.

As if I hadn't said anything at all the reaper continued on. "But in you, I find the exception." He chuckled again. "I find you quite … amusing."

My right eye twitched. "Well, I hope you're going to find it amusing when I force you to take me back to Six again. And I'm going to keep going back until I save him." Somewhere between the moment I witnessed my best friend sacrifice himself for a human and the arrival of the reaper, I'd made up my mind. I would not accept anything less than what I wanted, and what I wanted was Six alive again, and back by my side. Damn reality itself.

"Force me? As if you could."

Ignoring him, I jumped up and dashed into the building after the mother and child. They were already out of sight by the time I made it to the security desk. One of the guards maneuvered himself in front of me to demand an ID badge or name of who I had an appointment with.

Japanese spilled from my lips in response, the luna ability to speak and understand all languages coming in handy as I attempted to talk my way past security. Instead of offering me admittance, the guard pushed a button on his wrist, essentially conjuring several other guards to stand in my way.

Frustration coursed through my muscles, tensing them. "You don't understand," I hissed out between clenched teeth. "I need to– There's a bomb!" Surprised at my own words, I waved my arms around to hit home the notion of impending danger. "In fact, there are several bombs about to go off! I need to warn—" Swallowing the rest of the sentence, I whirled around, running from the building.

What the hell am I doing? I can't save that mother and child, let alone warn the humans about the calamity about to befall them. I paused, staring over my shoulder at the stunned security guards.

Then again ...

Reversing course, I reentered the building, my indecisiveness on full display. "Did you not hear me? There are bombs! You have to evacuate people! You have to—"

The closest guard lunged forward, tackling me to the ground. My breath left me in a whoosh, pain shooting through my shoulders as my arms were wrenched behind my back.

"The police are on the way, and they'll deal with you."

I choked in oxygen, gasping out, "Please, I'm not crazy. There are bombs!"

The low rumble, and then thunderclap of an explosion punctuated my exclamation. The pressure on my back released, and I staggered to my feet unencumbered. Chaos erupted as several more blasts seemed to shake the very foundation of the building.

"Fuck," I muttered. Whatever I'd been trying to do was pointless now. The tagged humans, including the mother and child, would die, if they weren't dead already. With my head hanging low, I shuffled outside, making my way back to where I'd left the reaper.

"Sometimes humans don't want to be helped," he said. "And sometimes they want to revel in the horror they bring on themselves."

Flopping onto the ground, I leaned my head against the sculpture and squeezed my eyes shut. I didn't want to see it anymore. Any of it. I was tired—mind, body, and soul. The grief of losing Six had eaten away at some unknown piece of me. And that child … he lost his life before he even got a chance to have one. It was the same with Six; in comparison to me, he'd been so young, only a mere three decades he'd been by my side.

"And there he goes," the reaper murmured, "trying to save the day yet again."

My eyes snapped open, my gaze instantly finding and tracking the human—the human whose body contained the same soul from my last three jobs. He didn't have anything physical that made him stand out, even to me, but I knew him instantly. He possessed the same singular focus or vibe each time I encountered him.

The man wore a police uniform, his features etched in lines of determination as he disappeared into the building. *Well, at least this time his job requires him to help, and it's not completely on his own volition. Of course, he did choose the job.*

"Aren't you going to go after him?" the reaper asked, his tone blasé.

I shrugged. "What's the point? He's not tagged, at least not yet, and it's his job."

"And your job is to ensure this fixed point in time, despite your best efforts to destroy the plan laid out for the humans here today."

I rolled my eyes. "Didn't make a damn bit of difference, did I? Maybe I never do."

"Humans hold all the power. You and I are merely here to guide and—"

"Kill them if need be. But never save." I heaved out a long sigh. "How am I supposed to save Six if I can't even save one little human child and his mother?"

"Giving up then?"

Shaking my head, I growled, "No. Not giving up, but definitely feeling very pessimistic about how long it's going to take me to get Six back." I sighed again. "Good thing I'm practically immortal."

The reaper's head fell back, his laugh abruptly filling the air.

I flicked my hand at him. "Uh-oh, there I go amusing you again."

A surge of energy danced along my skin, goose bumps erupting in its wake. *It's time.*

My wings flared out behind me, and I threw my head back as I rose into the air. Hovering between worlds, the recently dead souls passed through me one after another in lightning fast succession. I recorded their essences, making sure all that should be was. I couldn't seem to resist, even though a part of me wanted to—a part of me didn't want to do any of it anymore.

As the numbers of dead added up, the warmth their souls offered seeped into my bones. Or at least I tried to absorb the warmth like normal, but nothing about me or this day was normal. The delight my body usually hummed with was absent, so therefore the rest didn't follow. There was no contentedness, or satiation, no feelings of belonging, just vast emptiness and numbness.

In fact, as I finished recording the dead, my attention swayed to the soul in the police officer's body. I knew how much brighter it burned than the rest, and since he hadn't died this day, I wanted … I wanted—

I don't know what I want. To understand maybe? As if the knowledge of what drew me to that soul would give me answers about what drew Six to Tina's soul?

Whatever the reason, I found myself searching for the police officer's essence. *Ah, there you are.* He was helping an injured man from the rubble of the building, his face covered in dirt and soot. I inched forward, my body yearning to be closer to his.

I will find out what makes you so special, and I will find out why things have changed. For Six … and for me.

Chapter 10

The reaper peered into the large window, glancing at me, and then back into the window. "You might as well have your face pressed to the glass with how close you are."

Crouched near a large tree, I scrunched my nose at my unwanted companion. The reaper had tagged along on my … errand, completely uninvited. As if that wasn't bad enough, his constant commentary, most of it critical, was not helping the situation.

I glowered. "I never thought I'd say this to a reaper, but would you please shut the hell up? I can't think straight with all the yammering you've been doing. And I'm nowhere close to having my face pressed against the glass. I'm way over here."

"And what exactly is the rogue luna attempting to ponder that I need to be quiet for?"

"I'm trying to figure out what makes that human's soul so much brighter than the rest."

"And stalking him is going to fill in the blanks? Got it." He hummed with mirth.

Biting my tongue, I forced myself not to respond to any more of his baits. Instead, I shifted to avoid my legs from falling asleep and focused on remaining patient. The police officer had gone into a room not visible from my standpoint, so I had to wait until he came back into view or left his house.

The reaper paced back and forth in front of the window, setting my nerves on edge. "What do you hope to gain from this?"

"You already answered that question for me. I'm going to fill in the blanks."

He grunted, his hood falling forward as he continued to pace.

Wonder what that poor man would think if he knew a reaper and a luna were stalking him? A semi-hysterical giggle erupted as I continued to think about the ludicrous situation I currently found myself in. *Here I am, a nocturnal creature, one who thrives in darkness, and yet I desire nothing but the light. It's all I've ever wanted—needed.* And I wasn't referring to light in the literal sense, but light that shines on lives filled with happiness and love. Lives that had meaningful connections. *I can never have those things, not the way I want.*

No, that's not entirely true. Six and I had a meaningful relationship. He was a true brother, and not a distant sibling like the others of my kind. He was a friend—my best friend—who I shared everything with. We knew each other with an intimacy that went beyond romantic love. When you survive suffering with someone, the bond is … special. Unbreakable. *Which is why I know I have to save him. I'll never give up. Never.*

"Why do you think that figuring out what makes this particular soul special will help you with your Six dilemma?" The reaper's hooded face was scant inches from mine.

Startled, I swallowed a yelp. His close proximity was unnerving. "Because, it's all connected somehow, I can feel it."

This soul showing up at jobs around the same time Six had found Tina was no coincidence. It wasn't often lunas came upon the brighter humans, and somehow both of us had found one who drew our attention. I shook my head. *No, definitely not a coincidence.*

Or maybe I was wrong, my thoughts and judgment as cracked as my sanity probably was. Even so, I'd gotten lucky. I'd been handed a tool to help me, and I wasn't going to stare a gift horse in the mouth. Studying Tina would have been the obvious option, but somehow it wasn't the right choice. My gut was telling me the answers lay with this soul.

"Besides, you're the one who told me to wake up and look for answers. Since you're so chatty lately, how about you put all your cards on the table? In so many ways you steered me onto this path."

He shook his head. “Some things you have to figure out on your own.”

I threw my hands up in the air. “Then why are you even here? Your presence is absolutely pointless.”

“Probably. But yours isn’t since I find your antics so amusing.”

Clenching my jaw so tight it ached, I turned my attention back to the interior of the house. Nothing had changed. The police officer was still where I couldn’t see him.

Ugh. Being alone with my thoughts ... and the reaper is not my idea of a good time.

Speaking of the reaper ... I couldn’t figure out what his deal was. He couldn’t be following me around just because he found me amusing ... Could he? Was he mind fucking me for the hell of it? Was he bored with his immortal life, and looking for a distraction, one he’d conveniently found in me? If that was the case that would mean he’d throw up roadblocks to get in my way whenever he could to prolong his entertainment. Was he actually my enemy and not an ally after all?

“His car started. The soul you’re stalking—very badly—is about to give you the slip.”

My head whipped up. “What? How did he get past me?” I’d been able to see the front door from my hiding spot, and I hadn’t gotten a single glimpse of him on his way to the car.

The police vehicle backed down the small driveway

and pulled onto the street, it's lights coming to life a moment later. And just like that, he sped away.

"What the fuck?" I glared at the reaper. "Can't you follow him for me or something, tell me where he is?"

He shrugged. "I could, but I'm not going to. I want to see what you're going to do next."

Growling under my breath, I flopped down on the grass. "You want to know what I'm going to do next? Something super exciting. I'm going to wait some more."

"WHAT ARE YOU DOING?" *I peeked out from under my pile of blankets to watch Six move lazily around my room. He'd only come to the eclipse a short time ago, but quite surprisingly we instantly clicked. I never instantly clicked with anyone before.*

He grinned, his brown eyes twinkling. "Just snooping around. You know, trying to get to know you better."

The corners of my lips twisted up slightly. No one had ever gotten to know me better, and I never thought it was something I would want.

"Not much to learn," I mumbled.

"Ha!" Six exclaimed. "What are these?"

Slitting my eyes open again, I watched as Six poked at my stack of romance novels.

"Books. I'm pretty sure they're called books."

He stabbed the cover of the one on top with his index finger, laughing. "But what kind of books have a shirtless guy rippling with muscles and a—"

"There's nothing wrong with romance novels," I snapped, rolling over to face the other direction.

"Oooh, romance novels." He clapped his hands together. I rolled back over, curious about his reaction. He picked one up, and flipped to the back cover, scanning the blurb. "Is there a lot of sex in these?"

I giggled. "You sound like a human male!"

"Maybe we're not all that different from them."

"Don't be ridiculous. Now stop nosing around my room and let me rest."

My bed jostled, the weight of Six settling in beside me. "I might do some light reading while you're sleeping. You know, to figure out what this whole romance thing is about." He was quiet for a moment before saying, "Time travel romance, huh? Completely unrealistic, I think, but we'll see."

Jolting up, I swiped at the drool at the corner of my mouth. From the beginning of our friendship until practically the last day he'd been alive, Six had teased me about my addiction to romance novels. *Is it irony that he's the one who threw his life away for romantic love?*

Blinking bleary eyes, I glanced over at the reaper who was still pacing.

"Guess he hasn't come back yet?"

"No."

"Do reapers sleep at all?"

"There's no need."

"That doesn't answer my question though. Do reapers sleep or not? It doesn't matter if they need to … do they or don't they? Lunas don't need food, but we enjoy eating it when we get the chance."

I could practically feel his eyes roll within his hood. "Reapers sleep."

I shifted, letting my head fall back to lean against the tree once more. "Do they dream?" Night had fallen, and yet the stars and moon weren't visible from behind the clouds.

"This one does." His voice had gone low, barely audible, but I managed to hear the wistfulness behind his reply.

Huh. I wonder what he dreams about? Like he'd tell me though. "So, reapers have secret lives beyond what we lunas get to see?"

"Doesn't everyone?" he scoffed.

"Touché."

Silence fell over us once more, the gentle breeze swirling my hair around my face. I yearned to talk to Six about all of this. I knew he'd get a kick out of my sudden companion of a reaper.

Six. In my mind's eye, I saw his smiling face juxtaposed over his expression the moment before he faded into nothing. My heart twisted, a dull ache blooming in my chest. *There's so much I want to talk to you about. So much I need to understand. Why didn't you tell me about Tina? Why didn't you tell me about any of it? What else were you hiding? I thought we knew everything about each other.*

Apparently, the reaper was right, everyone had secrets,

even from those closest to us. Some just happened to be bigger than others.

A light flicked on in the police officer's house. Launching myself to my feet, I crept carefully closer to the big window, the cover of darkness making it easier to spy now.

The man was about five foot eight or five foot nine, late twenties to early thirties, and lithely muscular. He seemed to live alone, no evidence of any other person coming or going since the reaper and I had taken up temporary residence outside of the house.

"Why doesn't he have a family?" I muttered to myself, not expecting the reaper to respond.

Weirdly enough, he did. "Who is to say he doesn't? A family can be more than a spouse and children. Wasn't Six your family?"

I waited for the wave of grief to crash over me at the mention of his name, but it never came. *Huh.* It was then I came to the realization that it was because I'd stopped mourning Six. I, of course, still missed him, but I'd come to believe that getting him back was a definite thing, like a fixed point in time of my own making. *No sense in mourning someone who isn't permanently gone. Unless this is the denial part of things again. No. I am going to get Six back. Beginning and end of story.*

"Okay, well, he doesn't seem to live with family, blood or otherwise."

Attention riveted, I watched as the man sank down into the cushions of his couch, a steaming hot bowl of food in front of him on a small table. He bowed his head as he ate, his expression haggard.

I frowned. "He seems sad. Why would such a bright soul, one that feels such warmth from its existence alone, feel sad?"

The reaper pressed in closer, studying the same scene I was. "Just because lunas think the warmth of humanity alone would equal happiness, does not mean the same to humans. What you covet is something they take for granted."

"But he isn't a regular human. There's something special about him."

"Then what is it? What makes him special?"

"I don't know," I hissed, "that's what I'm trying to figure out."

The reaper's hood trembled as he exhaled loudly. "Why don't you forget about all of this and move on?"

My face twisted with astonishment, and my mouth fell open. "What? After everything you've done to put me on this path, you're now suggesting I abandon it? What? Get bored that quickly?"

"I'm beginning to think you aren't as interesting as I first thought, and that you're merely overly dramatic." He clicked his tongue. "Dramatics always get boring fast."

"Dramatic? You think I'm being overly dramatic? My best friend burnt up before my very eyes. Oh, and also he may have risked reality itself in the process." Although the jury was still out on that one.

"Everything dies eventually," the reaper stated. "It

never gets any easier for those left behind no matter the circumstances."

"Whatever, Death. If I'm dramatic, then you're a walking embodiment of depression."

"That does not make any sense. I'm not depressed, nor do I bring depression to others."

I tilted my head, the sudden urge to ask about a million questions washing over me. Even though the reaper was talking readily to me now, he remained an enigma. How long had he been a reaper? I guessed a very long time since his word choices were about as jumbled as mine. One minute he sounded modern, and the next he couldn't even be bothered to use a contraction. It was one of many signs of an ancient creature living in a modern world. Old habits die hard, so to speak.

I gnawed at the inside of my cheek. *It doesn't matter. You have better things to worry about other than the age of your own personal stalker.*

"Yeah, well—" I'd lost track of what we were talking about, my inner musings having sidetracked me. "Shhh … I'm trying to spy on the bright yet sad soul in there." I waved demonstratively at the window in front of me … and froze.

Staring at us from the other side of the glass was none other than my target.

His gaze locked with mine, eyes widening. "I know you. I dreamt … I dreamt of you." He tapped the glass right in front of my nose. "Don't go anywhere." He dashed for his front door, quickly shoving his feet into shoes before exiting.

My mind struggled to keep up. "How did he ... he saw us."

The reaper rose into the air, his robes billowing around him. "No, not us. You. I've been invisible this entire time."

"Whaaat?"

I'd completely forgotten that reapers couldn't be seen by humans unless they wanted to be visible. Obviously, this reaper wanted to remain incognito. I slapped a palm against my forehead. How the hell could I have forgotten? Of course, I knew the answer. I'd become so jaded to things that I stopped paying attention to the world around me a long time ago. How often did I do a job with only a mild sense of the year I was in? Being spotted by the human I was watching was merely another symptom of my carelessness.

Shit, shit, shit, shit, shit. What do I do now? I spun in a circle, considering and abandoning option after option. My wings itched at my back, and I wiggled my shoulders, the urge to take flight almost undeniable.

"Don't do it," the reaper said. "Right now you're merely a human outside of his window, who if seen running away is strange, but not—"

"Yeah, supernatural, I know." I gritted my teeth. "Although I don't think he had the forethought to grab his phone. If he doesn't get me on video it didn't happen."

"You don't know what kind of technology this future

time has. For all you know the phone is connected to his brain. He could ocularly record you."

"Don't be ridiculous," I growled. "Ocular recording? To what the brain? How would he—"

The police officer rounded the side of his house, halting a few feet from me. We both stood there, frozen in place, and staring at each other. The muscles in my shoulders spasmed, my wings seeking release from their flesh prison.

"Who are you, and why are you watching me?" the police officer demanded, breaking our silent standoff.

"How about you just make me invisible, too," I hissed out of the corner of my mouth at the reaper.

"Too late for that," the reaper murmured. "Not that I would, regardless. This situation promises to be entertaining."

My right eye twitched again. I opened and shut my mouth several times, my gaze darting warily around. *Run! Just Run! Nothing supernatural about that.* The option to will myself home was always there, but I was afraid if I left this time and place that I wouldn't be able to find this soul alive again. It did have a way of turning itself into a tagged human more often than not.

"Please," the tension in the police officer's expression eased, "I've had dreams about you all my life, and now here you are—watching me. Who are you?" He paused, the *what* are you hanging unspoken between us.

"It's a coincidence. I have one of those faces that looks like a lot of other faces …" My excuse trailed off into nothing as his eyebrows rose. "What did you dream?" I'd turn the tables, get him answering questions, so maybe I could get what I came for after all.

He narrowed his eyes and took a few steps closer. "I saw you, in different times, wearing different clothes, but there was always a disaster—fires, or accidents ... terrified people. But not you. You were calm—there just watching as if you knew it would happen."

I lifted my palms up and shrugged. "I have no idea why you'd dream about me. I don't—"

"Are you a ghost or a spirit of some sort? A deity or demon of some kind?"

The reaper laughed, his body lifting up higher as if his delightedness gave him extra buoyancy. I resisted the urge to acknowledge him, keeping my focus on the police officer.

Staring into the man's deep brown eyes, I forced a placating smile. "What's your name, Officer?"

He shuffled closer, gaze riveted by mine. "Youta," he said in English. "My name is Youta."

I nibbled my bottom lip. "Why did you switch to English. I speak fluent Japanese, which was proven by the fact that we've been speaking it until just now."

He smirked. "You are not Japanese, and I wanted to make you more comfortable."

I hesitated. I didn't want to give away more than I already had. Lunas were designed to blend in wherever we went. Because everything about us was neutral, we didn't stand out as any one race, but a mix of all. It could be said simply looking at me that I wasn't one hundred percent Japanese, but also by appearance alone, one shouldn't be able to tell that I wasn't at least part Japanese and not a local of some sort. Youta's switch to English was also not because my Japanese was anything less than perfect.

I quirked an eyebrow and crossed my arms over my chest. "You're guessing … or fishing for information. You didn't know I could speak English, but you wanted to see if I could." And damn if I hadn't walked right into that one. "I am fluent in many languages," I said, quickly switching to French.

"As am I," Youta fired back in near-perfect French.

I smirked. *I can do this all day.* "Do you speak Spanish, too?"

"A bit," he replied with an answering smirk.

Just who is this guy, some kind of secret agent? For me to know so many languages was nothing, but for him to know them meant he actually had to learn them, not simply have the knowledge placed in his head.

I switched back to Japanese. "Tell me why you think it's me you dreamt about."

Youta's lips pressed together, and the muscles in his jaw ticked. "It was you. I know it was you. Now tell me why you were peering into my window, having some kind of conversation with an invisible person."

"Wh-What?" I stammered. "I wasn't talking to anyone else. Just, you know, having a conversation with myself.

As one does when trying to talk themselves out of doing something stupid."

"Good try," the reaper murmured into my ear, causing me to stiffen. "But it seems as if this human is entirely too observant of even things he can't see with his eyes."

This whole situation is absolutely ridiculous. I lost control of my objective, and any hope of a plan the moment Youta spotted me. Yep, I have absolutely no chance of getting any kind of answers this way.

"Welp, gotta go!" I gave an idiotic half wave before pivoting on my heel to sprint as fast as I could in the opposite direction.

"Wait!" Youta yelled. "You can't go yet! Wait!"

A dense patch of trees loomed just a few feet in front of me, which I would use as cover to disappear in. I could hear Youta's footfalls pounding the ground behind me, but he wouldn't be catching me with my supernatural speed, even with it toned down a bit.

Surrounded by trees and the night, I squeezed my eyes shut. *Home. Home. Take me the hell home. Now.*

Chapter 11

Having caught the reaper's pacing disease, I shuffled back and forth across my room, nibbling on my thumbnail, my mind lost in thought.

How had Youta seen me at his window? I wasn't a human spying on him, and therefore I shouldn't have had to be any more careful than I am at one of my jobs. And yet, he'd spotted me easily.

How the hell did he notice me? I'm a luna, no one ever notices me. Even if some part of his brain registered my presence it should have moved on without a second thought, like when hearing innocuous background noise. Lunas didn't trigger any base human reactions such as fear or curiosity, at least not normally.

I threw my hands up in the air, muttering to myself, "Whatever makes his soul different must make him be able to notice lunas, too. So what is it? What makes him so special?"

As if on cue, the reaper—my reaper—or just Reaper, as I'd dubbed him in my head, appeared directly in my path. Stumbling back, a yelp escaped from me, and I clutched my chest. "Don't do that," I hissed.

Reaper inclined his head, his robes billowing around him. "Somewhat jumpy today, aren't you?" It wasn't really a question, but an observation.

Biting at my thumbnail again, I nodded rapidly. "Yeah. Yeah, I'm a bit out of sorts, jittery, I guess. But in my defense, I'm trying to figure out what the hell happened back there with Youta."

Reaper settled on the edge of my bed. "I will tell you what happened—you panicked and didn't handle the situation well at all."

I opened my mouth to fire a snappy comeback, but unfortunately even I had to admit he was right. "I didn't expect him to see us … or me since you were invisible the whole time." I gave him the stink eye before resuming my pacing.

He crossed his legs at the ankles, and leaned back, his robes rippling around him. *I swear, those things have a mind of their own. And who knows, maybe they do.* "What are you going to do now?" he asked, all casual disinterest on the outside, but I knew, just knew it was an act. After all, why else would he be back to pester me so soon if he was bored already?

I grimaced. "Not sure. That's what I'm trying to figure

out now. I've made a mess of things." Working outside of my comfort zone had proved to be fruitless so far, but I was going to have to get comfortable and fast if I wanted to save Six anytime soon.

"What do you think I should do next?"

Reaper leaned forward, his elbows on his knees. "You're actually asking my opinion? I have to admit, I'm quite surprised."

"Yeah, me too," I grumbled. The truth was, I didn't have anyone else to bounce ideas off of at the moment. Was Reaper a friend? No. But he was all I had, and if I wanted to accomplish my lofty goal then I was going to have to use any and all tools at my disposal … even a reaper who had yet to prove any kind of trustworthiness.

Pausing under the skylight, I let the warm glow from the moon filter over my skin. Closing my eyes, I tilted my head back. "Maybe I should fly for a bit to clear my head. After all, I am a creature of the night."

Reaper laughed, the deep rumble long and loud. "You remind me of that meme—the one with the tiny black kitten—and the kitten thinks he or she is darkness incarnate, but it clearly isn't." More laughter rolled out from under his hood. "This is what I was talking about with the luna dramatics. You're not any more a creature of the night than the kitten in the meme."

Scowling, I crossed my arms over my chest. "Um, yes I am. I—"

"Lunas are nocturnal if given the choice. That doesn't make you some, I don't know, Dracula type creature. All it means is that you prefer to sleep during the day and to be active at night. It has no dark and sinister meaning."

I narrowed my eyes at him. "Wait. You know about Dracula … and memes?"

"You find that surprising?"

"Well, yes, you're a reaper for crying out loud."

"And you're a luna, a creature of the night," he choked back another laugh, "but you know what a meme is."

"But … but you're a reaper." I couldn't seem to wrap my brain around how normal reapers were, at least this particular one.

"What do you suppose we do when not helping to guide souls on to the next life? Do you think we have no downtime, and that lunas are the only ones who entertain themselves with trivial things if we so choose?"

I blinked rapidly, still trying to process the weird turn of our conversation. "No? I mean, no. I guess not. It would make sense that you weren't—"

"Robots of death?"

It was my turn to choke back a laugh. "Robots of death? That … well, that's one way to put it."

Reaper leaned back on his elbows to recline across my bed. "Now that we have that cleared up, back to what I was saying. You are simply a luna. Nocturnal, yes, but a creature of the night, no."

I pursed my lips. "By definition alone, all nocturnal beings are creatures of the night."

"Creature of the night has taken on a different meaning over the years. Technically it still means the same thing, but language changes." He raised his hand, to stave off my response. "And I already know what you're going to say, you're old, you mean it the way it was originally defined, but that's not true as evidenced by how you say creature of the night with such a brooding tone."

I glowered. "Do reapers have a second job as lawyers? Or do you just like to argue?"

"That wasn't an argument of any kind, nor was it worthy of being compared to a lawyer's—"

"Yeah, okay, you like to argue." I quirked an eyebrow in challenge.

Reaper sighed. "Banter, maybe, not argue. Didn't hear you putting up much of a rebuttal."

"Whatever." Stretching my wings out, I once again closed my eyes, and tilted my head back. "I have more important things to worry about than whether or not you feel I'm dramatic."

Reaper didn't respond. Slitting one eye open, I peered at him through my lashes. His robe-clad arm was outstretched toward my nightstand, just the tips of his fingers brushing one of my romance novels.

"Hey!" I lurched toward him, slapping at his arm. "Don't touch my stuff!"

"I was curious to know what the creature of the night reads in her spare time." His tone was mocking, making me want to punch him.

Shoving at him, I loomed over his massive figure. "If you nose into my stuff again without permission, I will show you how much of a creature of the night I can be."

"Oh, I'm trembling with fear." Snatching a novel, he held it level with the open part of his hood, the barest hint of his jaw visible. "Ah, just as I suspected."

Sagging with defeat, I replied on a squeaky exhale, "What?"

"You don't merely yearn for the physical warmth lunas are denied, but for the emotional fulfillment of love you can never experience."

"I can love."

He tapped the cover of my book. "Not like this. Even if you were capable, what would happen if you fell in love with a human? You're immortal, humans age and die."

My attention reverted back to the situation with Six and Tina. "And Six threw away his eternal life to save a fleeting human one. What was he thinking?"

"I suspect he wasn't thinking at all."

"You certainly suspect a lot of things, but what do you actually know?"

"More than you."

Biting my tongue, I resisted demanding answers from him yet again. *No point in wasting my breath.* Since I didn't know what my next step should be, I supposed I would head back to Archives to track down another event Six recorded. I'd keep trying until I got it right.

Ignoring me, Reaper flipped through my novel, pausing overly long on certain pages.

Annoyance nettled me, my cheeks heating. "Can you please put that down? I didn't give you permission to borrow it."

"I'm not borrowing it, I'm perusing it."

I growled under my breath, "You are the most difficult creature I've ever come across. I'm pretty sure your appearance in my life is some kind of cosmic punishment."

He continued to scan the contents of the book, and I decided I was over it.

Whirling around, I made a big production out of leaving, making sure to stomp my feet and slam the door behind me. Hopefully, he wasn't too involved to notice I was gone so he would join me in Archives. I wasn't entirely sure, but I thought that he was an important part of the traveling process. *Unless he'd hitched a ride with me into the past, and not the other way around.* Quite possibly, Reaper was playing me for a fool. *Probably, not possibly. Shit.* But I couldn't exactly boot a reaper from somewhere it wanted to be.

Two, and Forty sidled past me in the hallway, two sets of brown eyes meeting mine solemnly for an instant before darting away. "Hi, to you, too," I muttered.

How was Reaper more friendly to me than my own kind? Could he have a point about reapers not wanting to chat up lunas because they were boring? Was that the real reason I'd only ever bonded with Six? So why were we different than the rest? Why—

It doesn't matter. Not really. Things are the way that they are, and the thing I have to figure out is how to get Six back. That's it. Nothing else. At least until I accomplish his rescue. Then and only then can I attempt to figure out the rest.

Shoving at the heavy wooden door, I strode into Archives with my head held high like I was supposed to be there. Because I was as far as I was concerned.

Silence encased me, the peace stifling instead of the calm I normally felt. I chose to ignore the tension pumping through my veins, focusing on what had gotten me results from Archives the previous time I visited.

Squeezing my eyes shut, I imagined Six's face and the way his brown eyes crinkled at the corners when he smiled. I spun in a circle, my arms stretched out searching … searching, searching.

Warmth, subtle and comforting, washed over me, and then …

Just like before … a tug, the smallest of pulls fluttered in my sternum, causing me to stumble forward, hands outstretched. My fingers curled around the supple leather spine of a book, and I lifted it to my nose, inhaling deeply.

Six, it smells like Six. Like home. I almost forgot. Or I was starting to forget.

My eyes still tightly squeezed shut, I opened the book, placing my palms on the smooth pages.

Take me here. Take me to this time and place—to Six. Take me to him again.

A feather-light touch danced across my cheek, and my eyes sprung open to take in Reaper before me, his robes swaying around him. He took my hand, squeezing it roughly, and my world fell away into oblivion.

Chapter 12

Thunder rumbled, and flashes of lightning illuminated the dark sky. Icy rain pummeled my face, plastering my hair into my eyes, making it difficult to see. As I trudged forward, using my wings for balance, knee-high water tugged at my legs, threatening to sweep them out from under me.

"Where are we?" I yelled over the roar of nature, my teeth chattering.

Reaper, seemingly untouched by the elements, glided forward without even a sidelong glance in my direction. I had little choice but to follow.

A row of beach houses, all of them dark except one, seemed to be our destination. *Why is Reaper leading me here? Is he helping or not? And where the hell is Six?*

Once we reached the house at the end of the row—a small, blue one, with pieces of aluminum siding missing—Reaper bent toward a small window, drawing my curiosity. Rising on to my tiptoes, I followed his gaze, noticing a couple on the couch wrapped in each other's arms.

Surprise zinged through my system, setting my heartbeat off at a gallop. *Six.* The male half of the couple was Six. *What the hell is he doing?* Glancing at Reaper, I attempted to speak to him again. "I thought we were going to another disaster. Specifically, the one recorded in the book I had. I specifically—"

Reaper's index finger pressed against my lips firmly, and he shook his head. *Okay. Guess he can't hear me or doesn't want to.* Returning my attention to Six, it was only then that I noticed the girl he was with was none other than Tina. *Of course it is.* And yet, I couldn't help the shock that vibrated through my system. *How is he here with her? And why? Okay, I'm pretty sure I know the why … so, again with how? Or maybe what I should actually be asking is—*

Reaper yanked my head back, pain shooting through my scalp. "Ow!" I grabbed at his hand, flailing.

He tapped at the windowpane, and then made a circular motion with his hand.

"Okay! What? What are you trying to say, you asshole?"

It was then I saw it. Directly behind Six and Tina was an oblong … thing just hovering there. Or maybe I should say it was a circular absence of—

Fuck. I slapped a hand over my mouth.

Grabbing the edge of Reaper's hood, I yanked him down so I could yell into where I thought his ear should be. "Please tell me that's not a hole in reality." He didn't respond. "When was this? Why hasn't Six noticed?" He still didn't respond. Slamming my fist against the window, I screamed, "Why won't you tell me anything if you know what's happening?"

Emotions warred within me. Recently, I began questioning reality itself, and the very purpose of it. I came to the conclusion that even as a luna I had no clue what reality actually was. So, if I didn't know, then why was I to be bothered if it fell apart? And yet—standing there, witnessing firsthand a sign of reality dissolving—my heart threatened to break free of my ribcage. *I can't let this happen. I was bullshitting myself to think that I could.*

Marching over to the door, I kicked it repeatedly with my booted foot. It swung open a moment later, Six's startled expression meeting my determined one.

"Eighty-nine, what ... how—"

Despite everything, I launched myself at him, throwing my arms around his middle, trapping him in a too-tight bear hug.

I fucking missed you, you idiot.

Even though he was there in my arms, alive, I knew that he would burn up in our shared future. In that moment, he was a twisted version of Schrödinger's cat, existing in two states simultaneously, me not knowing which one would win in the end. *No. I do know. I will save him. He will live despite his stupidity.*

"Simon? Who the hell is that?" Tina's voice snapped out from behind him, jealousy coiling within it.

Disentangling himself from me, Six turned toward her. "Tina, this is Eight– Emma, my best friend. I told you about her, remember?"

Emma, not Eighty-nine, okay. He hasn't revealed his true self as a luna to her ... yet. Which means ... fuck if I know what anything means anymore.

A sudden grin stretched across her face. "Oh! Emma! I'm so excited we finally get to meet! You came because you're worried about us being here during the storm, right?"

Shifting my weight from foot to foot, I shimmied back and forth. "Oh … um, yeah. I need to get you both out of here pronto." I snagged Six's gaze, narrowing my eyes with meaning. "It's not safe here."

"We'll be fine, Emma. You didn't need to come all the way out here," Six said, taking Tina's hand within his. "We'll be totally fine."

I raised my eyebrows, repeating, "It's not safe here." Glancing at the tear in reality, I swallowed around the massive lump in my throat. *Or possibly anywhere.*

A wave of nausea roiled my stomach, and the room spun. I staggered, clutching at the nearest wall.

"Emma, what's wrong?" Six's voice echoed, sounding far away.

Bile erupted up my esophagus, burning my throat. "I don't know." Dropping to my knees, I managed to turn my head toward the reality tear, the oblong shape rippling with colors. Raising a shaky hand, I pointed at it. "Don't you see it?"

"See what?" Six whispered near my ear. "What are you talking about?"

"The tear in reality." I waved my hand in its general direction, my body curling in on itself in pain. "It's right there."

"I don't see anything. Talk to me, Eig– Emma. What's going on?"

"Did she take something?" Tina demanded. "Is she on drugs?"

"No. She would never." Six's hand smoothed down my back, the motion meant to be comforting, but it only served to agitate me more.

"We have to get out of here now!" Bright light exploded from the tear, blinding me. "Six, please!"

Silence fell, followed by a ringing in my ears. I swiped at my eyes, colors slowly bleeding back into existence.

Screams saturated the air, stealing my attention. I swung my head around, taking in chaos, buildings burning all around me. Confusion kept me rooted in place, my breath stuck in my throat.

And then my gaze zeroed in on him ... *Six.*

Lurking in the shadows, where lunas preferred to stay, my friend watched the disaster unfold before him, his expression much like I imagined mine was at every one of my jobs—twisted between anguish and anticipation. I'd never witnessed another luna at work, and seeing Six before me, I realized we were every bit the outsiders I'd come to think of us as.

How does no one ever notice us when we're so out of place? It should be clear to any and all who glance in our direction that we don't belong in the human realm.

His eyes sparked red as he moved a few paces closer to the building directly in front of him. I moved in tandem, shrinking the distance between us.

Wait. I've done this before. This exact thing, even down to my thoughts. But my mind was fuzzy, filled with something akin to cotton candy.

A hand clamped down onto my shoulder, pinching painfully. "Be careful what you do next, for you are complicating things more than you can possibly fathom as is." The reaper stared down at me, his gaze burning from the depths of his hood.

"Why did you bring me here? Why are you helping me?" *No. You already said that before. Say something else. Do something else.*

He tilted his head, a low chuckle rumbling in his chest. "Am I helping you? Are you so sure of that?"

He was right. I had no idea if he was actually helping me or not. In fact, being that his kind usually never got involved in anything beyond escorting souls to the next realm, I was guessing he had an ulterior motive, one that had absolutely nothing to do with me, or my end game.

Stop! A memory ricocheted around in my skull, bouncing just beyond my grasp. *A beach, a storm, Six and ... someone else.* But my body refused to stop, or even pause. It was as if there were two of me crammed into my head, and the other one had complete control. I was just along for the ride, the feelings of déjà-vu and disconnect from myself overwhelming. Yet, there seemed to be nothing I could do about it.

I crossed my arms over my chest. "Different question then. Do your end goals align with mine?"

"Quite possibly. Hard to tell at this point."

"Whatever. I don't have time for your cryptic bullshit right now." Pivoting back in the direction of Six, I sprinted toward him.

"Six! Six, I have to talk to you!" I had no idea when or where we were, or how long ago in his timeline Six had done this particular job, but I knew I had to take him with me. I had to save him from whatever had stolen him from me.

You know. You already know what stole him from you. Remember—just remember so you can do it differently this time! But the more I grasped, pushing for what was just beyond my reach, the more I slid into my other-self. Soon, I would be completely lost—lost in someone who was me, but a different me. Someone who didn't know as much as I did, even though they were technically still me.

Six froze, every muscle in his body tensing, and just when I thought he was going to turn around, demanding how and why I was there, he ran across the street, and straight into the burning building.

What the fuck? How the hell didn't he hear me? It might be utter chaos around here, but I was just yelling his name less than two feet from him.

Dashing into the building after Six, the thick smoke ripped at my throat and welled up my eyes. I caught a flash of movement off to my left, and staggered that way, pulling my shirt up to cover my nose and mouth. Inhaling the smoke wouldn't kill one such as me, but it certainly could make things uncomfortable.

"Tina! Tina, where are you?" Six's familiar voice was strung tight with anxiety bordering on panic. "Tina! Please, answer me!"

I froze, fear spiking through my veins, and my heart thrashing painfully against my ribcage. *Why is Six searching for someone in here? It couldn't possibly mean what I think it does.*

A moment later, Six pushed past me with a girl his arms, completely oblivious to my presence. I trailed after them, my stomach twisting into knots. The girl was tagged, the bright orange aura of those marked for death visible even through the dense smoke.

No. He can't. It can't be what it looks like.

"Shh … Tina, I've got you. You're going to be fine." Six planted a tender kiss on her forehead before depositing her gently on the sidewalk.

Tina—the girl from the diner that Six had been so fixated on—squinted up at him, her bright green eyes brimming with tears. "Simon, I was so scared. How did you know? How did you get here?"

"It's going to be just fine, my tiny Tina." Six smiled, but the emotion didn't reach his eyes.

She doubled over as a coughing fit wracked her body, her lungs gasping for enough air to keep her breathing. Shuffling forward, I studied her, realizing that despite

Six's efforts she would die without immediate medical attention. Not only had she inhaled too much smoke, but her shirt and hair were saturated in crimson, evidence of her severe injuries.

Tina will die this day as she's supposed to.

Six palmed Tina's face between his hands just as her eyes slid shut. Her chest rattled out one last shaky breath before remaining still.

Dodging behind a car, I peered at Six over the hood, not wanting to interfere until he was ready for me to comfort him. I smiled to myself. *This is what happened. It has to be. He burned up from grief because I wasn't there in time to help him, but I am now. I can save him ... and change everything. It's all easier than I thought it would turn out to be.*

Six's wings flared out behind him, and his feet rose off the ground as he disappeared from sight. He was recording the calamity and the souls who died because of the disaster, invisible even to me until he was done.

My gaze dropped to Tina's body as I waited. Blood haloed her small form, the macabre scene oddly mesmerizing. When had Six met her, and why hadn't he given me any kind of clue about her? Sure, we both had occasional dalliances with humans, but it was clear that Tina was more to him than sex. There had been a moment when I'd actually thought Six was going to risk reality itself for her.

Six has a lot of explaining to do when we get home. But I couldn't even manage an ounce of anger with the jubilation rising up within me. I'd come so close to losing my best friend forever ... so close.

Six reappeared in front of me, dropping down to his knees beside Tina. A high-pitched keening sound filled the air, his glowing eyes casting shadows across her motionless features. He yanked her body into his chest, cradling her while swaying back and forth. A few minutes later he stilled, and then gently laid Tina back on the ground. His fingers danced along her hairline, smoothing a few wisps away from her forehead. Rocking back on his heels, he sucked in a sharp breath.

Move, move, move, this is the time. I have to talk to him now. Comfort him. Stop him from burning up. Stop hovering behind him like an idiot and save your best friend before it's too late ... again.

With lightning speed, Six exposed his wings and arched them forward. He bared his teeth in a grimace, ripping the delicate forms from his back. Blood spurted from the gaping holes in his flesh, his torn shirt billowing like a cape.

My mouth fell open, a scream bubbling up from my throat.

Six's head whipped around, our gazes clashing, his filled with determination, and mine with horror.

Golden energy blobs streaked out from Six's wings where they lay discarded on the ground. His attention shifted as he deftly plucked a blob out of the air, shoving it into Tina's chest before it raced away.

Tina jolted up, sputtering, her wounds fully healed.

My vision wavered. *What have you done?*

In a burst of flame, Six and his wings were gone.

Just like that, there one instant, gone the next.

"Simon?" Tina's hands passed through the empty space where Six had been. With a whimper, she fainted dead away.

Reeling back, I attempted to wrap my brain around what I'd just witnessed. Six sacrificed his life to bring back Tina, and in the process, not only broke the rules, but released the other fixed-point souls before a reaper could collect them. I wasn't sure what would happen to those souls, but I did know that Tina was alive when she wasn't supposed to be. That was a threat to reality itself.

My instincts as a luna drove me forward, my intent to put to rights the fixed point in time.

I halted mid-stride, several humans rushing to Tina as if conjured from nowhere. A flurry of questions ensued, all directed at her:

"Are you all right?"

"How did you get out of the building?"

"Was anyone else with you inside?"

"Did anyone else make it out with you?"

A paramedic with an oxygen tank and mask scurried to her side. "Here, ma'am, put this on while I check your vitals."

Backing away, realization settled in. Despite my and Six's paranormal display of otherness, no one had noticed us. Not one single person. It was how lunas were designed, but until that moment I'd nearly forgotten.

Wind tore at me, lifting me off my feet. My wings shot out, flapping uselessly as I tried to move forward, or at the very least not get blown away like a moth in a tornado. Screaming with frustration, I made mad grabs for anything to hold onto as I sailed through the air. My fingertips slipped from everything, the world blurring around me as I moved faster and faster.

Strong arms wrapped around my middle, not halting me in place, but anchoring me to a muscular body. Black robes whipped against my skin, the material abrasive. "I won't let go," Reaper bellowed into my ear, causing me to grimace.

"What's happening?" My legs and arms flailed helplessly, my wings flattened to my back by Reaper.

"I won't let go," Reaper bellowed again.

A strange kind of peace wound its way through my system. *No matter what's happening or where I end up, he won't let go. Reaper may not be a friend, but at least I won't be alone.* Sadly, for one such as me, presently having no one else in the world, that was enough.

Chapter 13

Groaning, I sucked in a burning lungful of air. I pushed up onto my hands and knees, squinting into blinding sunlight. Sweat trickled down my spine, my shirt sticking to my skin along my back.

Reaper reached under my arms, lifting me to my feet. "Are you okay? Or are you going to be sick again?"

Sick ... again? It was then the acrid odor of vomit assaulted my nostrils, the yellowish-brown biohazard splattered in the sand nearby. Blinking rapidly, my mind caught up next, the memory of what happened hitting me all at once.

"We were back at the time and place of Six's death, and I was trapped in the me that was there before—past me." Shaking my head, I rubbed my temples. "But I'm back to present me … or is it future me? The future me as far as that me was concerned. Shit. I never realized time travel was so complicated before."

Reaper grabbed my hand, leading me to a bench. We both sat down, and I let my gaze travel to the ocean. "Is this where we left Six and Tina? Time has obviously passed, but is it the same beach? And what about the reality tear?"

"It's not the same beach."

"Is it at least the same ocean?" I was looking for some kind of connection, hoping to make sense of something —anything.

"No, it's not."

"Well, shit."

"Reality is beginning to … implode, for lack of a better term. My best guess is that we ended up back at ground zero because all reality tears will lead there."

"All reality rips? Exactly how many are there?"

"They're springing up all over the place, the first one spotted yesterday, by us."

A dolphin danced merrily through a wave, and I found myself envying it. *Oh, to be enjoying the freedom of the sun and surf without a worry in the world.* "How do you know this when you haven't left my side since then?"

"I have my ways."

More questions he wasn't going to answer. Big surprise. "Why all of a sudden though? It seemed like reality was fine at first, but then if that's true—"

"There is much unknown about all of this, even by me."

"Oh." Translation: Even if he had a theory, he wasn't going to tell me.

My stomach fluttered, and an invisible thread attached to my sternum was yanked, drawing my undivided attention.

No! Not fucking now! I refuse! I refuse to go this time!

The location of my pending job appeared in my mind's eye despite my protests, along with every other detail I would need.

Before my last job, for the first time in my long existence, I had pondered the possibly of resisting the pull, to simply not go to the job. Now, I saw no point in it. Reality was already crumbling, and the payoff I usually got probably wasn't going to happen.

And yet … uncertainty still warred.

Even though I felt as if I'd hit rock bottom, both physically and emotionally, deep down—very deep down—a speck of hope remained. *If I can prevent Six from saving Tina, if I can stop the hole in reality before it starts, then things will go back to the way they were. Therefore, if I don't do my job, I could cause a second starting point for a reality issue.*

I sighed heavily. *Am I rationalizing because I can't manage to break away from what I've been doing my entire life, or is there actual sense to my thought processes?*

I sighed again, being every bit as dramatic as Reaper had accused me of being. *If I don't go to this job then I might as well give up on Six, and that's something I can never do. Never.*

Canada, here I come.

MY GAZE SKIPPED from human to human, barely managing to catalogue the tagged as I waited for the impending disaster, my thoughts pensive.

Humans are so fragile, so easily broken; not just their bodies, but their spirits as well. In a nutshell, human equals vulnerability, and yet the same flaw is the one that makes them so easy to love. Yes, humans can draw you in with sympathy, an urge to protect, but it's necessary to resist the urge because they are also quick to perish.

So why did Six let himself fall for Tina? Wasn't he afraid of the anguish the relationship would bring him? Because there would have been no doubt that it would, even from the beginning. Humans and lunas can't form romantic attachments, it simply can't work. The most we can hope for is what Six and I had—true friendship. Love, just not the romantic kind.

I yawned, weariness riding me hard. It wasn't the type of tired that could be solved with a few days of sleep though. It was the kind of soul-deep exhaustion caused by the need for peace. I supposed all lunas eventually developed the need for it all to end. To truly appreciate life, death must be part of the equation. Immortality doesn't offer such an end or the promise of peace.

Can that be the answer? Had Six just wanted a little taste of happiness before throwing in the towel? Maybe his constant optimism and good nature couldn't handle the harsh realities our life exposed us to, day in and day out. Perhaps he was too good for this world—the world of a luna.

A ghost of Six's laugh wormed its way into my ear. I sagged with relief having not completely forgotten the sound as I'd feared. The memory that followed was just as surreal, capturing my attention completely.

"My feet are hot." Six kicked off his shoes, leaving them outside of the small motel room.

"How can only your feet be hot?" I tugged on the blanket wrapped around his shoulders.

"I don't know, it's not like I can control it." He toed his shoes, lining them up perfectly with the wall. "There, now they can cool off for me."

Taking another swig from the bottle I was holding, I grimaced as the mystery liquor burned its way down my throat. "What the hell is this crap, and how did I let you talk me into drinking it?"

Six bumped my shoulder with his. "We needed to have one of our times," he slurred. "You know ... our times. It's been a while."

I grinned. "Yup. It has."

When not working, we tried to take in as many human experiences as possible. It had become somewhat of a tradition for us. We would see something in a movie, or read about it in a magazine or book, and decide to give it a shot. This time it was get shit-faced in New Orleans and crash at one of those dingy little motels that probably had a body count.

Six lurched to the side, ramming his hip into the doorjamb. "Good thing I'm difficult to break. Pretty sure I'm still gonna bruise." He rubbed at the point of impact, frowning. "Sometimes I get sad when I think about old people."

Sliding my arms around his waist, I helped him into the

room, kicking the door shut behind us. "Yeah, why is that?" The room tilted slightly, that last shot taking effect.

"Cuz nobody honors their elders the way they used to." He slumped onto his bed. "It used to mean something when you were old—all that knowledge. Now humans put too much value on being young. It's vanity over brains nowadays. Old people deserve better than what they get in these so-called enlightened times." He sniffled. "Poor old people."

"At least they get a chance to grow old."

He sniffled harder, repositioning himself to lie spread eagle on the small bed. "Poor people who die young then, too. Humans are so damn fragile, and even still ..." He went quiet, and I thought for a moment he'd finally passed out. "I would give almost anything to get a chance at being human. Young, old, anything in between, you know?"

Flopping onto the other bed, I stared at a crack in the ceiling. "Yeah, I know exactly what you mean."

Soft snores vibrated Six's lips, sleep overtaking him. Unfortunately, I wasn't as drunk, and my brain was going about a mile a minute. All my thoughts were random, dancing along brightly-colored threads that dissolved almost as soon as they formed. Thunder clapped, causing me to jump, the pitter-patter of rain tinkling along the roof.

Just as sleep had almost claimed me as well, I heard Six's teeth chattering. Lumbering over to his bed, I pulled the comforter over him and tucked it up around his neck. He immediately stopped shivering, and a small smile curled one corner of his mouth.

"Thanks," he mumbled.

I watched him for a moment, a small smile of my own forming. "You're too good for this world, Six. Too good for this world and too good to be my friend." I leaned over, pressing a gentle kiss to his forehead. "But thank you for being my friend. Thank you so much. I don't think you'll ever truly know how much I needed you when you showed up. You ... I want to be there for you as much as you are for me. I hope I am ... or can be." I stumbled back over to my bed. "I would die for you, you know that? I would if it would save you any pain. I know you're sleeping, but I hope on some level you can still hear me. I would die for you, Six, because you deserve to have someone love you like that. And I do—" I yawned again, "I totally do."

"It's gonna collapse!" A panicked voice drew me to the present, even as part of me continued on down memory lane.

"They're filled with water! Why did I think it was a good idea to leave them out here?"

I laughed, the sight of Six's waterlogged shoes hilarious in that moment even though I wasn't exactly sure why.

"It's not funny!" He lifted puppy dog-like eyes to me. "These were my favorite pair."

I stifled another laugh. "Like you can't get a pair exactly like them."

Lunas weren't paid, and the items we wore when not on a job and automatically shifted into the clothing, were simply taken. Going unnoticed applied to retail stores, and simply walking out with what we wanted was how we shopped. We also acquired things from the dead, because nobody ever noticed a pair of sneakers missing from someone's apartment when they were being grieved. We also sold pawn-able items to get cash for other things, like cheap motels in New Orleans, or a heaping bowl of chocolate ice cream.

"Not exactly like them. I don't even remember where I got these. Man, they were my favorite, too." Water splattered onto the ground as he emptied his shoes, his lips twitching despite his displeasure. "Guess we nailed the doing stupid things while drunk experience though."

Our gazes clashed, and laughter burst from both of us.

"I'm pretty sure I threw up in the middle of the night," I managed.

"Good thing we heal fast, because our hangovers would be brutal otherwise, I'm guessing."

I blinked away the rest of the memory, a dull ache blooming in my chest. That night—and others spent with Six—had made me feel almost human, almost warm in the way that they were. I didn't know what other lunas did in between jobs, at least not exactly, but I was absolutely certain they didn't have fun the way Six and I did.

The bridge about twenty or so feet in front of me whined and buckled, collapsing in a rather anticlimactic way. Silence settled around me, snow continuing to drift steadily down.

My wings flared out behind me, and I threw my head back as I rose into the air, the cold not affecting me in the least. Hovering between worlds, the recently dead souls passed through me one after another in lightning-fast succession. I recorded their essences, making sure all that should be was.

As the numbers of dead added up, the warmth their souls offered seeped into my bones. My body hummed with delight, the energy of the deceased an addictive force.

Hmmm ... yes. This is what it's supposed to feel like. The familiar wave of feeling satiated, content, full … like I actually belonged there … or anywhere, was back. I was whole, and nothing else mattered.

A moment of true peace.

And then it was over practically before it began.

Sinking to my knees in the snow, I swung my gaze to Reaper, who of course I was sure had been there the entire time, but had remained silent.

"It was like before … before the tear in reality. I mean, it felt the same. Do you think things righted themselves naturally? We were in the future, after all, and things seemed just fine there. And I guess it's worth mentioning that the bright soul wasn't here either." Or maybe another luna had already been tasked with righting the fixed point in time which had begun everything. Would that mean anything in regards to my plan to save Six?

Reaper inclined his head, the edge of his jaw visible. "What do you speak of, luna?"

"Oh, um …" Hovering off to the left was a second reaper, one that I was pretty sure was Reaper, and not the one directly in front of me. "Never mind. Ignore me. You have a job to do anyways. I don't want to distract you from that."

Fighting my way through the snow, I made my way to Reaper. "Oops, I thought he was you."

Reaper crossed his arms over his chest. I could feel his annoyance, the grating sensation hitting me in palpable waves. "What?" I threw my hands up in the air. "You all wear the same robe thingy. How am I supposed to tell the difference? Maybe you could wear a pin or something?"

He shook his head, sighing heavily. "We're not even close to the same height, our builds are also completely different. You shouldn't need for me to wear some kind of ridiculous adornment such as a pin to pick me out of a crowd."

I quirked an eyebrow. "Maybe you all look completely different to each other, and I'm guessing you all are different under the robes, but—um, hello? All I can see is the robe. You all look exactly the same to me. Maybe if the other reaper had been a woman—"

"This is a trivial matter. We have other more important things to deal with. I heard what you said to Bri– him, and I—"

"Why haven't you been pulled to any other jobs besides the ones you've come to with me? Why are you able to be my shadow through all of this?"

"You get distracted so easily. None of that matters. We need to deal with the cause of the tear in reality before it spreads."

Cocking my hip, I lifted my chin. "If you actually did hear me, then you would have heard me say that this job felt completely normal. The bright soul was even missing for the first time in a while." Which was a relief on a number of levels because I was already freezing in this frigid wilderness without the extra chill of letting the bright soul pass through me.

"Reality is imploding, which means exactly what it sounds like. There will be points which aren't affected at all yet."

"Do you know that for sure or are you just guessing?"

"Do you want to leave this all up to chance?"

"Guess that means you're guessing. Got it." I winked at him.

"It's an *educated* guess." The scowl that positively was under his hood had its own presence, surging through the space between us.

I rolled my eyes. "Mmm hmm. Sooo ... what do you suggest we do next then?"

"Don't you need to rest?"

I shook my head. "Weirdly enough, no. I don't feel drained like I ... shit. This job wasn't normal after all. I thought maybe because the bright soul wasn't here, but—"

Reaper scooped me up in his arms, throwing me over his shoulder.

"Hey!" I exclaimed.

"We need to do research while we still have the chance."

Everything blurred into white noise.

Chapter 14

One moment I was in a vast void of oblivion and the next color exploded into existence, causing spots to dance in front of my eyes. The reaper mode of transportation was not suitable for lunas such as me, I decided. It was similar to blacking out every time he took me anywhere. Pressing the fleshy part of my palms into my eyes, I grumbled as such under my breath.

Striding ahead of me, Reaper turned to glance over his shoulder. "Coming?"

"I need a second to get my bearings straight."

A tiny, all-white cottage sat nestled in a clearing in the woods. Reaper disappeared inside, leaving the door ajar as an invitation for me to follow.

Spinning in a circle, I took in the greenery stretching as far as the eye could see. It was an odd sensation to travel somewhere that I didn't automatically know where

I was, and now it had happened more than once while with Reaper.

Sighing, I trudged after him into the cottage. "Hey, Reaper …" My mind went blank, surprise pinging through my system. The inside of the cottage seemed to be some kind of massive library. The dimensions far exceeded what the outside appeared to be capable of holding. "Another Archive?" I breathed.

"Yes, but one very different than the one you're used to," Reaper said, his voice coming from off to the left.

Scanning the spines of the leather-bound books, I noticed the titles were in all different languages and fonts. "What does this Archive … archive exactly?" I pulled a book down from one of the shelves, the cover green with silver lettering. "I can't read this, and I'm supposed to understand every language there is."

Reaper appeared in front of me, snatching the book from my hands. "Not celestial languages. You understand all languages born of Earth. These languages are not." He slid it back onto the shelf and grabbed my arm. "Don't touch anything. You shouldn't be here, and I could get into a lot of trouble if anyone found out I brought you."

Huh. He'd seemed so casual about the whole deal, since he'd left the door open, and basically left me to my own devices for a few minutes. My eyes widened as I considered the situation further. "You could get into trouble? With who? What would happen?" Lunas had rules, intrinsic ones, but we didn't directly answer to anyone. The notion that reapers did too was mind-boggling.

"I don't have time to play twenty questions with you." Yanking me after him, he led me over a few aisles.

"When do you have time to play twenty questions with me? You never answer any of my questions."

Reaper flipped through a massive tome, the pages silent as they shuffled through his fingers. "I answer your questions, just not all of them."

"Please, I can't even count—"

"This is not the one I need." Shoving the book back onto the shelf, he grabbed my arm again, dragging me deeper into the Archives.

"What are you looking for exactly?"

"One of your favorite things … answers." He yanked several books out at once, flipping through one after the other.

"If you have such an Archive at your fingertips, then why haven't you been—"

His hand pressed over my mouth. "Shhh … someone's coming." In one smooth move, his robes engulfed me in darkness, the Archives disappearing from sight.

My heart quadrupled in time, my heightened pulse thundering in my ears. Inside of Reaper's robes was the very definition of pitch black, the complete lack of any kind of light, causing my panic to surge higher. *Who's coming? What's going to happen? How long do I have to be in here? It feels like I've been here for forever. I need to get out! Let me out!*

"Calm down," Reaper's baritone voice curled directly

into my ear. "You should be able to handle this, being a creature of the night."

I sucked in a sharp breath. *Did he—did he just mock me about that again? And now right in the middle of such a dire situation. Or, well, I think it's dire. It's quite possible—*

Abruptly I was standing in the Archives again, Reaper beside me as if nothing at all had happened. "They're gone, and we went undetected ... for now." He went back to flipping through books at lightning speed.

Narrowing my eyes at him, I bit the inside of my cheek to keep quiet. I didn't like how he took control of every situation, expecting me to simply fall in line. I had ideas of my own of how things should go. Sure, all of them so far had been shit, but everyone knows that wisdom is gained through making mistakes, so therefore I was due a brilliant plan ... and soon.

"This," Reaper stabbed a book with his index finger, the pale skin of his hand practically glowing, "this is what we came here for." He tucked the bright blue book into his robes.

"Do you have secret pockets in there, or—"

Everything went dark.

"DAMNIT!" I slapped at Reaper. "You need to give me a warning before you do that!"

We were back in my room in the luna realm. Ignoring

my outburst, Reaper reproduced the blue book and settled down on my bed with it.

I tapped my foot rapidly against the hardwood floor. "Are you allowed to have that book?"

"Define allowed."

Flopping down beside him, I peered at the pages as they flew by. "What will happen if you get caught having stolen it?"

Silence.

"You said the languages in this book are all celestial. How can you read them then?"

His fingers paused on a page mid-turn. "I'm a reaper."

I crinkled my nose. "Yeah, I'm well aware."

Silence.

"You still haven't answered my question. How can you read the celestial languages?"

"I'm. A. Reaper," he repeated slower.

I blinked at him expectantly. "Aaand, what's that have to do with—"

"Reapers are angels of death. How can you not know that?"

"I've heard that term, but I thought it was just—"

"We are angels. Of death."

My left eye twitched. "But you don't have wings."

Reaper set the blue book down on top of the stack on my nightstand, and rose, giving me his full attention. "I have wings. How do you suppose I fly?"

Squinting at him, I ran my gaze up and down his robe-clad body. "I've seen you fly, but never seen any wings." I spread mine wide behind me. "These are wings. See?" I flexed them up and down. "Wings."

"Reapers can maintain invisibility of their wings at all times, unlike lunas who can only hide them when not in use."

"But … but if you're invisible from mortals, why hide your wings from immortals? Why hide everything including your face behind robes all the time?"

He clicked his tongue. "We really don't have time for this, but I grow weary of your incessant questions that will surely keep coming if I don't answer some of them."

With a wave of his hand, his robes disappeared. I jerked away, hitting my shoulders against the headboard. "Y-You're … the most beautiful man I've ever seen." My eyes widened as far as they could stretch, absorbing the sight of him.

Reaper stood before me, all of him on display. And I do mean *all of him*. Naked as the day he was born—or created—he crossed his arms over his chest. "Go ahead, look your fill. I'm not ashamed of my form."

"Then why do you hide it?"

"We all have jobs to do, and reapers are the only angels to interact directly with other immortals. We do not wish to be distracting, although we are not half as distracting as other types of angels."

I gulped, my gaze running over his lithely muscled body, and his pale skin glowing with a kind of otherworldly sheen. Light blond hair hung in waves to his chin, framing a square jaw, and full lips. His eyes were a deep shade of lavender, with perfectly arched brows perched above them. Wings, black and feathered, swished behind him. I was ... discombobulated by his perfection. It was as if he was a living sculpture brought to life, created with such intense love no flaws dared exist.

Reaper smirked. "Are you quite satisfied?"

Sweat trickled down my brow. "Satisfied?" Did he know what he was saying? Was he trying to mock my reaction to him? What female, or male for that matter, of any species who was capable of lust, wouldn't stare? I had absolutely no control over it. *And, dear moon and stars above, did he say other types of angels are more distracting? How is that even possible? You can't improve on perfection. I'm lucky I didn't strip and throw myself at him.*

And that thought was like a bucket of ice water dumped over my head. Even if I did throw myself at Reaper, there was no way he'd ever be attracted to me—me, a plain luna, built to blend in wherever she went. *This isn't one of your romance novels, Eighty-nine, he'd never be attracted to you no matter the circumstances.* If capable of lust himself, Reaper would of course desire one of his own kind, one who possessed the same kind of stunning beauty.

Turning away, I flicked my hand in his general direction. "Fine, you made your point. Put the robe back on."

The bed shifted beside me as he settled back down with the blue book. "Reapers have the opposite problem as lunas—everyone notices us. We don't wish to be sought after for our appearance alone. However seldom it happens, if a connection is made, we want it to be a melding of personalities. A lasting lust develops from seeing into each other's souls, and loving the good with the bad, not from only desiring a physical form."

I grunted. I had no concept of what he was talking about, but I knew that every creature had a cross to bear. To feel as if you were only wanted for your appearance, and for no one to bother looking beyond to what really matters when it came to love … yeah, okay, reapers didn't have it any better than lunas.

"Do you think all immortals are cursed?"

Reaper turned toward me, and I could imagine his lavender gaze studying me with unnerving intensity. "What do you speak of now?"

My eyes slid shut as I willed myself to stop picturing what was hiding under his robes. I swallowed several times to return some moisture to my suddenly parched throat. "Well, it seems to me that all immortals have something that creates distance between them and a truly fulfilling life. We all have jobs, but beyond that, we've all been created with a barrier of some sort … so, yeah, do you think we're all cursed?"

Silence hung between us, think and full, before he said, "Perhaps."

"If Six had been allowed to cultivate his love with Tina, or really if lunas were able to have relationships of that nature with humans at all, then maybe none of this would have happened."

"There needs to be rules for ones such as us. We need to have distance from humans."

"But then why make it so that we can't have romantic relationships between each other either? Maybe if lunas weren't all like brothers and sisters ..." I punched my pillow. "I don't know how to fix the system, but I know it's broken."

Reaper nodded slowly. "Reapers also consider others of our kind to be siblings. Romantic love does not develop between us either. Or none that I'm aware of."

I bit my tongue to not say what sprung into my mind next. *Then who do you have sex with?* Surely reapers didn't get it on with humans like lunas sometimes did. Curiosity zinged through me. *Who do they—who can they without catastrophic results—have sex with?*

"I can hear the question buzzing in your mind, but I'm not going to answer it. I'm done placating you. I revealed my true self to you, something a reaper has never done with a luna, and now it's time to focus on the task at hand ... making sure reality doesn't completely implode."

"Yeah, I guess because of time travel, there's a part of me that has lost the urgency. I just want to make sure that when I save Six it sticks. You know, that I don't think I've saved him and then another luna is dispatched to fix something that screws things up for us in that regard." I stared at my feet. "I don't think I could handle losing him more than once."

"Fear of action will not fix anything."

"I'm not afraid, just uncertain of the next move. Or,

rather, I need to make sure my next move is the right move. I can't afford to make even one more mistake." My chest constricted, making it hard to breathe. *Maybe I am afraid ... afraid to fail once and for all. Because that would mean Six is well and truly gone forever.*

Reaper slapped his palm against the book, his long fingers splayed across the open pages. "Here. Here is what we've been looking for."

I raised my index finger in the air. "One more question. Why didn't we go to the other Archives to begin with? Why did you wait until things were this bad before researching there? And why does such a place exist? And what I mean by that is—why are there books with information about the possible implosion of reality? Or are they records?" I gasped. "Holy shit! Has this happened before?" He'd told me that it had never happened before, but maybe it had, and he just didn't know about it.

Reaper's head clunked against the wall, and he heaved a long sigh. "Usually I admire the quality of curiosity, but you ask too many damn questions. You remind me of a human toddler. Why? Why? Why? Learn to pay attention better. For someone who's purpose is to watch and record, you certainly aren't very observant."

I scowled. "I watch and record specific things, as you're well aware. My scope of knowledge is very limited, so yeah, maybe I am like a human toddler because this is all new to me, as life is to them."

My stomach fluttered, and an invisible thread attached

to my sternum was yanked, drawing my undivided attention.

Of course. Of course, this going to happen now.

The location of my pending job appeared in my mind's eye, along with every other detail I would need.

Resignation settled over me. I'd attempted to resist before, but now I knew when I got the call, whether I wanted to or not, I was unable to deny the need to go. It was the pull felt by all lunas. It was a fact that I'd known since my creation. You feel the pull of a job … you go. Beginning and end of story.

"We're going to have to finish this conversation after. Duty calls."

Reaper offered me his hand. I curled my fingers into my palm. "No thanks, this time I have my own mode of transportation."

He nodded, and I closed my eyes.

And here we go.

Chapter 15

A fine tremor rumbled under my feet, indicative of what was to come.

A man, the bright soul I'd encountered several times before, was attempting to herd people out of the small town. "Please, do you not feel that? The mountain is angry! We must leave!"

"The earth has quaked many times before. We were fine. And we will be fine now. Leave us alone," a second man shouted at the first.

The bright-souled man continued to make his pleas, going as far as to grab hold of several people, much to their protests. Unlike my other run-ins with my own personal pain in the ass, I wasn't concerned with his meddling attempts. Every human as far as the eye could see was tagged. In fact, all the people in this town, and all the villages and towns for miles from where I stood, would die today.

The tremor turned into a rumble, the rumble into a boom, long and low. Complete and utter chaos erupted … literally.

Closing my eyes, I waited for the worst to pass—for the screams of terror to be snuffed out with as great a power as any I'd ever witnessed.

After several minutes, deadly silence settled around me.

Opening my eyes, I took in the changes. Ash filled the air, coating everything in sight like grey snow. The heat from the volcanic eruption rippled the atmosphere, distorting my vision. The brunt of destruction to human life was over, the land itself still being reshaped by Mother Nature.

My skin was blackened, my lungs charred, and yet I was already healing, my immortality ensuring that I continued on. I glanced at the reaper beside me, and then at Reaper off to his right, neither of them bothered in the slightest by any of the earthly events.

Why are lunas subjected to such things when reapers aren't? Is it one more way to torture us? Or are they simply immune because they're angels?

A surge of energy danced along my skin, goose bumps erupting in its wake. *It's time.*

Shaking my wings out, I threw my head back as I rose into the air. Hovering between worlds, the recently dead souls passed through me one after another in lightning-fast succession. I recorded their essences, making sure all that should be was.

As the numbers of dead added up—the many, many numbers—the warmth their souls offered seeped into my bones. Of course, as I now expected, one of the souls burned brighter, hotter, its essence familiar. The urge to hold onto it was there, just as it had been before, but I knew it wouldn't work, that I'd be forced to relinquish it in the end. Still, I clung to it longer than necessary—eventually letting it slip on into the reaper's grasp.

Shivering, I wrapped my arms around my middle.

Reaper placed a hand on top of my shoulder. "The bright soul was back, I see. And the rest?"

"Just like before." My teeth began to chatter. "I need to finish this job, get to Archives, then we can continue our conversation from before."

Nodding, he squeezed my shoulder.

Turning from him, I willed myself home. Even though it didn't really feel that way anymore without Six being there.

"LET ME GET THIS STRAIGHT—" I shifted under my pile of blankets to face Reaper, who was comfortably lounging on the bed next to me. I ignored the lump in my throat, and the hollowness in my chest at my recovery companion being him and not Six.

My mind veered off into a memory.

"There," Six said, "that's every last blanket that you have. You need to sleep now."

I rubbed my socked feet together and yawned. "What are you going to do while I sleep?"

"Sit here with you, of course." He settled down beside me, stretching his long legs out.

I yawned again. "It's a waste of your time, all I'm going to do is sleep."

He shrugged. "Nothing better to do."

I laughed. "Well, thanks, I think."

Six leaned over, our noses almost touching. "When you wake up, let's go to the human realm for some junk food."

"Yeah, okay." My eyes slid shut, suddenly too heavy.

"And then if we have the time, maybe to an amusement park."

"Mmm hmm."

"Or we could go to the ocean. At night of course. I know how much you hate the beach during the day."

"You don't exactly enjoy all that sun either," I mumbled.

"I'll take the beach—any of them—any way I can get them. I'm not as picky as you."

"Mmm hmm." He said that now, but then he'd be whining about the brightness after about three minutes. We were lunas after all.

Six shifted, jostling my mound of blankets. "Or we could go somewhere else. Up to you."

"You choose. You're the one who has all the ideas today."

"The world is our oyster, there are so many fun things to do in the human realm."

I sighed. I wasn't sure if I envied Six's optimistic view of our lives or pitied him. Probably a mix of both. I wondered if the shine of things would ever wear off for him, or if he'd always remain so exuberant about ... everything. I had a feeling his sunny disposition was part of his personality, and not something that would be leeched out of him over time as a luna. Even my first day as one of the hundred I hadn't been anything other than myself, the same luna I was at present moment. Sure, Six had brought me out of my shell a bit, but nothing about my personality had changed.

Fingers snapped in front of my eyes, jolting me back to the present.

"You didn't hear a word I just said," Reaper stated.

I cleared my throat. "Sorry. My mind has a tendency to wander when I'm like this."

"And how much more time do you need to be ... like this?"

My gaze darted to the skylight, the silhouettes of my brothers and sisters dancing across the sky. "Depends." It only then occurred to me that my time with Reaper possibly wasn't all that private. Lunas, in general, didn't peek into each other's rooms while in the air, but usually, nothing very exciting was happening within them either.

"Are you visible right now? Can the other lunas see you in here?" I was fairly certain that none of them had seen him naked because there would have definitely been a commotion of some kind.

Reaper turned to follow my gaze. "No. Only you can see me right now."

"Oh, okay. I guess talking to myself is the better alternative."

"Than what? Being seen with a reaper in your room?"

"I don't want anyone to know what's going on. They might try to stop me from using the Archives to save Six. I don't trust any of them."

"Maybe you're wrong, quite possibly a few of them would be willing to help you."

"Doubtful. Most lunas only worry about themselves." Was I any different? Could my desire to save Six be purely selfish? He'd made his choice, one that I possibly had no right to interfere with. But I was going to change his choice because I missed him—because I couldn't deal with not having him in my life.

Stop. Yes, you're being selfish, but no friendship is completely selfless. The desire to be with another person is heightened because of how they make you feel. If you didn't miss them then why bother with the friendship? Of course, it was a tad more complicated than that, emotions usually were, but the bottom line was: I shouldn't feel guilty for wanting to have Six back in my life. I shouldn't feel like I was doing something wrong because I wanted to save him from himself.

As if reading my thoughts, Reaper said, "So you only worry about yourself as well? Then how would you explain your desire to save your friend?"

"It's selfish. I'll admit it. I want him back in my life, he made everything easier, better. I miss him."

Reaper's gaze burned into mine even from beneath his hood. "It's surprising how honest you are with yourself sometimes, and completely clueless others."

I fluffed my pillow and closed my eyes again. "We all have our moments." I yawned. "Okay, now tell me about what you discovered in that book of yours, and I promise not to ask any more questions until you're done explaining what little you think I should know."

Sleep claimed me then, my worries temporarily lost in my unconscious world.

Chapter 16

Coming to instant awareness, a few things immediately occurred to me: one, I fell asleep before Reaper had a chance to share the discoveries from the blue book, and two, things were vastly more urgent than I'd been letting myself admit. It was now painfully obvious to me, even though I'd made excuses before, well thought out excuses I might add, that it wasn't just fear of making a misstep when it came to Six's rescue.

It all bubbled down to denial. I was in denial on how dire the situation surrounding us was. None of it was simple in the least, no matter how much I told myself it was. And also, despite my not wanting to acknowledge it, there was a very real possibility I would fail. Not only was Six's life on the line, but the existence of reality itself.

The more I considered the complications that could arise and the complete lack of scope I had about any of it

… I sank deeper and deeper into the ocean of panic inside of me.

Staring at the night sky, and yet unseeing, my eyes filled to the brim, everything around me blurring. The band that had taken up residence around my chest constricted painfully, breathing made nearly impossible. Staggering to my feet, I opened and closed my mouth like a fish, gasping for oxygen that wouldn't come. My heart thundered against my eardrums, and my body trembled violently.

"Reaper," I croaked, clutching at my throat. "Can't —breathe."

But he was no longer there, and I was left to deal with … whatever was happening to me alone.

Stop. Lunas can't have heart attacks or die like this. It's some kind of panic attack. You've read about them. Humans have them all the time.

But what if something actually is wrong with me? What if I'm the next thing reality is going to mess with? What if my body is being unmade? Which means if I'm not here then I won't be able to fix anything, and I'll cease to exist.

My arms and legs tingled, and I dropped to the floor, curling into myself.

You're not dying. You're going to be fine. Just breathe. You can do it. Take in a deep breath, one after another.

My lungs burned, shallow breaths the only thing I could manage. My heart felt like it was going to explode from my chest at any moment.

You're not overreacting. You're in denial about this, too.

You're being unmade. You're being unmade right now as you lie here and there's nothing you can do about it. All those memories of Six, all those simple moments, ones that seemingly meant nothing, they mean everything and you're never going to make another one with him again. It's all going to end, and no one will ever know you were here. You're going to die just like you lived, silently and alone, with no one noticing.

My vision blurred, my entire body convulsing.

This is it. The end. I wish I could have done more, known more ...

The clock on my nightstand ticked steadily, and I waited.

Tick, tick, tick ...

And waited.

Tick, tick, tick ...

And waited some more.

Slowly, my lungs filled to capacity, and then my breathing evened out. My vision cleared as my heart slowed, and my shaking halted.

I'd thought it was over, the end, and yet—

"I'm not being unmade." Fresh tears tracked down my face, burning my chilled skin. "There's still a chance to fix things."

Weariness, a kind of mental exhaustion I wasn't accustomed to, weighed down my limbs. With a herculean effort, I pulled myself to my feet.

No more denial, and no more distractions. You don't have all the time in the world to fix things, time-traveling luna or not. You need to give this your all, and if you do fail, and you could, at least you'll know it wasn't because you hesitated. No longer will you be your own worst enemy.

With a renewed determination, I marched out my door and headed to Archives. I didn't have time to wait for Reaper, nor did I need to rely on him the way I had been up until now. He'd conveniently shown up when I needed someone or something to turn to and aid me. His help would be greatly appreciated, as much as he could give, but I didn't need him in order to continue on with my plans. The only thing I needed was me.

Shoving open the black door to Archives, I strode in with purpose, my head held high. Ignoring several other lunas who passed me, I made my way to a secluded corner and squeezed my eyes shut.

Just like the previous attempts to track down one of Six's recorded events, I imagined Six's face and the way his brown eyes crinkled at the corners when he smiled.

Warmth, subtle and comforting, washed over me, and then…

A tug, the smallest of pulls fluttered in my sternum, causing me to stumble forward, hands outstretched. My fingers curled around the supple leather spine of a book, and I lifted it to my nose, inhaling deeply.

Six, it smells like Six. Home. It's like home. He'll always be home.

But I'm losing it. Losing him. I can't forget this scent. I can't let it become nothing more than a distant memory.

My eyes still tightly squeezed shut, I opened the book, placing my palms on the smooth pages.

Take me here. Take me to this time and place—to Six. Take me to where I need to be.

Vertigo hit, spinning my world. My mouth opened in a silent scream of surprise as darkness blotted away everything.

AS IT TURNED OUT, I didn't need Reaper's help to travel back after all. I was fully capable of shifting through time to a Six event all on my own. I smirked, more pleased with myself than I probably had a right to be. But you know, baby steps and all.

As I scanned my surroundings, I couldn't help but wonder where Reaper had disappeared to. He'd been like a second shadow for several days, and then without a word, poof, gone. *Not that it really matters. I can work without him, and will, but it would be nice if I had the information from the blue book.*

Shaking my head, I forced myself to focus back on the task at hand. I had to be fully present, and to no longer let denial and distractions, fear and inaction rule my decisions. Six's death had shattered me to pieces, and maybe a part of me had died right along with him. But I was slowly rebuilding myself, fashioning a new Eighty-nine, one who was stronger, one that could save the day without help from anyone else. Six always had my six, and it was time to prove that I had his. *Death can't sever a true friendship; it can only put a tad more distance within it.*

Wind whipped my hair around and rustled the leaves on the nearby trees. I was in an old cemetery, most of the stones worn down and misshapen. *I don't get it. Why am I here? These people are already dead. Six wouldn't be here to record anything.* Uncertainty niggled. *Maybe I didn't successfully travel back. I could be anywhere.*

Soft sobs rent the air, curling into my ears eerily. Turning toward the forlorn sound, I followed it across the cemetery, halting abruptly when I spotted its origin.

Six was hunched over a grave, a surprisingly fresh one. Apparently, there was a newer side with modern headstones, and the recently deceased. There my best friend mourned some unknown human; at least they were unknown to me.

Moving silently, I crept closer. Reaching for Six, I paused, my hand hovering just above his shoulder. "Six?"

Slowly he turned, his face a mask of anguish. "I wish I could have saved him."

Kneeling beside him, I pushed his hair back from his forehead. "Him who?"

Six pressed his palm to the headstone, sagging forward once again. "He was just a little boy." He sniffled. "You should have seen him … so smart. He was so smart, smarter than most adults, I swear."

"Okay. But who was he?" I tried to read the name etched into stone, but Six's hand blocked half of it.

"How did you find me?"

"I-I …" *Should I just come clean now? Or not say a word and sweep him back to the present with me? Could it actually be that simple? Or maybe I should find out if he's met Tina yet?*

"It doesn't matter." Pulling me into a hug, he pressed his wet face into my shoulder. "I'm glad you're here." He choked on a silent sob.

Rubbing small circles along his back, I hugged him to me as tightly as I could. Even like this, Six was a gift to experience. "Tell me who the little boy was. I need to understand." More than he knew.

"He was only fifteen years old. Do you know that? Fifteen years old. And he gave his life to save her. He loved her so much he didn't even think twice about it."

I didn't correct Six. Fifteen was not exactly a little boy, but to someone who was immortal, I could see how it might seem that way. Funny how I was older than Six, and I didn't view the boy that way. Clearly, Six had witnessed something that had affected him profoundly. Although it made me wonder why he never shared this with me either. I would have remembered such a story if he'd ever told me. How much of himself did he keep hidden from me? Was he afraid to show his true sorrows because he thought I expected him to be the optimistic one all the time? But why would he think that?

Continuing to hold him, I asked, "What happened? Tell me everything."

"He loved her so much. I've never seen anything like it before. It … it changed everything for me. Absolutely everything."

Wind whistled past us, picking up speed. "What does

that mean exactly? What did it change for you?" Craning my neck, I saw a reality rip hanging almost directly above us. This one was shaped like a deflated football, colors rippling across the surface like it was made of water.

Swallowing back the bile that erupted up my esophagus, I tightened my arms around Six. "Listen to me. We have to get out of here. Now."

Shaking his head, Six only sobbed harder. "I don't want to leave yet. Not just yet."

Staggering to my feet, I managed to pull him to his without letting go. "We can come back later, I promise. But right now we need to get out of here."

"Why?" Six mumbled. "Why does any of it matter?"

I threw my head back. "Don't you see it? The tear in reality?"

Ignoring me, Six crumpled to the ground, his legs buckling. I dropped back down beside him, roughly grabbed the side of his face, and forced his gaze up toward the rip. "It's right above us. Don't you see it? Feel it?"

"I don't know what you're talking about." He reached for me, taking my hand within his. "Just stay with me for a bit, Eighty-nine, please. I feel like I can't hold myself together anymore, and I need you to do it for me for a while."

My heart dropped into my stomach. "I'll do whatever you need me to do to help you feel better. Anything. We'll get through this." I slid my hands under his arms, pulling up. "But we have to get out of here. We can't do it here."

Fumbling for my hand again, Six bowed into himself.

"I've never seen that kind of love before. It was right out of a movie or book. But this was senseless. I don't understand why he had to die at all. Who decides who's tagged and who's not?" He jumped to his feet. "We need to find her. What if ... what if she can't live without him? What if—"

"Yes, we'll find her. Right now. Let's go."

Bright light exploded from the tear, blinding me.

Silence fell, followed by a ringing in my ears. I swiped at my eyes, colors slowly bleeding back into existence.

Screams saturated the air, stealing my attention. I swung my head around, taking in chaos, buildings burning all around me. Confusion kept me rooted in place, my breath stuck in my throat.

And then my gaze zeroed in on him ... *Six*.

Lurking in the shadows, where lunas preferred to stay, my friend watched the disaster unfold before him, his expression much like I imagined mine was at every one of my jobs—twisted between anguish and anticipation. I'd never witnessed another luna at work, and seeing Six before me, I realized we were every bit the outsiders I'd come to think of us as.

How does no one ever notice us when we're so out of place? It should be clear to any and all who glance in our direction that we don't belong in the human realm.

His eyes sparked red as he moved a few paces closer to the building directly in front of him. I moved in tandem, shrinking the distance between us.

No. No. I've done this—twice before? Yes, twice now. This

exact same thing. Think, think, think. What's going on? How did you end up here again?

Cemetery ... the reality rip. Shit. I can't let my future self get sucked into my past self. I have to fight this time. Fight to do it differently. This is my chance. I can save Six and end all the insanity. But just like my first repeat of the event, my mind was fuzzy, filled with something akin to cotton candy.

A hand clamped down onto my shoulder, pinching painfully. "Be careful what you do next, for you are complicating things more than you can possibly fathom as is." The reaper stared down at me, his gaze burning from the depths of his hood. *Is his future self trapped in there, too? Is he fighting himself like I am, even as we speak the exact same dialogue?*

"Why did you bring me here? Why are you helping me?" *No. You already said that before—twice now. Say something else. Do something else. Start small, change something. Anything.*

He tilted his head, a low chuckle rumbling in his chest. "Am I helping you? Are you so sure of that?"

He was right. I had no idea if he was actually helping me or not. In fact, being that his kind usually never got involved in anything beyond escorting souls to the next realm, I was guessing he had an ulterior motive, one that had absolutely nothing to do with me, or my end game.

Stop! You can't let yourself be absorbed into your past self again. There has to be something you can do!

I crossed my arms over my chest. Grimacing, I forced my

arms back to my sides, but then I crossed them again. *Damnit! How are you supposed to do anything different when you can't even position your arms differently? Okay. Okay. Say something else. You can do it! You were already lost by this point last time.*

My lips contorted, twisting, but the same words as before still fell from my mouth. "Different question then. Do your end goals align with mine?"

"Quite possibly. Hard to tell at this point."

"Whatever. I don't have time for your cryptic bullshit right now." Pivoting back in the direction of Six, I sprinted toward him. *Argh. No. Stop. Stop running!*

I slowed, my steps jerky, but I still made forward progress toward him. *No. Please. You have to change things. You have to somehow.*

I halted, freezing in place. *Yes! Yes, that's right. You can do this! You can—*

Black spots danced in front of my eyes, and my ears rang. Shaking my head, I tried to remember what I was doing.

Six. You have to go after Six. Why are you just standing here?

"Six! Six, I have to talk to you!" I had no idea when or where we were, or how long ago in his timeline Six had done this particular job, but I knew I had to take him with me. I needed to save him from whatever had stolen him from me.

Six froze, every muscle in his body tensing, and just when I thought he was going to turn around, demanding how and why I was there, he ran across the street, and straight into the burning building.

What the fuck? How the hell didn't he hear me? It might be utter chaos around here, but I was just yelling his name less than two feet from him.

Dashing into the building after Six, the thick smoke ripped at my throat and welled up my eyes. I caught a flash of movement off to my left, and staggered that way, pulling my shirt up to cover my nose and mouth. Inhaling the smoke wouldn't kill one such as me, but it certainly could make things uncomfortable.

"Tina! Tina, where are you?" Six's familiar voice was strung tight with anxiety bordering on panic. "Tina! Please, answer me!"

I froze, fear spiking through my veins, and my heart thrashing painfully against my ribcage. *Why is Six searching for someone in here? It couldn't possibly mean what I think it does.*

A moment later, Six pushed past me with a girl in his arms, completely oblivious to my presence. I trailed after them, my stomach twisting into knots. The girl was tagged, the bright orange aura of those marked for death visible even through the dense smoke.

No. He can't. It can't be what it looks like.

"Shh … Tina, I've got you. You're going to be fine." Six planted a tender kiss on her forehead before depositing her gently on the sidewalk.

Tina—the girl from the diner that Six had been so fixated on—squinted up at him, her bright green eyes brimming with tears. "Simon, I was so scared. How did you know? How did you get here?"

"It's going to be just fine, my tiny Tina." Six smiled, but the emotion didn't reach his eyes.

She doubled over as a coughing fit wracked her body, her lungs gasping for enough air to keep her breathing. Shuffling forward, I studied her, realizing that despite Six's efforts she would die without immediate medical attention. Not only had she inhaled too much smoke, but her shirt and hair were saturated in crimson, evidence of her severe injuries.

Tina will die this day as she's supposed to.

Six palmed Tina's face between his hands just as her eyes slid shut. Her chest rattled out one last shaky breath before remaining still.

Dodging behind a car, I peered at Six over the hood, not wanting to interfere until he was ready for me to comfort him. I smiled to myself. *This is what happened. It has to be. He burned up from grief because I wasn't there in time to help him, but I am now. I can save him ... and change everything. It's all easier than I thought it would turn out to be.*

Six's wings flared out behind him, and his feet rose off the ground as he disappeared from sight. He was recording the calamity and the souls who died because of the disaster, invisible even to me until he was done.

My gaze dropped to Tina's body as I waited. Blood haloed her small form, the macabre scene oddly mesmerizing. When had Six met her, and why hadn't he given me any kind of clue about her? Sure, we both had occasional dalliances with humans, but it was clear that Tina was more to him than sex. There had been a moment when I'd actually thought Six was going to risk reality itself for her.

Six has a lot of explaining to do when we get home. But I couldn't even manage an ounce of anger with the jubilation rising up within me. I'd come so close to losing my best friend forever … so close.

Six reappeared in front of me, dropping down to his knees beside Tina. A high-pitched keening sound filled the air, his glowing eyes casting shadows across her motionless features. He yanked her body into his chest, cradling her while swaying back and forth. A few minutes later he stilled, and then gently laid Tina back on the ground. His fingers danced along her hairline, smoothing a few wisps away from her forehead. Rocking back on his heels, he sucked in a sharp breath.

Move, move, move, this is the time. I have to talk to him now. Comfort him. Stop him from burning up. Stop hovering behind him like an idiot and save your best friend before it's too late ... again.

With lightning speed, Six exposed his wings and arched them forward. He bared his teeth in a grimace, ripping the delicate forms from his back. Blood spurted from the gaping holes in his flesh, his torn shirt billowing like a cape.

My mouth fell open, a scream bubbling up from my throat.

Six's head whipped around, our gazes clashing, his filled with determination, and mine with horror.

Golden energy blobs streaked out from Six's wings where they lay discarded on the ground. His attention shifted as he deftly plucked a blob out of the air, shoving it into Tina's chest before it raced away.

Tina jolted up, sputtering, her wounds fully healed.

My vision wavered. *What have you done?*

In a burst of flame, Six and his wings were gone.

Just like that, there one instant, gone the next.

"Simon?" Tina's hands passed through the empty space where Six had been. With a whimper, she fainted dead away.

Reeling back, I attempted to wrap my brain around what I'd just witnessed. Six sacrificed his life to bring back Tina, and in the process, not only broke the rules, but released the other fixed-point souls before a reaper could collect them. I wasn't sure what would happen to those souls, but I did know that Tina was alive when she wasn't supposed to be. That was a threat to reality itself.

My instincts as a luna drove me forward, my intent to put to rights the fixed point in time.

I halted mid-stride, several humans rushing to Tina as if conjured from nowhere. A flurry of questions ensued, all directed at her:

"Are you all right?"

"How did you get out of the building?"

"Was anyone else with you inside?"

"Did anyone else make it out with you?"

A paramedic with an oxygen tank and mask scurried to her side. "Here, ma'am, put this on while I check your vitals."

Backing away, realization settled in. Despite my and Six's paranormal display of otherness, no one had noticed us. Not one single person. It was how lunas were designed, but until that moment I'd nearly forgotten.

Wind tore at me, lifting me off my feet. My wings shot out, flapping uselessly as I tried to move forward, or at the very least not get blown away like a moth in a tornado. Screaming with frustration, I made mad grabs for anything to hold onto as I sailed through the air. My fingertips slipped from everything, the world blurring around me as I moved faster and faster.

Wait. Isn't this where Reaper is supposed to grab onto me? Tell me that he won't let me go?

But he didn't come, and I was swept away. Oblivion claiming me before I reached my destination.

Chapter 17

Perplexed, I tilted my head back and forth, studying Six's costume. It consisted of a box hanging in front of him from a string around his neck, and several objects glued onto the surface, a digital clock, a small lamp, and a box of tissues. "What exactly are you supposed to be?"

"I'm a one-night stand, as in a singular nightstand. It's a word pun." He pointed to the objects on the box. "See, these are things you might find on a nightstand."

"You're a one-night stand." I rolled my eyes. "Why would you pick that for a costume?"

Six and I enjoyed Halloween more than the other human holidays because it gave us a chance to blend in like we normally did by way of dressing up, and yet we could stand out a touch more than usual. We didn't break any rules by donning a costume and interacting with humans since there was no risk of anything being remembered for more than what we wore.

Six faux scowled at me. "Because, Eighty-nine, I like word puns, and it oddly fits me because of the whole luna thing."

"You mean because all you can ever have with a human is a one-night stand?" I chuckled. "No one will get that part of the joke but me."

He slipped the costume off, setting it down on his bed to scrutinize. "Do you think adding a box of condoms would be too much?"

I flicked his ear. "I swear you're a human male sometimes with the things you think and say."

He continued to scrutinize his costume, rubbing at his ear. "Yeah, you're right, condoms are probably a bit douchey." He turned to me, eyes twinkling. "Have you decided what you're going to be this year?"

Flopping onto his bed, I curled on my side to watch him. "Not yet. I keep changing my mind."

"Well, you better get on that before it's too late."

I grunted, already re-considering my tentative decision to be Cat Woman. "Maybe I should just be Rain—"

"Don't be Rainbow Brite again this year," Six interrupted, knowing exactly what I was going to say.

I pouted. "But I already have the costume, and it's so ... so colorful."

"It's played out. Do something new."

"I don't know if I'm in the mood to figure out something new."

Six launched himself at me, fingers wiggling. "I'm not letting you be the same thing again. Anything. Pick anything else."

Rolling around the bed, I squealed, managing to dodge him. "Don't you dare tickle me, Six! You know I hate it!"

He laughed. "That's why it's so funny."

"I seriously hate you sometimes! Just leave me alone and let me wear what I want for Halloween!"

"Never! I'll never leave you alone!"

The ghost of Six lived on in my memory, haunting me with our past any time I wasn't on guard. It was the simple things I missed the most. The little moments that passed without fanfare when they'd happened, holding so much importance now.

I fucking miss you so much, Six. I knew I loved you, but I never understood how much until you left me. I wish I could tell you right now how much you mean to me. Maybe you didn't understand—maybe that's why you threw your life away so easily: you thought I'd get over it. But I won't. I'll never get over losing you. Never.

Lying on my stomach, I managed to lift my head a few inches, barely enough to spit out the sand filling my mouth. When I was done, I sank back down, listening to the calming crash of waves. I felt like a starfish washed up on the beach, not really wanting to be there, but lacking the ability to get where I needed to be. I didn't even have the energy to will myself home, which was probably a mental thing.

My chest burned, and a lump formed in my throat. I'd visited the scene of Six's death a grand total of three times, and of those three times, I'd made absolutely no difference. *No, that's not entirely true.* I managed to scar myself with the memory of watching him die, over, and over … and over again. All I had to do was close my eyes to see it with perfect clarity, I didn't need to witness it again, and I would avoid a fourth visit if I could. *But I have to save him somehow, so I have to go back.*

Finding Six's events through Archives had been fruitless, having only delivered me to one actual calamity out of all the trips. I didn't understand why I ended up at the beach in the storm, and then at the cemetery. And why did I end up at a different beach after Six's death? None of it made any sense.

Hopping through time for jobs had always been a bit unusual, but it had order to it. Go to the job, fix any problems, record the events and souls, pass the records of the events into a book in Archives, recover … rinse and repeat. Now my life had taken on a distinctly dream-like quality, nothing having rhyme or reason. Even when I visited Six in the past, he felt like an echo of himself, and not actually tangible in some weird way. I could interact with him, but some unquantifiable thing was missing. My memories with him seemed more vivid.

I was sinking deeper and deeper into the depths of despair the more I considered my situation. *What's the point in any of it? If you can't change Six's death scene, and you get lost in your past self there, then you can't save him that way. So, yeah, what's the point of any of it?*

I was going 'round and 'round in circles, contradicting myself from moment to moment. It seemed unavoidable, though; my warring emotions twisting my thoughts up in knots, even the ones that attempted to be rational. I'd questioned the definition of reality before, wondering if letting it crumble wasn't the way to go, and yet I'd swung the other way, deciding I had to save it, and Six. If I could only find a way to fix reality and not rescue Six from himself …

What's the point of reality without my best friend in it? Maybe I should just let go. Forget about all of it and fade away into nothing when I'm eventually unmade. Not even bother fighting anymore.

"You going to lie there all day?"

"Reaper!" I exclaimed, rolling onto my back. He loomed over me, blotting out the sun. My mood instantly buoyed, the flame of hope flickering to life, and I wasn't even sure why.

"Where the hell have you been? I went back in time again, and then was sucked into Six's death scene … again … and then I was thrown onto a beach … yep, again. It's almost like a very bad version of *Groundhog Day*." I squinted up at him. "You know what *Groundhog Day* is, right?"

"The movie *Groundhog Day*? Or course."

My lips twitched up. I wished I could share that little tidbit with Six. A Reaper, and me, on a beach, talking about *Groundhog Day*. Sounded like the beginning of a bad joke.

Pushing up to a sitting position, I glared at Reaper. "So? Where were you?" I tried not to sound too annoyed. After all, I'd decided I didn't need him for anything, but all the same, I didn't appreciate him ditching me without explanation either.

He crossed his arms over his chest and lowered his hooded head to be level with my face. "You're not the only one who has a job to do."

"I just figured with how you've been my constant shadow lately that you had a little bit more leeway than lunas did." Grabbing a handful of sand, I sifted it through my fingers. "Why do you suppose I keep ending up at a beach after being sucked through the RR?"

Reaper shrugged. "No idea. And is that what you're calling the rip in reality now? RR?"

"Yep. I'm calling it, or them, RRs now." I didn't tell him it was in Six's honor. He loved abbreviations that let him feel like he was in the know. It was just another quirk equal parts annoying and lovable that I missed about my best friend.

Reaper reached into his robes and pulled out the blue book, waving it in front of my face. "I thought you would have already started drilling me with questions since you fell asleep before I could tell you what I found in here."

I gazed up at him steadily. "Do you think we can actually pull this off? The whole fixing the hole in reality thing?"

"Yes."

One word. No hesitation.

His certainty steeled my resolution once more. *I can do this. And ... and ... maybe it's silly and naïve to think that I can do all of this by myself. Even the most successful people need help sometimes, and I shouldn't begrudge Reaper his, if that is in fact what he is doing—helping me.* Yet, somewhere along the line during the short period of time since I met Reaper, I'd come to trust him. I didn't think he was trying to screw me over, even if I was still unsure about what his end game originally was. Things had changed for the both of us since the RR had appeared.

"Okay, so what did you discover?"

"You are unable to change Six's death because it happened at a fixed point in time. He gave his life for Tina, who was one of the humans scheduled to die that day. Him, being a luna—the luna assigned to that job—locked his decision into place along with the event. When you go back all you can truly do is observe."

My heart thudded loudly in my chest. "Th-That doesn't sound like anything but bad news to me." *If Six tied his death into the fixed point in time, then it was fixed—* "But wait. That soul, that bright soul I keep encountering changes his status of being tagged or not. And I did more than observe, Six saw me, he reacted."

Plus, I was fairly certain lunas didn't have the power to lock down fixed points in time. Unless it was something we did automatically without conscious thought, kind of like breathing. *How is it possible that I know so little about my job?* I've been doing what I've been tasked with for millennia without bothering to delve deeper into the minutia. Sure, I had questions, idle musings, but I'd never followed through on any kind of research.

"There's still hope." Reaper tapped the top of my head.

"We merely have to find a loophole and a new plan of attack. What we've been doing won't work no matter how many times you're thrown back into that scene."

He started pacing. "Maybe the key lies with past Tina."

I brought my hand up to shade my eyes. "Past Tina? But how will we get back to her since Archives is how we've been going into the past up until now? She's not a luna and doesn't have books."

"There are ways. Although they're riskier when not dealing with a fixed point in time. We could end up making things worse than they already are."

"Worse?" I grumbled. "How is that even possible?"

"Ever hear of the butterfly effect?"

"Sure. Who hasn't? But it's a human concept when it comes to messing with time. A theory."

Reaper came to stand directly in front of me again. "A theory that actually holds some truth to it."

I nibbled on my thumbnail. "If that's the case, then me attempting to save Six could have the same negative results."

"Creatures such as us live outside the rules of time and space to a large degree. We have our own problems to watch out for."

Oh, yes, we definitely had our own problems to watch out for. "Since you're the man, or reaper with the plan, what do you suggest our next step be? Time, or really, reality is running out. Or it will be soon."

He resumed his pacing. "I'm not quite sure yet."

"I know why I haven't asked any of my kind for help

with any of this, but why haven't you asked any reapers? Seems like they might want to, since, you know, they have a vested interest in reality."

Ignoring my question, Reaper paced back and forth in front of me, kicking up sand.

My eyes widened. "Or did you? Did you ask and none of them cared?" Could Reaper be more of an anomaly than I realized? His involvement in all of this, even his interest in me, had seemed out of character for his kind from the beginning.

"We've discussed this before," Reaper snapped. He cut his hand through the air. "I'm not doing it again."

I crinkled my nose, resisting the urge to stick my tongue out as well. "We did not. We only talked about why I wasn't asking other lunas to get involved." *At least I think we only talked about that. It's possible I'm a bit distracted, my mind focused on other things.*

My stomach fluttered, and an invisible thread attached to my sternum was yanked, drawing my undivided attention.

I'm not even surprised anymore. This keeps happening at the most inconvenient times, and a lot more frequently than it used to.

The location of my pending job appeared in my mind's eye, along with every other detail I would need.

Standing, I brushed sand off of me in rough strokes. "Duty calls. Again."

Reaper tilted his head. "Inconvenient."

"Just what I was thinking," I grumbled. "But when I feel the pull—"

"You must go."

I nodded.

California, here I come.

Chapter 18

Airport employees bustled around the plane, loading luggage, and doing last-minute maintenance checks. I lingered near the right wing, studying the faces framed in the small windows. All of them were tagged.

In my peripheral vision, a reaper appeared, recognizable by his power signature and dark garb.

"Is that you, Reaper?" I hissed out of the side of my mouth.

The reaper slowly turned toward me. "Do you speak to me, luna?"

Shit. Not him. Where the hell did he go this time? "What? Why are you talking to me, reaper? I didn't think any of you actually had vocal cords."

Without responding, the reaper glided a few feet farther away. I internally chuckled at how easy he was to scare off, so to speak. I wasn't sure if it was a compliment of my quick thinking or an insult to my species as a whole.

The loud thump of the baggage compartment, being slammed shut and locked, drew my attention back to the plane. I was now alone on the tarmac, save for the reaper, as the plane's engines roared to life.

I heaved a long sigh. Usually, at this point, I would be eager to feel the warmth the soon-to-be-dead souls would offer me as I recorded them. There was none of that today. I knew I couldn't resist the pull of a job, but when all was said and done, I wouldn't receive the same reward that I, as a luna, had come to expect. The physical warmth would still be there, to be sure, but the emotional satiation would be lacking. I wouldn't have even a moment of peace. That would only come once I figured out how to save Six.

A man in a bright orange vest rushed past me, arms flailing. *Ah, I'd wondered if he'd make an appearance at this event. And there he is, the bright soul, and pain in my ass, right on schedule.*

"Wait! There's something wrong with the plane!" He danced around the front of the cockpit, trying to get spotted by the pilots.

Frowning, the co-pilot spoke into his radio.

A few moments later, a security cart screeched to a halt near us, two guards hopping out. "Hey! Are you an employee of this airline? What are you doing out here?"

The man, tall and lanky, dark skin with dyed pastel blue hair, was obviously not an employee. If his hair wasn't the first clue, then his ripped jeans was another. Although, I wasn't sure what year it was, so the dress code could be laxer than I was used to seeing.

"There's something wrong with the engine! You need to get the people off that plane!"

Moving in unison, the guards approached him cautiously. "Are you trying to do something to that plane?" one of them demanded.

"No! I would never! I just know something is wrong with the engine! Please, you have to trust me!" He dodged both guards, sprinting toward me. His eyes widened, the whites dwarfing their color. "You! I know you! What are you doing here?"

Groaning, I froze in place, unsure of where I should go. If I took off running, despite being a luna, I would be noticed. Plus, I had to be there to do my job. Glancing down at my clothing, I confirmed that I was wearing an employee vest. "Here he is! Get him out of here!" I jumped in front of the man's path, slowing him down enough for the guards to grab hold of him.

"He just got here, so he definitely didn't have time to do anything to the plane." It didn't hurt to add that on. It wouldn't help me get my job done if the security guards decided to investigate for possible tampering.

Ignoring me, the man was dragged to the security cart, fighting the entire way. "No! You don't understand! I'm trying to save all those lives!"

Numbly, I watched as the three of them drove off. Since they weren't tagged there was nothing else for me to do. The bright soul would probably get the blame for the disaster in the end. It seemed that his fate was to suffer no matter whether he lived or died in every one of his lives.

I again was left alone on the tarmac with the reaper. The plane turned, slowly taxiing to the runway. The engines revved as it set off, picking up speed.

The explosion was instant, the wave of heat striking me a millisecond before the sound.

Unfazed, a surge of energy danced along my skin, goose bumps erupting in its wake. *It's time.*

Shaking my wings out, I threw my head back as I rose into the air. Hovering between worlds, the recently dead souls passed through me one after another in lightning-fast succession. I recorded their essences, making sure all that should be was.

As the numbers of dead added up, I barely noticed the warmth their souls offered me. I knew the payoff wouldn't be there like normal, but I also hadn't realized that it wouldn't give me any kind of reprieve from my plight as a luna. My cravings to touch humanity would not be dulled at all with this job. The only reason why I'd complete it at all was because I knew I had to. I wouldn't risk messing up reality any more than Six already had, otherwise I would make it even more difficult to fix.

Souls recorded, I turned, my gaze following the path the security cart had taken. I'd whiffed the last time the bright soul walked away from a disaster, unable to discover what made it special, but maybe this time would be different.

"Going after him again, are we?" Reaper's sardonic tone caused me to jump.

Clutching at my chest, I said, "I should expect you to do that. I don't know why you startle me every time. I swear you wait for just the right moment when I'm lost in thought to just pop right in."

"You seem to be lost in thought a lot lately then."

Was that an actual observation or a covert jibe from him? Sometimes it was hard to tell since I couldn't read his facial expressions. I relied on that social skill more than I'd ever realized until Reaper came along and decided to shadow me.

I cleared my throat. "Well, I'm going after the bright soul again. You can do what you want."

"I think it's a waste of our very valuable time."

"Our time isn't linked in any real way. You can do what you want, and I can do what I want. We don't have to do anything together. Therefore, it's not our time."

Reaper swung around to block my path. "We should follow the past Tina lead. This bright soul has no proven link to the reality problem. It could simply be a coincidence."

Notching my chin up, I crossed my arms over my chest. "You going to tell me, as a reaper, you actually believe any of this is a coincidence anymore?"

The dark cavern of his hood stared back at me, his lavender eyes glinting like twin flashlights from its depths. "Maybe. Maybe not."

Well, the eye glowing thing is new. Quirking an eyebrow, I decided to let it go without question. I had other things to worry about. "I'll take that as a no." Why was he being so obstinate about this? It was a better idea—safer—to follow up with the bright soul than past Tina. Even Reaper had acknowledged the dangers of messing up reality more than it already was with his plan. "Again, the bright soul has presented itself at one of my jobs. He's here, and the RRs all seem to be centered around Six for now. We still have time."

"We still have time ... until we don't."

As usual, Reaper was right. We had no idea how much time we actually had to solve the reality problem. And even if we did have some kind of number ... would that number apply to the linear progression of human time, or to a cumulative amount accrued by us starting at the event horizon? The only thing we could do was to muddle through with a bit of urgency. There was no point in panicking when time travel was on the table. Of course, with fixed points in time, butterfly effects, reality tears, and possible paradoxes involved as well ...

Pinching my nose, I picked up the pace. "We follow this bright soul to try and figure out why it exists, and maybe we'll get some much-needed answers."

My stomach fluttered, and an invisible thread attached to my sternum was yanked, drawing my undivided attention.

"Fuck! No! How is this even happening so soon? It's never been like this before!"

Reaper whirled around, robes billowing dramatically

around him. “Another job?” Surprise of his own was laced into his tone.

I nodded, the location of my pending job appearing in my mind’s eye, along with every other detail I would need.

“Th-This isn’t a coincidence either. None of it is.” What I was wondering was how far back the links had begun. I had a suspicion further than I could fathom. “But duty calls. Again.”

“I’ll be right behind you,” Reaper said.

“Hmm … whatever.”

Here I come, ready or not, you humans better be prepared to die.

Chapter 19

Is it because I didn't get those feel-good vibes from my last job that another was handed to me so quickly? Are jobs handed out like heroin from some divine dealer to keep lunas hooked? And I'm dangerously close from slipping free? Or are the number of jobs increasing as a side effect of the RR? After all, there are only one hundred lunas, and all of space and time to manage.

Coughing, I surveyed the desert wasteland surrounding me. Nothing but sand, sun, and a spattering of vegetation as far as the eye could see. Oh, and of course the several military tents lined up at the base of a dune.

A reaper hovered beside me. Again, a stranger and not the Angel of Death I'd become so familiar with. *Wonder how and why Reaper keeps himself hidden from the other reapers?*

A desert-camo-colored vehicle lumbered over the dry terrain in the distance, drawing closer and closer to where

I stood. Even though I was clad in military gear of my own, I still wondered how my presence at places like these were explained away by the human mind. Appearing as a soldier who was supposed to be in the area, what was my excuse for being out in the desert alone the way that I was? *Hmm ... just more things I'll probably never get the answers to.*

I swiped at sweat gathering on my forehead with my sleeve. No anticipation battled my nerves; instead, I found myself annoyed by having to do another job so soon after the last. I hadn't even had enough time between the two events to stop at Archives. I'd never created more than one book in a visit before. *Lucky you gets to experience a lot of firsts lately.*

Gnawing on my lower lip, my mind began to wander, going to another first.

Heading up the stairs, having just returned to the luna realm with a stash of several new books, a dull thump sounded at the front door. Pausing my climb, I turned to ascertain what the noise had been. Another dull thump sounded, followed by a kind of scratching sound.

What in the world is that?

The door creaked open, and Six, the new Six, staggered through. Upon spotting me, he threw his arms up in the air. "Welp, I did it. I went to my very first job and recorded everything like I'm supposed to." He shuffled closer to the base of the stairs, his lower lip quivering slightly. "Is ... is it always like that?"

I frowned, my gaze darting across his visage. "Like what?"

He sniffled. "So horrible. All those deaths."

I'd only known the new Six for a few days, and a huge part of me wanted to ignore him and go about the day I had planned for myself. I even half turned to go.

His eyes shimmered with unshed tears as he stared up at me, waiting for a response.

Just walk away. He's a luna, and he'll figure it out eventually without any help from you.

His stare was unwavering, all open vulnerability even as his teeth began to chatter.

Shit. Shit. Shit. Don't do it Eighty-nine. Don't do it.

He suddenly slumped forward, as if someone had unplugged him. Without thought, I rushed down the stairs, shoving my shoulder under him before he hit the ground. Grunting, I managed to get my arms around him to give him full support.

"Thanks," he mumbled.

"Come on, I'll help you down to Archives, and then get you to bed. This ... the cold, the emptiness, it's all part of it, and you'll get used to it after a while."

"But what if I don't want to get used to it?"

"You're a luna, it's what you were created to do."

That was the moment I first let Six into my life. After that, he'd simply decided we were going to be friends, and I'd been powerless to resist. And I definitely tried to resist.

I chuckled to myself, other memories shuffling through my brain, bringing a myriad of emotions with them. Six was this force of nature that swept me along for the ride. I couldn't remember how many times over the first few months of getting to know him that I told myself it was a mistake and I should run away.

You were the best mistake I ever made, Six. Our friendship gave me new life ... or a life at all.

Clearing his throat, the reaper sidled up beside me. "Luna, are you going to do your job? I cannot do mine until you complete yours."

Swallowing a yelp, I pulled myself from my inner musings, to discover that it was indeed time for me to do my thing.

I didn't feel the surge of energy this time. I always feel the surge like an early warning system.

Releasing my wings, I threw my head back as I rose off the ground. Hovering between worlds, the recently dead souls passed through me one after another, creeping along, slow as molasses. Studying each one, I let them hang in my consciousness before moving on to the next.

You were going to propose to your girlfriend when you got home. You were so excited and so nervous. You hold so much regret now that you'll never see her again.

You were going to retire after this tour of duty. You wanted to spend time with your wife, your children, and grandchildren. You wanted to have a quiet life in the country. You have no regrets but you're sad you won't get to grow old the way you wanted.

You were only here because you needed money for college. Your family was so proud of you, of the future you were working toward. You feel like your life is over before it really got a chance to begin. You regret all the lost dreams. You wanted to fall in love someday.

I'd never felt the thoughts and emotions of souls so clearly before. It had always been more of an impression or imprint.

Heat surged through my veins, and I stretched out my limbs, the souls' regrets consuming me, burning me from the inside out. I wanted to scream, I wanted to cry, but beyond anything else I wanted it to stop. All of it. The pain—not just the physical pain I was experiencing, but the pain of the recently departed, the pain of the entire world.

Dropping to the ground, I sobbed. Humans suffered so much. They were given so much opportunity, the ceiling for them high, but the risk of failure, of anguish just as high. *And to think I crave what they have.* I wasn't so sure I did anymore.

"I can't do this. I just can't do this anymore." Chills broke out along my skin, my body bereft after the souls had scorched their way through me.

I sensed Reaper's presence just as he swept me up in his arms. "Hold on, little luna, I'll get you out of here."

"They were all bright this time. Every single one of them. They set me on fire from the inside out." I closed my eyes, sand abrading my corneas. "Am I burning up? Is this it for me? Or has the RR finally decided it's time for me to be ripped to pieces and unmade?"

"There's no reality tear here as far as I can tell." His

long fingers dug into my flesh. "But something isn't quite right either."

Wind howled past us, blowing sand into my mouth and nose. "What's happening?" Fear spiked through me, mingling with my confusion.

"I spoke too soon. There is a tear."

Prying my eyes open, I was greeted with what appeared to be a sandstorm. "How can you see anything at all?" I gripped him tighter.

Please don't take us back to Six's death scene. Please don't take us back to Six's death scene. If I had to witness it again on the heels of the two jobs I'd just handled, I might very well rip myself apart and offer up my molecules to be remade into anything but me—anything but a luna.

"Hold on to me tight. I think we're getting pulled back into the—"

Bright light exploded, visible even in the cloud of sand.

My world blurred to nothing.

Chapter 20

Coming to instantly aware, panic caused adrenaline to surge up my spine, and my heart fisted with dread. Gasping for oxygen, I practically choked on my own tongue, expecting to be at Six's death scene.

Instead, I found myself surrounded by books and an unnatural silence.

I knew exactly where I was: Archives.

And I was alone.

Unfurling myself from the floor, I rested against a bookshelf while trying to get my bearings. Reality was imploding or unraveling, or any verb anyone wanted to use to describe the complete and utter fucked up state of reality as we all knew it. I couldn't help but wonder if the RRs were now sucking people up from one place and depositing them in another with no rhyme or reason. At least before they seemed to be linked to Six, but now that rule no longer applied, just like a lot of others didn't either.

What am I supposed to do? I didn't have many choices. My plan of following the bright soul seemed pointless now, and something I could have done before the severity of the situation escalated. There was still the option of tracking down past Tina, but without Reaper I didn't have the means to so do. Going directly to Six's death scene was also out since I'd merely get trapped in my past self and be unable to change anything. Only one option was left as far as I could tell … go back in time, and grab past Six before he can do—

Fuck. No. No, no, no, no, no. If Six locked his death into the fixed point in time like Reaper said, then that means he now has to die there. He has to die, but …

I tore at my hair. *He's created a paradox. Six has created a goddamn paradox. How the fuck didn't either Reaper or me figure out that glaringly obvious tidbit?*

Six created a RR by locking his death into place at a fixed point in time where Tina should have been the one to die. The fixed point in time now has to happen that way, and therefore if we stop it from happening that way, boom, new RR. But if we don't stop it from happening that way, boom, the current RR destroys us all.

I silently laughed. *Well, Six, you really FUBARed this one up, didn't you? Yep, you never did do anything half-assed, huh? Why would you start now?*

Dropping back down to the ground, I stared blankly at

the books in front of me. *Reality is going to be destroyed either way. There's nothing I can do about that part. The question now is: Which way do I want to go out? With Six by my side, or a pathetic loser who dies alone?* When I thought about it that way, the answer was clear. It also wasn't a complicated task anymore. If all I wanted was to not die alone, then I could find Six in the past, and simply stay with him there.

Jumping to my feet, I squeezed my eyes shut, and spun in a circle. I imagined Six's smile, the way his brown eyes crinkled at the corners, and his laugh, how he sounded like a wounded donkey when he thought something was extremely funny …

Warmth, subtle and comforting, washed over me, and then …

A tug, the smallest of pulls fluttered in my sternum, causing me to stumble forward, hands outstretched. My fingers curled around the supple leather spine of a book, and I lifted it to my nose, inhaling deeply.

Six. Home. He'll always be my home.

My eyes still tightly squeezed shut, I opened the book, placing my palms on the smooth pages.

Please, please, please ... Take me here. Take me to this time and place—to Six. Take me to where I need to be. Let me be with him at the end. Please.

Strong arms wrapped around me, the rough texture of Reaper's robe abrading my cheeks just as darkness swallowed me whole.

WE WERE at some kind of power plant. I wasn't sure what kind because the information hadn't been placed in my mind since it wasn't my job. There were large coils and lots of fancy-looking equipment. I shrugged. None of it mattered. Reality was imploding, and I only had eyes for Six.

He was a few feet in front of me, attention consumed by his work, gaze riveted to a platform above him.

I guess I'll let him finish. I mean it's all pointless in the end, but he could probably use the energy fix from the soon-to-be-dead souls.

Reaper placed a hand on my arm, stealing my attention. "You figured out that he created a paradox, I see."

My mouth actually swung open, hanging there for a few moments, before I regained enough composure to speak. "You knew? You knew about the paradox and you didn't say a word about it?"

He glided in front of me, crossing his arms over his chest. "Of course I knew. I'm an Angel of Death."

I slapped at him, unable to restrain myself. "Then why didn't you tell me? Why with all the cryptic bullshit, and then pretending like we had a chance to stop it? I don't understand why you did any of it. And why are you even still here?"

Lavender sparked within his hood before he turned his head. "I have my reasons."

"Don't you have better things to do than follow around a luna when we're all about to be wiped out of existence?"

"Existence or reality, whatever you call it, has been destroyed many times before. And in the ashes of destruction, something new is always born."

My lips curled into a snarl. "So what you're telling me is that reapers, or maybe all angels, aren't going to be affected by this. Humans, and lunas, and who knows who and what else, will be erased, but you don't care because other things will be created in our wake."

He rose up into the air higher. "Basically."

"So all of your help was a lie." *I guess I got my question answered once and for all.* Reapers wouldn't help and didn't care. In fact, they didn't even actually have a horse in the race at all.

"No. My help wasn't a lie."

Speaking through gritted teeth, I said, "If you knew about the paradox, and you were just tagging along with me because I'm amusing, then yes, everything you said and did was a lie."

"That is a false claim. The things I did were done for a specific reason. Whether or not I helped in the end, remains to be seen."

My gaze swung to Six, and then back to Reaper. "Did … did you take pity on me or something? Did you help me get back here to Six so I wouldn't die alone?"

But none of that made sense either. If he'd merely wanted to grant me a last boon before my death, then why all the subterfuge? Why not just take me back to Six after his death? Unless he thought I had to come to the paradox conclusion on my own. No. Why not point it out to me after the first trip back to Six's death scene?

My right eye twitched, the left doing the same a moment later. "None of this makes any sense whatsoever."

"Things rarely do when one doesn't have all the information to paint the full picture."

I shoved past him, no longer wanting to spend even another millisecond in his duplicitous presence. *I'll wait outside for Six.*

After exiting the power plant, I scuffled around in the parking lot, trying to wrap my mind around the conversation I'd just had with Reaper. He knew about the paradox, if not from the very beginning, pretty damn close to it. And yet he'd even gone as far as to take me to a celestial Archive to make it seem like there was hope. In fact, he'd repeatedly been the one to motivate me, to push me along when I'd been willing to give up. Was it pity, or some twisted game? I wondered again what his end game was.

"Aaargh!" I kicked the curb, jumping back as pain shot up my foot. "What the hell is wrong with him?"

Sirens flared to life, and people came flooding out from several doors around the power plant. I backed up, crouching down near a car.

"Shut it down! Shut it all down!" a feminine voice bellowed from somewhere.

"It's too late!" a masculine voice answered. "Shutting it

down won't help! We need to complete the evacuation and notify—"

Fire erupted from the top of the building, the ground vibrating with the force of it. Debris rained down, and everyone in unison seemed to crouch and cover their heads, even the employees wearing hard hats.

A woman was the first to her feet, head swinging around in panic. "Who was still in there? We need to count off or something."

"Just the emergency crew," someone else said.

The rest of their voices faded into the background as Six stumbled out of the front door. His arms were wound tightly around his middle, and his expression was stricken.

I made a mad dash for him. "Six!"

Surprise lit up his features. "Eighty-nine? What are you doing here?"

"It doesn't matter." I pulled him into a hug. "I'm here."

"Okay. I just want to go home."

Home. The luna realm. Shit. I hadn't thought about that. What if I run into past me? When I decided to go back in time, I imagined spending my last hours or days with Six, but I hadn't considered what I would do if I ran into myself.

"How about we do something fun? We're going to recover at a fancy hotel this time. With room service and the works." I injected as much false cheer into my voice as I could muster.

Six grunted, which I took as agreement to my plan.

"All right. Just hold onto me, and we'll get you warm soon." Glancing over my shoulder, I saw Reaper gliding along behind us. "Get out of here," I hissed.

"What?" Six mumbled. "Who are you talking to?"

"No one. Absolutely no one."

Chapter 21

Yawning, Six wiggled under the stack of comforters I'd piled on top of him. I'd made a stealth purchase—aka stolen a bunch of hotel comforters right out from under the unobservant employees.

"What about Archives? I haven't made my book from today's job. I've never gone right to recovery mode without doing that first."

I nibbled my thumbnail. I was already two behind on my event to book situation, but I wasn't concerned in the slightest since I knew that reality was crumbling as we sat there. But what to tell him? Filling him in about going back to spend time with him at the so-called end, not necessarily something I wanted to do. I hated the idea of lying to him, but there was also the issue of upsetting him so that we couldn't enjoy ourselves. As it was, I was going to be struggling with putting on a happy façade. If both of us were down in the dumps it would be hopeless.

Lie it is then. "I've done it a few times before. Back when the other Six was around. As long as you do it soon, you'll be fine."

Six yawned again, snuggling deeper under the fluffy mound. "Oh. Okay." His eyes slid shut, and his mouth fell open, soft snores vibrating his lips.

I couldn't hold back a laugh, which distorted into a snort. The amusement over Six's sleeping habits was short-lived though.

Melancholy, sudden and acute, drowned me in a sea of despair. Several times now, I'd pondered the upside to letting reality dissolve, not knowing what actually was waiting for the majority of us at the end of the road. Reaper had confirmed the destruction of old realities, but that didn't mean much. After everything we'd experienced together, Six and I would be gone, these versions of us erased forever. The amount I didn't know about the universe was infinite in comparison with what I did know. Our lives could end, but did that mean our souls would dissolve into the cosmic ether? Or would we simply be remade into something else?

The fear of the unknown warred with the hope of discovering something better. My life as a luna could end, with a new, brighter life beginning as some new creature —or my torment could be multiplied exponentially. Until it actually happened, I'd have no way of knowing, nor did I know if I would even remember being a luna in the first place. I could have been many things before becoming what I am today …

Sometimes when things evolve and change, where it's been is forgotten, which can be good in some cases, therefore it doesn't really matter. In others, knowing the path makes all the difference in the world. For instance, what if whatever I was in a past reality made being a luna seem like a walk in the park? Because I didn't remember the experience, I couldn't appreciate what I'd gained.

Knowledge may be power, but it also means pain. *Like now. I'm experiencing emotional angst because I know the world, as we all know it, is coming to an end. Six, who doesn't know, is sleeping peacefully.* Maybe becoming something else—something ignorant of the way things are or were is a reward. Because ignorance like that can be bliss.

Slumping beside Six, I stared out the huge window, the twinkling lights of the Vegas Strip not even capable of ensnaring my full attention. My thoughts were jumbled, my perceptions twisted, my brain addled from regrets.

A dark human-shaped silhouette hovered outside of the window, long fingers tapping on the glass. Scowling, I turned my head away. *There's not a chance in hell I'm talking to Reaper now. I'm not even going to acknowledge him.* Any fond feelings I'd developed for the Angel of Death evaporated the instant I found out he was playing me for a fool.

What could he possibly have left to say to me?

I could still see him in my peripheral, bobbing around in the wind like a demented balloon. *Demented balloon?*

Okay, so maybe your brain is going to be unmade before your body. It could already be happening.

Reaper tapped on the glass again, and I jerked my head farther away in a clearly demonstrative motion. *I'm not going to acknowledge you—you stupid asshat!*

He materialized directly in front of me, inches from my face, the dark cavern of his hood blotting out the light. I yelped, and scrabbled to the side, falling off the bed in a heap.

Six shot straight up, eyes as wide as saucers. "What's going on? What happened?" He peered over the edge of the bed, taking in my prone form. "Why are you down there?"

"It's nothing. Go back to sleep. I rolled off the bed and startled myself."

His eyebrows shot up to nearly his hairline. "Were you asleep?"

"Umm … no." Reaper had made himself scarce again, apparently not wanting to show himself to Six. *Interesting.*

"Then how'd it happen?" Six muttered, settling back down under his comforter mound.

"Thought I saw a spider."

Six sniffed with annoyance. "You're acting weird, even for you. We're going to talk about it when I wake up." He closed his eyes, already half asleep.

"What are you going to tell him?"

Slapping a hand over my mouth, I stifled another yelp. "What the hell is wrong with you?"

Six grunted as he rolled over.

Jumping to my feet, I scurried into the massive bathroom, shutting the door behind me. Reaper, of course, took that as an invitation, the twisted creature that he was.

Leaning on the inside of the door, he steepled his hands in front of where his face would be. "So, what are you going to tell him?"

I slashed my arm through the air. "My days of having conversations with you about … well, anything are over. Done. Finished."

He crossed his arms over his chest. "Is it me or have you grown more dramatic since I first met you? Not an easy task."

Shooting him with my best death glare, I spoke through gritted teeth. "If I knew how to kill a reaper, I swear on all that is holy, I'd do it right here and now."

He clicked his tongue. "That answers my question well enough."

"Why won't you leave me alone? The jig is up, I know you were lying to me about everything, so there's no point in pretending anymore."

"I have my reasons for being here."

I bared my teeth in a snarl. "Just go away. I don't want to see you anymore."

Poof, he was gone. There one minute, gone the next. The thing was, I still sensed his presence. "Oh, okay. We're going to play the literal game, are we? I may be dramatic, but you're like a five-year-old."

The only response I got was the door opening

seemingly by itself. Despite Reaper now being invisible, I could still see him in my mind's eye just hovering there all smug. I never had to see his expressions to pick up on his attitude. It was always there, rolling off of him in palpable waves.

"You know," I stage whispered, "whoever created reapers must have used up all their energy on making you physically perfect. By the time they got to personality they were like whatever, they're so pretty they can be assholes."

Silence.

"I know you're still there. I can feel you."

More silence.

"Yep, total and complete asshole. Too bad you won't be erased with the rest of reality. It would almost be worth it just for that."

Anger simmered, my body primed for a fight. It was only made worse when Reaper still pretended he wasn't there anymore.

"What are you going to do? Stealth stalk me?"

More silence.

"I hate you." I wanted to punch him in his perfectly formed face more than words would ever be able to express.

I can't exactly make him visible again. I can't force him to do anything. There's absolutely nothing I can do about him, in fact. I growled under my breath. *Fine. If he wants to play it that way, I'll just pretend he's not here. Permanently.*

Creeping back out into the main room, I peered over at Six, who was thankfully snoring again. A part of me wanted to wake him up so we wouldn't waste another millisecond of time together, but I knew he'd be dead in the water if I didn't let him recover.

Settling into the space on the bed beside Six, I stared out the window again. I had a lot of things to consider. Time didn't flow in a straight line per say, but now that I'd traveled back to be with Six, I wasn't sure what that would mean for past me. I'd looped back in my own timeline, so just like in a convoluted time travel movie, in order for me to be here at all the past had to have happened the way that it already did. Buuuut ... by me interfering in the past, I'd changed it.

I rubbed my temples, a headache blooming. *Ugh. I don't know why I'm making any kind of attempt to figure this out. Even if I screw something up, it doesn't matter, reality is already crumbling.* But I couldn't help it. Curiosity was a huge part of what drove me through life.

There's also the job thing. *Will I get pulled to any, and will I be able to resist now? And what about any jobs Six gets pulled to? I can't exactly tell him not to go, if either of us can actually resist.*

Oh, good god, why can't I turn my brain off for even two seconds? I eyed the room service menu on the end table. Food could help. Yep, I could force myself into a sugar coma, and then maybe my thoughts would switch off for a bit.

Leaning over, I grabbed the menu, and the phone as well. My lips curled up slowly as I scanned my options. *Mmm hmm, yep, this is the best plan you've had in a long time.*

Chapter 22

"Okay, now I'm convinced something is going on with you for sure." Six's brow furrowed, his gaze darting over my prone form and then to the empty plates strewn around the room. "I know you only binge on that kind of level when something's wrong." He leaned forward, his eyes narrowing. "Sooo … spill."

Groaning, I rolled over onto my side, rubbing my belly. *Immortal I may be, but impervious to stomach issues, I am not.* Apparently, even I could eat to the point of pain. "I had a few cravings."

Six snorted, his eyebrows shooting up. "You think?"

"Just trying to get into the celebratory mood."

"And what exactly are we celebrating? Because this whole thing is weird. First, you show up at my job, something you've never done before. And sidebar, something I didn't even think was possible. Then you whisk me off to Vegas before I even get the chance to visit Archives, and while I'm asleep you eat all of the food in the hotel."

"I didn't eat all of the food in the hotel."

He picked up the phone, room service menu in hand. "Well, we're about to find out."

I burped, remnants of that last bit of chocolate cake making an encore. Just when I thought my mutinous digestive track was about to settle down, my stomach cramped, and I made a mad dash for the bathroom. Hunched over the toilet, sweat erupting out of every pore on my body, I revisited some of the things I'd stuffed into my face to avoid my feelings. *Gross.*

My hair was gathered off my face, removed from the danger zone. As I continued to retch, Six settled in next to me.

"You really are in rare form today, Eighty-nine."

"I might have eaten too much too quickly." I reached for some toilet paper, my fingers spinning the roll without capturing the end.

Six shooed my hand away, and then placed a few crumpled squares into my palm. "So, again I'm going to ask you, what's going on?"

I wiped my mouth and sat back to lean against the wall. Six flushed the toilet, his gaze never leaving mine.

I sighed. Lying to Six when he knew me so well was going to be difficult. That's why sticking to as close to the truth as possible was my best bet. "I've had a really shitty couple of days, and I miss you."

He pursed his lips. "Okay. I just saw you a few hours ago—"

"No, listen to me. With the way things have been going it—it ... well, it just seems like it's been forever since we've had one of our adventures. I miss our time together."

His gaze softened. "Yeah, it has been a while. I could use a Six and Eighty-nine adventure right about now."

I flicked my gaze away. "I know I don't always say it, and I'm not as good as you at showing it, but I need you to know how much I love you. I—"

"Eighty-nine, why are you—"

"Just listen to me for a second, okay?" He nodded, his lower lip tucked in between his teeth. "You're my best friend, and you mean the world to me. I honestly don't know what I'd do if I ever lost you for good. Nothing makes sense without you. I may be older and wiser than you," I chuckled, and he grinned, "but it feels like we grew up together. You're not only my best friend, but you're like my brother, and yet so much more. I just want to make sure you know all of that."

An image of him engulfed in flame just before he disappeared popped into my mind unbidden. My tongue suddenly weighed a hundred pounds, and a boulder had taken up residence in my throat. "I love you, Six," I croaked.

He pulled me into his arms, resting his head on my shoulder. "I'm not sure why you're being so sentimental today, but if it makes you feel any better, I know you love me. You're just old and cranky sometimes." I laughed. He squeezed me tighter. "I hope you know I love you just as much."

"I know."

"What are you, Han Solo?" he joked.

Shoving at him, I pulled away to swipe at my eyes before I did something really sappy like shed any tears. "Okay, I'm done. Let's go get our Vegas on."

Six bowed his head, appearing sheepish. "I agree, we need to have one of our adventures, and soon, but I have a few things to do first."

I fought a petulant pout, my lower lip trembling with the effort. "Like what?"

"Like hitting up Archives for one. I simply won't be able to relax until I get things squared away like I'm supposed to. It's our job, the entire reason for existing."

I couldn't exactly argue with that, unless I came clean about my real reasons for wanting to avoid the luna realm. "Yeah, I guess I can see your point."

"Okay, then let's head home, and when I'm done, we can plan our next adventure."

"Not Vegas?"

He shrugged. "I'm cool with Vegas, I guess. But I don't want to rule anything else out either."

I narrowed my eyes at him. "Mmm hmm, okay. Where do you want to go if not Vegas?"

He picked at his jeans. "Nowhere in particular."

Crossing my arms over my chest, I nudged him with my foot. "Six."

"I said nowhere in particular."

I kicked at him. "Just tell me already."

"Okay, fine. I thought we could go out to some cool little local bars."

"Local to where?"

A grin stretched across his face. "You'll see."

I sighed, and rolled my eyes, playing along with our normal interactions. If I gave in too easily, he would focus in on something being wrong with me again. I couldn't let him know that I would do almost anything he wanted without any argument at all. Dealing with the knowledge of the impending end of reality tended to make me a tad more agreeable, apparently. Why sweat the small stuff when the small stuff won't be around for much longer?

Standing, he offered me his hand, pulling me to my feet. "Okay, home, and then I'll reveal the super cool place I want to go."

"Yeah, sure, whatever." I hid my smile until he turned his back to me.

It wasn't long ago that I'd wished for even five more minutes with Six. It was the small, seemingly inane things I missed the most about spending time with him, and there we were, together again like nothing had separated us to begin with.

I bet Reaper is having a ball spying on our private moments. He probably thinks I'm so amusing. My sappy moment in the bathroom especially entertaining.

Six waved. "See you there." He closed his eyes and vanished.

Raising both middle fingers, I spun in a circle. I knew

Reaper was still there, lingering … spying. "Don't follow me anymore. I'm warning you."

I closed my eyes and willed myself home. To Six.

SIX'S GAZE was fixated on the moon, his hands resting on his belly. "Did you ever wonder why our clothes morph to whatever we need on a job, but when we're … say here, we can't just mentally conjure an outfit of choice onto our bodies?"

Picking at a few blades of grass, I shoved my nerves away the best I could, although my eyes kept darting around furtively. I was hoping to not run into past me since we were in one of our favorite spots in the luna realm. I inhaled a few deep breaths, my heart continuing to thud erratically. "I mean, sure, there are lots of things I've wondered about over the years, that's one."

"It's just one more thing that doesn't make sense, unless it does …" Six sat up on his elbows, peering down at me. "Unless it's meant to make things more difficult for us."

After everything I'd been through lately, I wouldn't be surprised. "And where do our personal clothes go when we change into period-appropriate clothing? They just pop back on us when we leave. Oh, and our wings, we don't need to make wing holes in anything, they—"

"Just kind of pop right on through, but the hole

disappears when our wings aren't in use," Six finished for me.

I sighed. "Our lives definitely don't make sense, of course neither do reapers'."

"Reapers? What do you know about them, despite the obvious?"

I know they're duplicitous assholes, who like to get their kicks by lying to give false hope to lunas, and then expect them to just be okay with it. "Umm … I'm just saying, you know, that they probably have confusing things along the same lines as we do."

"Yeah, I guess." Six flopped back down, gaze reverting to the moon.

Just think about the now. Enjoy your time with Six. There's no point in worrying about things you can't change. Breathing deeply, I soaked up the majesty of the cool night. Twinkling stars, and a full moon, throwing pale light over a lush land filled with active wildlife. There was something simple, pure, and absolutely invigorating about the night. It was when I felt the most alive both mentally and physically. I'd often wished for all realms to be held in the permanent state of night like the luna realm. Soon, I'd get my wish of the daytime being banished, but of course everything else would be ripped away as well. *Maybe the next reality will be better for whoever gets to live in it.*

Restless, unable to fully lose myself in the now because our time was finite for the first time in my existence, I poked at Six's shoulder. "I thought we were going to go on one of our fun times after you went to Archives."

"Yeah, I still want to, but I guess I just need a bit more recoup time first." He waved his hand in the air. "Did you ever wonder about the moon here?"

"What about it?"

"It's always full, so it can't be the same one we see when in the human realm."

"Sure, it can. Our realm probably just follows the moon around like some kind of floating bubble."

Six chuckled. "Now I'm never going to be able to get that image out of my head."

Six was the only luna I could have weird conversations with, and not hold any fear that I would be judged for sounding silly or stupid. Both of us asked *what if* and *why* a lot, things that other lunas didn't seem to care much about. In fact, I'd never encountered another creature as curious as Six; even I wasn't on his level.

"Six?"

"Yeah?"

"Wherever we go for our little adventure, can you make sure it's night there?" I didn't want to spend my last bit of time in anything but an optimal situation.

"Of course. I told you I had a place in mind, and in order—" Six jerked up, his eyes glazing over. "Shit. Well, duty is calling again."

"So soon?" I squeaked. My jobs had been getting closer and closer together, but I didn't remember any of Six's jobs being stacked so close on top of each other in our past. And this was the past, all of this had already happened, so it shouldn't be changing …

Yes, it should. Reality is crumbling.

Winking, Six saluted me. "We'll get to go have fun soon, I swear. I don't think I'm going to get a third job right after this one."

I gulped. *I wouldn't be so sure.* "Of course not."

He disappeared without another word.

Shit. Shit. Shit, shit, shit. Kicking a rock, I glared at the spot where Six had just been. How could I have been so stupid? So naïve? Again? If I didn't come clean with Six about what was going on, how could I expect him to act any differently?

"You didn't think any of this through, again … did you?" Reaper's baritone voice coiled into my ear.

I'd been beginning to think Reaper had actually packed it up and was no longer hanging around playing at being my invisible stalker. Of course, I should have realized I wouldn't be that lucky when it came to him. "Oh, so that's how it is now? Stay invisible and make snarky comments?"

"Not a snarky comment, just an observation. What are you planning to do now?"

I threw my hands up in the air. "I don't know." *Why are you talking to him? There has to be a cure for your word vomit. Although, what difference does it make now, since the world is ending regardless of what intel Reaper garners?* I didn't want to admit to myself that my conversation with Reaper was probably largely to do with my loneliness. Even though my best friend had temporarily exited stage left, as long as my reaper was near, I wouldn't die alone if the end came sooner than expected.

I hung my head from the defeat by my own insecurities. "I guess I'm going to wait for Six to come back from his job and hope reality doesn't dissolve before then or that I don't get spotted by my past self. She's around here somewhere." The hairs on the back of my neck rose, morbid anticipation settling over me.

I needed to find a place to hole up in until Six's return. But where? Anywhere I might go to instinctually could already hold my other-self. "I'm going to Archives." It was the safest place I could think of. I'd also be able to spot myself if I entered and make a hasty retreat into the stacks. Plus, I could wait for Six there.

Moving as stealthily as I could without risking the attention from any other lunas, I headed inside to Archives.

Chapter 23

Striding casually into Archives, I heaved a sigh of relief when the massive, wooden door closed silently behind me. No other lunas were in sight, so I took the opportunity to scurry into an isolated corner to begin my stakeout. I could see the entrance perfectly, but from my position, someone would have to bend down to spot me.

Crossing my legs, I perched my elbows on my knees, and readied myself for a moderate wait, knowing Six would stop in after his job, and that's when I would join him, pretending I was also fresh off a job.

A face appeared directly in front of mine, and I teetered backward, landing in a half sprawl, the scream I let loose swallowed by the magical silence. Resting my hand against my chest, my pulse vibrated against my ribcage, felt but not heard. Inhaling shallow breathes through my nostrils, I focused on my surprise visitor, a tall woman with dark skin and amber eyes …

Wait … there's nothing neutral about her.

Which can only mean …

Holy shit! An architect! I'd never actually seen an architect even though they were the only beings that used Archives except for lunas. From what I understood, they were invisible, moving silently and anonymously around us, not wanting their work to be interfered with or to interfere with ours.

If I'm seeing an architect now that means she wants me to see her.

My eyes widened, and I clamored to my feet, almost knocking my forehead into hers. Raising her eyebrows, she backed up a few paces. I opened my mouth and immediately snapped it shut again, realizing I was rendered speechless because of our location.

Snatching me by the forearm, the architect yanked me along after her, heading for the door. I didn't put up a fight. If one such as her had something to say to me I would listen.

Once outside in the hallway, her gaze darted around as she ushered me into a small alcove that would keep us from being easily spotted, although definitely not a secure meeting place.

"What do you think you're doing, Eighty-nine?" Her eyes flashed with anger.

I rocked back on my heels in a useless attempt to gain a bit of personal space. "Um … I'm not sure what you're talking about." First Reaper and now an architect. I had to wonder why I was drawing all the attention of creatures who normally didn't interact with lunas.

"You're not supposed to be here."

It wasn't the first time I'd gone into Archives when I had no actual job-related reason to be there, and yet this was the first time anyone seemed to have noticed. "I was waiting for Six to get back from his latest job. Since he'd barely recovered from his last, I know he's going to be dra—"

The scowl that tugged her pretty features down was thunderous. "That's not what I mean at all. You are not supposed to be here. In this time or this place."

How does she know? Okay, she's an architect, and I'm not versed in their full job description, but why show herself now after all the other stuff I've done? It's probably a good time to play stupid. Scratching my head, I stared at the ground. "I don't know what you're talking about. I'm a luna, and this is the luna realm. Why am I not supposed to be here?"

"Don't you dare play stupid with me."

A low chuckle swirled around us, carried on a gust of unnatural wind. Narrowing my eyes, I glared at nothing, knowing it was Reaper letting his presence be known.

"And you, Alistar … I know you're here, too," the architect grated, stabbing her finger to the right of my shoulder. "You're not exactly being subtle."

Reaper appeared, the tilt to his head combined with his crossed arms belligerent and challenging. "Betha, I would say it's a pleasure, but then you'd know I was lying."

My head swung back and forth between the two of them. Not only was an architect arguing with a reaper, but I was now suddenly privy to both their names. Betha who I'd just met, wasn't as big a deal as Alistar.

Alistar, does he look like an Alistar? I replayed his full monty surprise from my room rapidly in my mind a few times, nodding to myself. *Yep, Alistar seems like a good name for someone like Reaper.*

I resisted the urge to fan myself. Even the memory of his physical perfection did weird things to my hormones, and I refused to regard him that way … ever. He was too much of an asshat to deserve anything other than mild dislike at best from me. It was definitely a good thing he kept himself under wraps in his reaper garb. That way I was able to suppress any lingering lust by burying the memory of his appearance.

Yep, my brain is definitely being unmade for me to be thinking about such a thing now. My id must be one of the only things left, or at least it's running the show now, leaving nothing but romance-novel-induced musings to work with. If lunas even have ids like humans. Who knows? I pinched a bit of skin on my arm, focusing back in on the present.

"You've been interfering with things you have no right to interfere with, Alistar, and you've dragged Eighty-nine into your games."

"And what games would those be, pray tell?" Re–Alister hissed.

"You're the one playing with reality itself. I'm merely

attempting to make things ... work out in the end," Betha snapped.

"Reality is falling apart, and we're scrambling to try and fix it, but as you well know, the only way to do that is to somehow undo the paradox."

"Paradoxes can be undone?" I interjected. "How? What needs to happen?"

Crossing her arms over her chest, Bertha sighed heavily. "These are things not meant for luna ears, as Alistar well knows. Although, if things turn out the way that I think they will, then it won't matter what you find out here today. However, if they go differently," she sighed again, "I'll have more work than I want to deal with."

Jumping to my own conclusions, I assumed she meant that it wouldn't matter how much I learned if reality unmade me. It also sounded like she was in favor of that outcome. But why? Why would an architect, whose entire purpose was to help maintain reality, want it to implode? *Unless that's not their entire purpose at all. Or since a new reality would be born, it was possible she had no real preference for which one survived.*

Alistar hooked his arm around my waist, yanking me into his side. "I won't let you do this, Betha. I've worked too hard to have it end another way."

What the hell is he talking about? If Betha wanted reality to crumble, and Alistar was opposed, then that meant he'd been working for a different outcome all along, even though he made me believe that the paradox prevented anything from essentially changing.

"Reaper … I mean, Alistar, tell me what all of this means."

His hood tilted forward, his lavender gaze sparking with light. "I thought you didn't trust me anymore, so why would you believe anything I have to say about any of this?"

I shrugged. "The devil you know and all of that?" The truth was, I didn't know why my instincts told me to trust him over Betha. But they did, therefore I would.

His fingers dug into the tender flesh at my waist. "Would you do something I asked of you then? No questions asked?"

"I-I guess." *Shit. What have I gotten myself into? It's the naked Reaper thing, I know it. I'm agreeing to do whatever he wants because his glorious perfection left what's left of my brain lust addled. Beautiful creatures really do get whatever they want for nothing! Damn him! He can never know!*

Alistar shoved me forward, jolting me out of my inner chastisements, propelling me toward the Archive door. "Run! Hide! Find a book to escape into now!"

A litany of swear words, as creative as one might imagine a creature known as an architect could construct, fell from Betha's mouth.

Pumping my arms and legs as fast as they could go, I crashed back into Archives, focused on finding one of Six's books.

Six. Think of Six. Don't let anything else distract you.

Unlike the times I searched before, the connection was almost instantaneous, and I leapt for a shelf a few feet above my head. My fingers slid from the supple leather, and I crashed to the ground.

Several architects popped into existence, just as Alistar and Betha raced across the threshold into Archives.

My stomach dropped into my feet, my heart beating as fast as a hummingbird's wings. I knew, just knew if I didn't make my getaway now that there wouldn't be one at all.

Forcing my body into submission, I launched myself at the book again, white light exploding the instant my fingers made contact.

Chapter 24

Four white walls surrounded me, no windows or doors. In front of me on one of the walls was what appeared to be a movie of some sort, the images flickering as if from a projector. I leaned forward, only then realizing I was sprawled on the floor, my legs and arms akimbo. My mind blanked as I was sucked in, completely consumed by the drama playing out before me. Sounds filtered in a moment later to help navigate what I was seeing.

A woman, somewhere in her late twenties or early thirties, loaded a small girl, a toddler, into a car seat in the back of an SUV. The vehicle was in a parking lot of a retail plaza of some sort. Once done, the woman got into the SUV and drove away.

The setting blinked out, flickering back into focus a moment later. The same SUV was on the side of the road, glass and twisted metal snatching my attention immediately.

The nearly transparent woman hovered above the vehicle, her face contorted with sorrow, and her flowered sundress drenched in blood. "It's my fault. It's all my fault, " she wailed. "I didn't see the truck. I just didn't see it."

A reaper offered her his hand, just his fingertips poking out from the depths of his robe. "It's time for you to move on, Mia. Don't you want to join your loved ones? It's time for you to find peace—to move to the next plane of existence."

"No!" Her voice cracked. "I don't deserve peace of any kind. I don't deserve to be with my loved ones. I killed us. I killed my baby! I should be punished!"

The reaper reached this time, his palm coming to rest carefully on her shoulder. "You did nothing wrong—nothing punishable. Humans are not infallible, they make mistakes. None of this is your fault."

Ignoring him, the woman continued rambling, "I'm supposed to protect her. And I didn't. I tried, I tried to swerve out of the way once I saw the truck—" Her head whipped to the side. "Where is the truck? Where is it? Where is the person who was driving it?"

The reaper dipped his head in acknowledgement, a man not much older than the woman appearing beside him. "I'm helping this soul to move on as well."

Mia flew at the man, hands out like claws. "You don't deserve peace of any kind either!" She passed right through him.

The man's eyes welled with unshed tears. "Ma'am, I didn't see you there. You have to believe me, please. I would never purposely hurt anyone, let alone a mother and child."

"But you did, you killed us!" Mia's slight frame shook as she began to sob again. "And I couldn't protect her! It's my fault … and it's your fault. You killed her, but I let her die."

The reaper shook his head. "You will understand that none of this is true, you will grasp the truth of things once I ferry you to the next—"

"No," Mia screeched. "I already told you, I don't deserve peace. I deserve to be punished for failing as a mother. I failed her!"

"Listen to me," the reaper said. "You are not a punishable soul. You made a mistake, that is all. Humans make mistakes. It's unavoidable."

A black hole opened up above Mia, and her spirit was sucked into it, dissolving instantly.

The man stared in disbelief. "Wh-What happened to her?"

"Sometimes a soul feels the need to punish itself, and when that happens there's nothing I can do."

"Where did she go?"

"That I cannot answer. She is beyond a reaper's reach."

"No. There has to be a way to find out … to help her. I have to help her. That's all I ever wanted to do before, was help people, but I got sidetracked … and now look at me.

Lord, please, let me help her!" A black hole opened up above him, sucking him away as well.

The reaper's arms fell to his sides, and he remained motionless, hovering there above the SUV for several moments before he also disappeared.

My awareness slowly returned, and I blinked the white box into focus, temporarily forgotten because of how riveting the scene with Mia had been. I had no idea when it happened, or if it even actually had, or why I'd been shown it to begin with. The incident couldn't have been one from an Archive book because only three people had died, not enough to warrant a luna.

I don't understand any of this. Why am I here? And how do I get out?

Pain exploded behind my eyes, and the scene with Mia began playing again, but this time in my head.

Stop. Stop. Why am I being shown this?

Or maybe I'm not. With reality falling apart I could have accidentally ended up here.

I watched Mia and the man getting sucked into oblivion again and again.

Again and again.

Until my thoughts strayed to where they always did recently: Six.

I need to get out of here and find him. Reality's collapse seems to be progressing faster than before. It probably won't be long before neither one of us exist anymore.

But it all seemed futile, something I'd been wrestling with since the beginning, yet I couldn't let go of my fear of dying alone. I wanted to be with Six at the end, whether it made any kind of sense or not, whether it made any kind of difference or not.

Please, let me go to him wherever he is. If I touched one of his books before I ended up here, then there has to be a remnant of the path I was on. Mind over matter. Mind over matter.

"Six always has your six, Eighty-nine. Remember that." His voice echoed in the white box, ripping a laugh from my chest. *Even now that cheesy line can bring a smile to my face.*

Clasping my hands together, I rolled my eyes heavenward. I believed in a higher power, although I never prayed, the concept pointless to a luna. *But today is different. I'll pray to whoever and whatever god or gods is listening. Please let me go to wherever Six is.*

White light exploded, temporarily blinding me. The sensation of weightlessness took over, hurtling me through time and space. With a grunt, I was deposited in a heap, colors slowly unfurling around me.

Lifting my head, my brain came back online fully to reveal my new setting. I was outside of a small apartment building in what appeared to be a largely residential area. It was nighttime, crickets and tree frogs filling the air with their chatter. I had no idea what year it was or even what country I was in, although I took a wild stab and guessed it was in the south somewhere, since the humidity was thick enough to cut with a knife.

Swiping at the sweat already covering my upper lip, I

managed to get to my feet. *Okaaay ... where is Six? Or did I end up in another seemingly random place?*

As if conjured by my thoughts, Six strode casually past me, whistling what I thought was a Green Day tune.

Sagging with relief, it took me a second to gather myself enough to sprint after him. "Six! Six, wait up!"

He halted, his back to me, as he scanned the apartment building. "Any time now," he mumbled.

Sniffing the air, the faint scent of smoke was barely discernible. I hesitated. If Six was on another job, I didn't want to interrupt him. I also had no way of knowing if this version of Six was the same one who just left me in the luna realm or a Six from years ago. *Time travel really is a bunch of timey wimey bullshit. The Doctor had that right ... not that he put it that way exactly. Too bad my problems can't be wrapped up conveniently like at the end of an episode of one of my favorite TV shows.*

Backing up, I partially concealed myself behind a massive Ford truck. *Why did Six not hear me yelling at him from a few feet away, just like at his death scene? Was there some kind of block between him and me when I traveled back to him doing a job? Maybe since he'd technically already done the job then I wouldn't be able to interact with him until it was over?* I rubbed at my temples.

A reaper appeared beside me. "Is that you?"

Long fingers grabbed and dug into my arm, hauling me farther back from Six. "I don't understand how you still can't tell the difference between me and other reapers," Alistar growled.

Slapping at him with my free hand, I shot him with my best death glare, but apparently, he was impervious. "How many times do I have to explain to you that you all wear the exact same robes? I think it's ridiculous that you keep expecting me to spot you right off the bat. It's not like I have X-ray vision or anything to help me see underneath all that swirling black." *Thank the moon above. Constantly seeing his perfect form wouldn't do either of us any favors.*

"I can spot you right off the bat, as you put it. Even when there are other lunas around."

"We may all have neutral … well, everything, but we look different. Every single one of us has different features and …" I pursed my lips. "I see what you're trying to say, and it's not the same thing at all."

He tilted his head, and I imagined a smirk on his perfectly sculpted face. "Isn't it?"

"Not even the tiniest bit the same." My nostrils flared as I forced myself to breathe normally. "What happened with Betha, and how did you find me so quickly? Are those architects after me? And what did Betha mean by what she—"

An alarm pierced the night, drawing my attention. Smoke billowed out of the bottom floor apartments, lights coming to life on the above floors.

I shook my head. "Another fire. I wish humans knew how often these things happened. It would save a lot of lives. I swear, most of my jobs lately are fire, fire, fire, fire. It's like humans discovered it, but never quite understood its destructive power."

"There are a lot of things that humans don't understand the destructive power of. Lunas too," Alistar murmured.

I threw my hands up in the air. "Well, maybe if we all had more information about … all the things, then we wouldn't be flying around blind and potentially cause the end of reality itself." I stabbed my index finger into Alistar's chest. "Now, tell me what exactly all of that was back in Archives with Betha, and all of the others. And for one last time, I'm going to ask you: What is your end game?" Although I wasn't sure if I'd ever actually asked him that question out loud. *No matter, I did now.*

"As I've informed you before, some things I can't share with you. It's not because I don't want to, trust me on that. It's because if I reveal what I know it could have catastrophic results."

I squinted up at him, trying to see into his hood. "More catastrophic than the breakdown of reality? Okaaaay … Why am I trusting you again? I'm not so sure I should. I did on good faith to begin with, at least to a certain extent, and then you proved me a fool for doing so, or I thought that was the case … and now I just don't know anything at all. That situation with Betha was … um, yeah, it was something."

"Eloquent as always."

I rolled my eyes. "My speech is a fair bit better than the stuff being produced inside of my head lately, let me tell you. I'm pretty sure my brain is being unmade before the rest of me. Or quite possibly it got fried somewhere along the line, and although I think I'm functioning fine, I'm working off a distorted perception. For all I know I'm making incoherent monkey noises at you right now, and merely think I'm forming complete words and sentences."

I tapped my fist against my forehead, hoping what I'd just said wasn't actually the case. But who knew? "Are Betha and the rest of the architects going to be able to track us?"

"No," Alistar said. "Or not in the sense you believe. They can view what we're doing after the fact, like a delay in video, but they can't find us in real-time."

"Interesting." No matter the situation, and the irrelevance to the grand scheme of things, the questions just kept on coming. I'd probably be pondering the order of the universe even as I was being broken down into nothing more than molecules.

"Six is preparing to head back to the luna realm, a place you can no longer return to if you don't want to be contained."

Contained? Six. Oh, shit. I'd been so focused on Alistar that I missed Six completing his job. *Stupid reaper causing more problems than he's worth.*

Whirling around, I spotted Six stumbling from the building, unnoticed by the first responders. "Six!" I hollered. "Hey! Six!"

He vanished without even a single glance in my direction.

"Nooo!" *Now what am I supposed to do?* I couldn't follow

him back to the luna realm, and without Archives, I couldn't track him to another location. *Or could I?*

Eyeing Alistar speculatively, I approached him again. "Can you take me to Six? Do you have a way of doing that? I mean, you pop up everywhere I am, so you must have a way to track me. Can you track him in the same manner?"

"No, I can't."

I balled my fists in frustration. "Why can you track me and not him?"

"But an alternative travel mode just arrived." He pointed over my shoulder, his robe billowing around him dramatically.

Peering over my shoulder, I spotted a fresh RR, one that most definitely hadn't been there a few seconds ago. It pulsed with color and light, beckoning to me. "But it's going to just take us back to Six's death scene like those things always do. There's no point in going there."

Alistar shrugged. "I have no other suggestions for you. Take your chances going through the RR or go to the luna realm."

My stomach twisted. "Neither way is going to end well."

Did I go back to Six's death scene and hope when it was over to get spit out somewhere good, or did I risk facing the architects? Both options seemed like a waste of time, something I wasn't sure how much I even had left.

"I pick secret option number three."

Alistar tilted his head in question. "I wasn't aware there was a third option."

I quirked an eyebrow. "Which is why it was a secret." I grabbed his arm, tugging him after me. "Hurry up, we need to get going before that RR sucks us in against our will." Already the winds had picked up, the subtle pull not going to be so subtle soon.

"Why do I have a bad feeling about this?" Alistar mumbled.

"Oh, shut up and quit complaining."

Please let this work. If only to prove Alistar wrong.

Chapter 25

I'd deduced from Six's clothes, and the feel of our surroundings, that we were in a relatively recent timeline. Which meant I merely had to go somewhere Six would probably show up when traveling to the human realm. There was the risk of running into my past self if she accompanied him, but there was also a strong possibility that Six would show up by himself.

I positioned myself in a corner booth, where I could see most of the interior of the diner, along with the front door. I'd ordered a steady stream of coffee, and an array of desserts. But I wasn't sure how long I could keep it up without raising suspicions. I didn't have anything like a phone or laptop to pretend I was working either.

Lifting the steaming cup of coffee to my lips, I pretended to take another sip. My hands trembled noticeably as I placed it back down on the table.

Alistar drummed his fingers along the edge of the faux

wood. "This plan has proven to be very fruitful." His voice dripped with sarcasm. "So glad I decided to tag along for all the excitement."

"Shut up," I hissed. "I can't sit here and talk to myself. I'm already the weirdo in the booth who is staring at the front door."

"No one is paying any attention to you, as per usual." Picking up the saltshaker, he spun it idly.

I grabbed it, placing it back on the table. "Stop it. I'll tell you what will get me noticed, if stuff on my table seemingly is levitating."

The bell on the door chimed. *Finally.* It wasn't Six, at least not yet, but it was the person I was hoping would draw him here. *Tina.*

If I can get lucky, just this once, Six would have already met or discovered her, and he'll show up sometime during her shift.

I studied Tina as she made her way through the diner, green eyes observant, and a smile for nearly everyone. I noticed again that she held a vibrancy about her, a certain *je ne sais quoi.* I wasn't sure if she was an actual bright soul like the one I kept running into lately, or if she simply had charisma. In the end, I supposed it didn't matter. Six was drawn to her all the same.

My mind wandered as I continued to watch her. *Speaking of bright souls* … I'd never gotten any kind of answer about the one who'd been plaguing me. I'd been convinced he was linked to the Six situation somehow or held a clue to the mysteries surrounding all of it, but as it turned out, there didn't seem to be a connection at all.

I mumbled to myself, picking up my coffee cup again. "That can't be right." The bitter taste rolled over my tongue, giving me a jolt of energy.

That can't be right. That bright soul showing up on job after job can't be a coincidence. It can't be.

I took another sip of coffee, my thoughts crystallizing into an internal argument of sorts.

That soul had answers, I know it.

But it doesn't matter. Reality is about to be caputs.

But what if that soul held a bigger revelation? One that could save everything?

Don't be ridiculous, one soul isn't going to save anything. Especially not a human one. Abnormally bright or not.

Although he did have the power to break out of the pattern, to alter his own destiny.

Altering one's own destiny is not the same thing as unlocking some kind of secret to the universe.

The coffee cup was unceremoniously yanked from my hands, clattering to the table. "That's enough coffee for you," Alistar stated. "You're about to vibrate right out of this booth." He shoved a plate holding pie in my direction. "Eat more."

Reaching for the coffee, my lip curled up. "Maybe I want to vibrate out of this booth. Not your call. And for the last time, stop moving stuff around when you're invisible."

Sighing, he steepled his fingers in front of his hood. "Whatever you say."

The bell on the front door chimed again, and an

older couple entered, the two of them holding hands with a small child who was in between them. I was guessing grandparents taking their grandchild out to spoil him.

My heart clenched, something akin to wistfulness curling through my system. *What would it be like to have a family? To grow old with them?*

The bell chimed again, but my attention was still focused on the family who just entered a moment ago.

What would it be like to die knowing a part of you lived on? What would it be like to share in that kind of multigenerational love?

Alistar flicked the center of my forehead. "Six is here."

Ducking down in the booth, I peered over the edge of the table. Sure enough, Six had entered the diner, his gaze already riveted to Tina, who thankfully wasn't working the section I was sitting in. Which meant Six probably wouldn't even glance my way, he was so enthralled with her.

How many times had he come here to ogle her before something actually happened between them? When Six had brought me to the diner, what seemed like an eternity ago, I'd thought he was attempting to draw her attention. Did he stumble upon her here at this diner, or had he met her somewhere else and somehow tracked her to her place of employment? Trying to figure out the timeline was nearly impossible.

I rubbed my temples, a headache blooming. *None of it matters. What happened, happened, and you know you can't change the paradox he created. You're only here to spend time with Six before neither one of you exist anymore.*

I looked at Alistar, who's attention was on me. "What?" I muttered.

"Well, he's here. Are you going to go talk to him?"

Six made his way over to Tina's section, the girl who worked the front waving him on to seat himself since the diner was fairly empty. As soon as his butt touched the chair, he was already scanning for Tina again.

I rolled my eyes. "Geeze. He's like a little lost puppy or something."

Reaching for my cup of coffee, I realized Alistar had slid it to his side of the table. Glaring, I grabbed the edge of the cup, pulling it my way. "Hey, I told you to back off about my caffeine consumption."

Before the porcelain could touch my lips, Alistar snatched it back. "Your heart is beating faster than it should."

I leaned over the table, grabbing for the cup. "I'm immortal, too much coffee isn't going to do me in."

"Can I get you anything else?" my waitress, Chelsea, asked, causing me to jump about a mile. The coffee cup slipped from both Alistar and my hands, clattering to the table.

I grimaced. "I'm so sorry." Gathering a stack of napkins, I blotted at the mess. "I don't know why I'm so clumsy today."

Chelsea barely concealed her annoyance. "No problem. I'll get you a fresh cup." She eyed the various dishes of desserts laid out in front of me. "Can I take anything away for you? Or get you anything else besides the coffee? The bill perhaps?"

She obviously wanted me gone, despite her nearly empty section. *How about that? I finally get someone's attention and it's not positive. Surprise, surprise.*

"Eighty-nine?" Six stood just behind Chelsea, shock etched into his features. "What are you doing here? I thought you just left for a job?"

Ah-ha. So he thought to sneak off to ogle Tina when I was away, making sure to be back before me so I'd never be the wiser. I attempted nonchalance, waving him off. "Oh, that. I already finished up."

He slid into the booth across from me, forcing Alistar to skooch over. Somehow my second shadow, and coffee policeman, was only visible to me. *Aren't I the lucky one?*

"Really? That was faster than you've ever been before." Six picked up a clean fork and took several bites of what I think was key lime pie. "And what about recovery? I've never known you … or any luna not to need it."

"This particular job didn't take much out of me, and you know, coffee, lots of coffee made up the difference."

Eating more of the pie, he spoke with a full mouth. "Uh-huh. Yeah, I can see you've had too much coffee. You're about to vibrate right out of here."

I flicked my gaze to Alistar, daring him to say something. Although, I was hoping he wouldn't blow his cover, forcing me to explain his presence to Six. "I'll be fine. Too much coffee never hurt any immortal."

Finished with the key lime pie, Six moved on to blueberry cobbler. "Why'd you order all these if you weren't going to eat them?"

I smiled at how easily he was distracted. "I was planning on eating them, just hadn't gotten there yet. Needed the coffee first."

Chelsea returned then, placing another cup of joe in front of me. "Anything else?"

Six motioned at the empty key lime pie plate. "Yeah. Two more of those, please."

"Sure, whatever," she muttered, already moving away from the booth.

Six snickered. "She really doesn't seem to like you. What'd you do?" Tina walked past the booth, and just like that, Six was once again ensnared.

I snapped my fingers in front of his face. "Who is she?"

The tips of his ears flushed. "No one, a waitress here. Her name is Tina."

Why does he not want to tell me about her? Ugh. "She's pretty. Have you introduced yourself?"

His cheeks pinkened to match his ears. "No, of course not. The best I could hope for is a one-night stand, and you know it." He sighed heavily, propping his chin up on his hands. "And she's … well, she deserves better than that."

Okay. So I'd somehow ended up back in the timeline before Six had begun his relationship with Tina. This is where it got tricky. I couldn't prevent him from being with her, or it would destroy the fixed point in time where he dies. That would create a different reality tear. *Damn paradox.* I had to figure out a way to progress things in line with how they were supposed to, and still spend time with Six.

Wait. None of it matters. I can do whatever I want because reality is going to be destroyed either way. I don't have to encourage Six to do anything.

Six sighed dramatically. "She's beautiful, you know. More beautiful than anyone I've ever seen."

I choked on some coffee, spewing it back into the cup. "Who, Tina?"

"Yeah, Tina. Who else have I been talking about?"

He'd been talking about her? Shit. I must have missed what he was saying when I got lost in my thoughts. "You are one lovesick little luna."

Six merely grunted in response, his eyes glued to Tina wherever she went. Biting my lower lip, I counted to ten. I'd come all this way to spend time with Six at the end, and unless I wanted to burst his bubble by telling him the end was nigh, I had to play along with him. And there he was mooning over Tina. I couldn't stand to see him pining after her when our world could end at any moment. *What do I have to do to get his undivided attention?*

"If I could just get her to notice me, for real notice me, it would make my entire existence."

Staring at Six, while he stalked Tina with his eyes, my heart twisted with remorse. I wanted to spend time with Six, but I also wanted him to be happy about it. If he was obsessing about Tina the entire time, we'd both be miserable. Perhaps … perhaps, I could help him out to give him a little boost before we set out on our adventure. The one he didn't know about yet.

Jumping to my feet, I beelined straight for Tina. "Hey, excuse me."

She rewarded me with a pleasant smile. "Yes, do you need me to get Chelsea? Or is there something I can help you with?"

I pointed over my shoulder at Six. "See that guy over there? He's my best friend, and I've had to listen to him go on and on about how you're the most beautiful person he's ever seen. Would you give him your number or something?"

She peered around me, expression softening. "He's been coming in here for a while now, usually sits in my section." She ran her gaze up and down, assessing. "He's … he seems like a good soul. There's something sweet and special about him." She reached into her apron and produced a slip of paper, which she scribbled her number on. "Tell him not to be so shy." She winked at him before heading into the kitchen.

Returning to the booth, I slid the paper with her number on it at Six. "There you go. She also told me to tell you not to be so shy."

Six's mouth hung open. "I-I can't believe you just did that." He stared at the paper, his fingers curling and uncurling above it like he was afraid to touch it, but desperately wanted to.

Alistar waved his hand in front of my face, pointing

toward the ladies' room. "Who else was going to do it if not me? I was getting tired of your sad puppy eyes."

Shoving to my feet again, I hastened to the ladies' room, calling over my shoulder, "I'll be right back."

Once inside of the restroom, I checked the stalls to make sure I was alone.

Alistar leaned against the door, sagging as if weary. "Why did you interfere? You have no idea what you could have caused."

"What difference does it make? Our reality is about to be caput. It doesn't matter if I cause any more problems, or hell, even if I cause another paradox."

Alistar rushed me, and I let out a yelp, stumbling into a stall door. "It always makes a difference. Now I have to figure out what to do next."

Regaining my composure, I shoved at him, storming over to the sinks. "There's nothing left to figure out, you've made that perfectly clear."

"Have I, Eighty-nine? Or is that just how you've interpreted things?" Muttering to himself, he said, "What did I expect of a luna? Of course, she'd only see the worst of everything." Straightening, he addressed me again, "You're going to fix this. Somehow."

"Fix what? There's nothing I can do to—"

He engulfed me, and my world disintegrated into black.

Chapter 26

Light exploded into existence, and I wobbled away from Alistar. "What the hell was that?"

We were in an alley, an overflowing dumpster behind us, the not so tantalizing aromas of rotten food and other garbage hanging heavy in the air.

"Don't worry, we're behind the diner a few minutes after I entered the restroom with you."

I squinted up at him. "Why? If you didn't take me to some other time or place, then what's the point?"

"You need to follow Tina."

"What?"

"You heard me perfectly clear. You need to follow Tina. Her shift will end in a few hours and this should be the perfect starting point."

Pressing my arm over my nose and swallowing back bile, I glared at him. "What about Six? That's why I'm here. To spend time with him. I don't plan on waiting for a few hours, by a dumpster no less, when he's right inside of the diner."

Alistar grabbed me by the shoulders, shaking hard. "Either you trust me or you don't. The time for anything in between has passed."

Damn it. I hate it when he's right. I have to decide right here and now if I'm going to trust him or not. I'd previously thought he'd proven himself reliable, but then I'd also thought to have discovered his treachery. The truth was, I had no idea where his motivations truly laid. I wanted to trust him, but it was easier not to. *Which is it, Eighty-nine? Do you give him the benefit of the doubt or not?*

"Sometimes you just have to take a leap of faith." Six's voice echoed in my head.

"What if I fall?" I asked.

"And what if you don't?"

Scowling, I knew my subconscious was attempting to communicate with me, and it was poignantly making its opinion known. I cleared my throat, gagging again as the garbage stench made its way past my arm barrier. "I'll trust you. I mean, what do I have to lose? Reality is coming to end after all."

Alistar crossed his arms over his chest, the dark cavern of his hood aimed right at me. "No takesy backsies, as the humans say."

A sudden laugh overtook me, and I doubled over with the force of it. "And what humans would those be? Fifth graders?"

His hood tilted back, a glint of lavender flashing. “Possibly.”

How was it that with the limited gestures he could make in his robe, and a hidden face, that I’d somehow begun to be able to read Alistar with ease. It was almost as if I could sense his moods and nonverbal responses. “Yeah, fine, whatever. No takesy backsies.” I snorted, unable to resist.

Checking the brick wall behind me for any kind of sludge, I decided to lean against it when I didn’t spot any. “So why are we going to be following Tina?”

“I have my reasons.”

“The more things change the more they stay the same,” I muttered.

Boredom almost instantly set in since I was attempting to keep my mind from wandering to the places it normally went. “Wanna play a game?”

Alistar turned toward me. “Let me guess, you want to play twenty questions?”

My eyes widened. “Was that a joke?”

“It’s only a joke when it’s not true.”

“That’s not exactly how jokes work. It’s usually the opposite, in fact.”

He grunted, the sound a not so subtle plea for me to shut up.

“Sooo …” I wanted to demand for him to tell me why he’d gone about with his bizarre plans when everything was pointless. Had he pitied me? Been attempting to give me false hope? Or—

No. Do not think about all of this again. "You know what? I'm going to go be with Six. I didn't tell him I was going anywhere and—"

"You don't think he doesn't assume you went to another job? If you go back now after your odd behavior before, you're going to have a lot of explaining to do."

"Maybe I should just come clean."

Alistar crowded into my personal space, looming over me. "Have you not put the pieces together yet? Six is on a crash collision with his death fixed point in time. It's almost as if he has become said point in time. He is the eye of the storm. It's why no matter what you do you haven't been able to pull him off course. He doesn't even hear you calling for him at certain events."

My mind conjured the memory of the last job I saw him on just before going to the diner. I had thought it strange that he hadn't heard me calling his name from how close I was. But no, I hadn't put those pieces of the puzzle together. I resisted the urge to cringe, pressing my face harder into the inside of my elbow.

"It doesn't make a difference. Why should I give myself a headache over all of this when I can't change a damn thing?"

"You can't change Six's part, but there might be a possibility that you can change something else."

I ground my teeth together so hard, a sharp pain spiked up my jawline and then down my neck. "If Six is going to die in the end, I don't care about reality dissolving. Without him, there's no point in this plane of existence continuing on."

"Are you really so selfish that you would let the world crumble because you lost your best friend?"

I nodded. "Yes, absolutely."

Silence fell over us after that, my words hanging heavily between us. I felt them to be true when I uttered them, and yet, if I was faced with that actual choice, I wasn't sure if I would actually react that way.

I shifted and sighed, leaning heavier into the wall. *How much time has passed already? When the hell is Tina getting off work? Ugh. Tina. I don't like her.* I was neutral at first, then I kind of saw the appeal from Six's perspective, but now … now …

Fine, I more than don't like her ... I hate her.

If Six had never met her then none of this would have happened. I wanted Six to be happy, but in the end, Tina didn't deliver that to him. Ultimately, it was her fault reality was being destroyed. *I hate her so much. Tina with her big, green eyes, and spattering of freckles across her nose. Tina with her easy smile for everyone. Blech! I bet she's an evil bitch under there somewhere. Look what she did to Six. Moon above, I hate her.*

"She's just a human female. I don't think they can actually be evil," Alistar stated, his tone bored.

Wait. I said some of that out loud? How much? All of it? Or just the last little bit? "Ha! You've obviously never been to high school."

"Neither have you. All you know of human high

schools you've learned from books and movies. We both know humans love their over dramatizations."

"Maybe, but I've come across enough evil humans over the years, and Tina is definitely one of them."

Alistar chuckled. "Is she now?"

"Yes, she is! And stop asking all your non-question questions with that sarcastic, Mr. Know-it-all tone. You're seriously getting on my nerves."

He bowed dramatically, his robes swirling around him in a flourish. "Yes, your majesty. I will endeavor not to annoy you in the future."

I rolled my eyes, something that I did often, but more frequently around him. "Just shut up and watch for Tina."

Stupid Tina. I should be hanging out with Six waiting for the world to end. Not waiting in a stinky alleyway with a reaper. If only—

"There she is," Alistar stated, interrupting my inner tirade. "You follow her from a safe distance, and I'll stick closer in case you lose her."

"Why can't you just follow her and tell me where she ends up? Why do I have to be involved before the end either way?" The option for him to do that hadn't even occurred to me. *Yep, the holes in my brain are getting bigger by the second. I'll be a slobbering mess in no time. Maybe I won't even be cognizant enough at the end to realize I'm about to die.*

But Alistar was already gone.

Muttering under my breath, I skulked out from the alleyway, heading in the direction I saw Tina go. I saw

Alistar first, his dark form gliding through the air behind her, but a good couple of feet above anyone else. It was kind of like following a reaper balloon in a crowd.

Keeping a decent distance behind them, I wasn't sure what to do when Tina hopped on a bus going in the opposite direction. *See, it was completely pointless.* I resisted the urge to stick my tongue out at Alistar as they zoomed by. I was an ancient immortal, after all, not a human teenager.

I lingered near the bus stop, waiting for my own transportation to return. When what seemed like an eternity passed, I decided to head back to the diner to hopefully find Six again. *Even if he left already, another cup of coffee wouldn't be the worst thing. My hands aren't even trembling anymore.*

Directly in front of me, a slash of light flashed, and a RR appeared, rippling with colors like the surface of the ocean. Wind whipped around me, pushing and pulling at the same time.

Dropping to the ground, I crawled away from the oblong shape.

"Are you all right, miss? Are you ill?"

"What's wrong with her? Is she drunk?"

"Should I call the police? Or nine-one-one?"

Ignoring all the not-so-helpful bystanders, I continued to crawl, knowing that I most certainly appeared insane, since none of the humans could obviously see or feel the RR or the chaos it unleashed around it.

Strong arms wrapped around me. "I've got you,

Eighty-nine." Alistar lifted me off the ground, holding me tightly to his chest. "I think we're going to have to do this the old-fashioned way." He moved slowly away from the RR, his struggle evident in his heavy breathing, and rapid pulse thrashing against his ribcage.

"Can the humans see us?" Because weirder than me crawling would definitely be me seemingly floating through the air. That would definitely be a viral video right there. Not that it would be relevant once reality dissolved … even still, some knee jerk reactions were ingrained, and the thought of making a stir didn't sit well with my luna sensibilities.

"No," he grunted, "you're cloaked within my invisibility aura."

I gasped as we slid a few steps back, being pulled by the RR. "And why exactly are we doing this the old-fashioned way?"

"I fear if I transport us to our destination, we'll be trapped in the magnetic pull of the the tear, and we'll end up precisely where we don't want to be right now."

Digging my fingers into his shoulders, I kept my gaze focused on the undulating portal. Bits of paper and trash flew toward it, disappearing into the void.

"It's because of Six, isn't it? Because he's like the eye of the storm like you said? But why haven't I seen one of those everywhere he is?"

"I don't know," he grated.

"And why—"

"Will you please shut up? I can't deal with your blathering right now."

I shut my mouth with an audible click. I wanted to argue with him, but he did have a point. He was exerting all of his physical and probably mystical strength to keep us from being sucked into the RR, and I was asking him questions irrelevant to our current plight.

"I can feel its reach," he said. "If we can get to the top of the hill, then I should be able to transport us to the hospital."

"The hospital?" A woman screamed as she was knocked off her feet, and yanked into the portal. "Oh, shit. That thing is eating mortals for lunch now."

"Bound to happen," Alistar muttered, leaning forward farther.

Inch by inch we drew closer to the top of the hill. I held my breath, hoping for the best, but expecting the worst.

With something akin to a battle cry, Alistar drove us up the last little bit of pavement, and darkness swallowed me whole.

Chapter 27

Doubled over, clutching onto something solid and unknown, I breathed through my mouth, waiting for the dizziness to pass. "I'll never get used to that," I muttered.

"And you won't have to," Alistar stated.

Blinking our surroundings into focus, I noticed an empty hospital bed, in an otherwise empty room. It was then I remembered Alistar's offhand comment about getting to the hospital. "What's Tina doing here? Visiting someone?"

Alistar glided toward the door, obviously expecting me to follow. Reluctantly, I did. "She volunteers here. Seems you were right about her being evil."

My nostrils flared with annoyance. "Volunteering at a place like this is exactly what an evil person would do. It's a blatant cover-up."

"Why don't you like her? Aside from her stealing Six's focus away from you?"

"That's not what it is at all." We casually strode down a long corridor; it also empty. I was guessing we were in an unused wing or one that was under renovation of some sort. "I don't like her because it's her fault reality is dissolving."

"And how did you come to that conclusion?" Alistar held a door open for me, and I stepped through it ahead of him.

"If Six would have never met her then he wouldn't have thrown his life away. If he hadn't exchanged his life for hers, then the paradox wouldn't be there."

"How do you know some other paradox wouldn't have sprung up somewhere else involving him?"

I scowled. "I just do."

Ignoring my answer, he pointed at another door just ahead of us. "That one leads to the main part of the hospital. The last I saw Tina she was delivering food to patients on the third floor."

I nodded. "Third floor, got it."

Shoving through the door, I was dropped right into the middle of controlled chaos. Nurses bustled by, some with patients and others on a mad dash to get somewhere important. Codes were called out, and people were paged over the intercom. The situation was perfect to slip through unnoticed.

Moving slowly, and with purpose, I made my way to the elevators. I got on with several other plain-clothed people, all who were heading to the third floor as well. To the staff, I was merely another visitor. Alistar stuck close to me, hovering like a second shadow. It was odd how people always gave him a wide berth even though they weren't aware he was there … at least not consciously.

Once on the third floor, I scanned for Tina, but of course, she was nowhere to be seen. *Great. Nothing can be easy anymore. Is it too much to ask to for her to have been walking right past the elevator exactly when the doors opened?*

"Search the rooms," Alistar ordered. "If she's not still on this floor then she's probably on the fourth."

"Or," I hissed out of the side of my mouth, "I could simply go to the fourth floor and wait for her to come up. Why are you always trying to make things more complicated? Is it because you're ancient?"

"I'm not sure what ancient has to do with any of this, but I'm not trying to make things more complicated, you are merely lazy."

"Lazy," I scoffed. "Lazy and working smart are not the same things. Why would I do something the hard way just for the sake of it when I don't have to? It seems plain ridiculous to me."

I nodded at a nurse as she passed, hoping she hadn't seen what appeared to be me talking to myself. Her uncertain smile hinted that she had.

"Why can't you be visible when we do these things? It would make things so much—"

"Simpler? Yes, I'm aware. But I would terrify the

humans if what they think of as death itself or the Grim Reaper was floating around, especially in a place like this."

Peering into a room on the right, I sighed when I didn't see Tina. "Couldn't you make yourself look like a human?"

"No."

I shuffled across the hall and peeked into the room there. *Damn, no Tina.* "Couldn't you just remove your robe?"

"I showed you my true form, in a sense, and obviously that would not be wise either."

"You couldn't turn down the effects or something? Change your— wait, what do you mean *in a sense*?" I narrowed my eyes. "Either you showed me your true form or you didn't. Which is it?"

"The entirety of my true form would cause you to disintegrate on the spot, so I showed you what I could."

Moving stiffly to the next room, I clenched and unclenched my fists. "What you mean is that you lied to me again. You claimed that was your true form and that you'd never showed it to a luna before." I wasn't exactly sure why I felt betrayed. It didn't matter if he'd lied about what he looked like under his robe or not. But I did—I felt betrayed. I supposed it might have been because it made me feel special to know something most creatures didn't. And for a luna to feel special was … priceless.

"I didn't lie. When I show my true form to any creature other than an angel, I will appear as the viewer's ideal version of perfection. It's the only way my true perfection can be perceived by one such as you."

This gave me pause. "What I saw was what I perceive as the ideal physical specimen of a male? What I think of as the perfect man?" *Huh. I wasn't aware I'd been pining for some kind of golden god in my subconscious. And that also explained my lustful reaction to him.*

"I was a more refined version of the cover of the—"

I slapped my palm against my forehead. "How did I not see it? You did look just like the cover of my book." *Well, shit. Wonder if I'd been reading something else if I would have seen someone different?*

"If you showed yourself to someone like Six, would you appear as a female?"

Alistar shook his head. "No. I would appear as his definition of the perfect male. Sexual preference has no effect on any of it."

I scanned another room, again coming up empty on the Tina front. But something inside of this particular room—room 313—snagged my attention completely. Nestled in separate beds, but close enough to link hands, was an elderly couple, man and woman, both with snowy white hair, and the shriveled appearance of those who had been sick for some time.

Scooting a few steps closer, I studied them with interest. They were whispering to each other, the tone of their words filled with love, and devotion. Beeping monitors kept me from discerning exactly what they were saying though. Even still, I was enthralled.

"They will both pass on soon," Alistar stated, his attention on them as well. "They have lived a long and happy life together, and are relieved to be together even now."

"You knowing that is a reaper thing?" It was a question, but I was certain I was right.

"Yes, I can read souls close to death." He waved his arm in their direction. "Theirs is a true love in all senses. They've weathered the good and the bad life had to throw at them, never wavering from their dedication to each other. They accepted each other's faults and have even grown to appreciate them." He nodded more to himself than me. "Their souls have entwined. They are what books are written about and movies made. It isn't as flashy as some would have it be ... but the truth usually isn't."

"That ... that's true love?"

A part of a past conversation with Six rose up in my mind unbidden.

I cleared my throat. "Have you ever seen true love outside of fiction? How do we know it even exists?"

Six grinned. "I love you, but I'm guessing you mean romantic love, right?"

"Yes, of course, that's what I mean. In all the jobs I've worked over the years, I've never seen anything even hinting at true romantic love, but I have seen the love of parents, of friends, stuff like that." I squeezed his hand. "And I hope you know I love you, too. You're my best friend and I don't know how I got by before you became Six."

He shifted, staring straight ahead as if he was suddenly somewhere else. "I've seen it. I've seen true love, and it changed me. It changed everything."

My mouth opened and closed a few times before I could form words. "You've seen it? When? What do you mean it changed everything?"

"Yes," Alistar said, "that is true love."

Mesmerized, I crept as close as I dared. Although I didn't think the couple would notice me, between me being a luna, and them being consumed within each other's gazes.

Something foreign bloomed in my chest as I stared at them. An ache of sorts, but also a ghost of warmth. As if their love was so powerful it could physically affect me. They filled the room with unspoken things such as intimacy, and trust beyond my comprehension.

And they're dying.

"What's wrong with them? Are they both definitely going to die? I mean, I guess that's good that they die together. Better than one dying and leaving the other behind. But why can't they both live? If they could possibly find a new treatment—"

Alistar's palm slid over my mouth, and he leaned in close, murmuring against my ear. A chill ran up my spine from his proximity. "Reality is breaking apart. They will cease to exist along with everything else. Or have you forgotten?"

Sadness overwhelmed me, and I sank into Alistar, needing some kind of physical support in that moment.

"But that kind of love should live forever." My words came out muffled against his hand.

"It will."

"Not if it technically never happens. If reality implodes then none of this, including their love, will ever have happened."

"But it did happen."

I shook my head. "It happened, but then it won't have happened."

Conflicting emotions warred within me. I believed reality was pointless if Six wasn't in it, but what if I was wrong? What if my selfish nature had failed to realize that there are other things that deserved to exist? Things like the elderly couple's love. What if I somehow could save something as precious as their priceless connection, but still lose Six in the end? Could I go on in the world knowing I'd be empty, yet at the same time knowing I'd let others be whole?

Realization hit, and I lifted my chin up, staring into the darkness of Alistar's hood. "Six was right, seeing it firsthand changes everything."

Ushering me back into the hallway, Alistar pointed at the next room. "Tina. You still need to find Tina."

Even though I was no longer in the room with the elderly couple physically, mentally I was. It was something so simple, the way they laid next to each other, their withering hands entwined. And somehow it was the world—or rather it had changed my world.

I want to save this reality, I admitted to myself with

shock. *I don't want to sit back and be passive anymore. If I die alone so love can exist in all its forms, then that can be my legacy. In a weird way, even if no one ever finds out that I saved love, so to speak, my actions will be remembered, and I would be known. I could die alone, and I wouldn't be forgotten. My gift to the humans would be felt every single day. Maybe, in the end, we all die alone, and what you do when no one is watching is the only thing that counts.*

It was then, while my mind was a million miles away, that Tina exited a room on the far end of the hallway, headed our way.

Leaning to the right, I hissed through the side of my mouth, "Okay, I found her. Now what?"

But Alistar was no longer there. *Shit, shit, shit, shit, shit.*

My stomach fluttered, and an invisible thread attached to my sternum was yanked, drawing my undivided attention. The location of my pending job appeared in my mind's eye, along with every other detail I would need. Surprise warred with dread.

The pull to go where I was being lured, summoned, or whatever you could call it now, was still an undeniable force. It felt as natural as it always had, despite the change in circumstances. But I didn't want to go. And beyond that, there was no reason to go. Not enforcing a fixed point in time at the current stage in reality collapse wouldn't change anything. All it would possibly accomplish would be to take me somewhere I didn't want to be, to deal with things I didn't want to see. Add in the fact that I couldn't return to Archives either.

Yep, I can't go. I'll just resist. If humans can overcome their addictions, then so can I.

Averting my gaze, I waited for Tina to walk past me, then I turned to trail behind her. *Alistar may be gone, but he'll be back, and in the meantime, I'll just do what he wanted me to.*

Ugh. I can't believe it's come to blindly following his plans.

Chapter 28

As it turns out, having what appears to be some kind of health ailment, like appendicitis or kidney failure, in a hospital, is not the best way to go unnoticed, even for a luna.

"You need to sit down." A nurse guided me to a nearby empty wheelchair. "Tell me exactly where it hurts."

"I'm fine. Just a stomach cramp—" her frown deepened, "I mean tummy ache. It's something I ate. I'm fine, or I will be soon."

"You're pale and shaking, and you can barely stand up straight. It seems a tad more serious than you're letting on." She pressed her thumb into my wrist, pausing for several moments. "And your heart rate is definitely elevated."

"I was just here visiting … my friend, and I was upset, so there's no need to worry about me. Like I said, I'll be fine."

Ignoring my protests, the nurse pressed me back into the wheelchair and stood. "Well, it's lucky for you that you were here when this happened then."

How did this happen? Weren't nurses usually overworked and busy with patients that actually wanted or needed to receive care? After all, we were in the United States of America in modern times, and everyone, even the supernatural world knew the medical system was a mess. Not the doctors, and especially not the nurses' fault, but how and why was I getting special attention all of a sudden?

Opening my mouth to mount more of a protest, a squeak of pain erupted up my throat, escaping past my lips instead. *Damnit. Turns out resisting the call to a job is a bit more complicated than I thought. If I want this to stop, I need to get away from this nurse, go somewhere private, and just get the stupid job over with.*

I white-knuckled the arms of the wheelchair. "I'm telling you, I'm fine. Please, just let me go home."

"Now, honey, you may not think there's anything serious going on with you, but you'll thank me later. Trust me."

"Doubtful," I grumbled. My gaze landed on a restroom, and my arm shot out. "Bathroom—I mean I need to go. Badly."

The nurse regarded me with skepticism, her dark eyebrows halfway up her forehead. "All right. But I'll be right here waiting."

"I'm well aware."

Half limping, half sprinting, I managed to make into the restroom and shut the door behind me. Closing my eyes, I willed myself to where I had no choice to be.

LURKING in the depths of the submarine's engine room, I watched crew members move with practiced movements, all of them with an edge of panic. None of it would do them any good, no one would survive. This military submarine was under attack, and soon the opposing force would make a deadly hit.

I glanced down at my uniform and grimaced. Being here was the price I had to pay for ending my pain. My mind kept wandering back to the elderly couple, and because of them, I couldn't help but wonder who of the crew had wives, husbands, or any kind of love connection. How dearly would they all be missed? Would any of their deaths result in the ruination of another's soul?

A reaper appeared next to me, and he placed his hand on my shoulder. Forcing a smile, I said, "See, that's a good way to let me know it's you. You're the only reaper who would touch me in any way."

"It's a better option than wearing a pin."

I sighed. "I tried not to come here. But here I am."

"You are what you are," he stated, his tone gentle.

"And if I don't want to be what I am? If I don't want to

do any of this anymore? Six was right. Seeing true love changes everything."

When I said it out loud it seemed ridiculous, but it was something I felt, and emotions were hard to explain sometimes, especially when whoever was feeling them couldn't quite decipher them. I knew seeing the couple had altered me in a cataclysmic way, but the more I attempted to pick apart the reasons and quantify the moment, the more the answers I was looking for eluded me.

"Your confusion is written all over your face, little luna."

"Yeah? I don't doubt it. I've never had to work at hiding my emotions since I'm a luna, and no one besides Six ever noticed. And with him … well, I didn't try to hide them either."

"That's a lie."

"What?"

"You heard me. That's a lie. No one is one-hundred-percent honest with anyone else all of the time. "

He was right. Again. I resisted the urge to growl at him like a rabid dog. "Fine. I didn't tell him everything, and I may have used white lies from time to time. But that's not the same thing as being outright dishonest."

"They're two sides of the same coin."

"How is it that you keep getting assigned the same jobs as me?" There had been a few times since I'd met Alistar that another reaper had shown up to the scene, but most of the time it was my second shadow who was called to task.

He answered me with silence.

"Right. More things you're not going to share with me."

Reverting my attention to the crew members, my stomach twisted. I couldn't shake the thoughts of their unknown families, and the loss they would feel. Fortunately, the pain would be short-lived since reality wouldn't be around all that much longer. "I don't want to do this anymore. I want to save humans, not ensure their deaths."

Alistar's hand hovered over my shoulder once again but dropped away before making contact. "You don't ensure their deaths. You maintain the fixed point in time surrounding their deaths. It might not seem like a big difference to you, but it is."

"Whatever. I still don't want to do it. These men on this submarine are going to die no matter what I do. I see no bright soul to offer help to them, and escaping when they're in the middle of the ocean, who knows how far down …" I shook my head. "I don't actually even need to be here."

I made the decision then. I didn't want to be there, and so I would leave. *But where will I go?* I couldn't return to the luna realm.

Six. I can find him again. But how? Without being able to use the books in Archives, how would I track him? And also, without hopping back to the luna realm to make sure

I was synced with the current human realm timeline, if I went to the diner again … well, hell, it might not even exist yet.

I eyed my uniform, and then the crew again. *Yep, I feel like this is in the past. So what do I do?*

"The wheels are turning. I can practically see the smoke," Alistar said, mirth covering every syllable.

"I've decided I'm leaving. I don't want to be here, so I won't be." I tucked my hair behind my ears. "But I don't know where I'm supposed to go from here."

He nodded slowly. "I can assist you with that."

I swung my arm in an arch. "What about all these souls? It's pointless for me to be here because they're all guaranteed to die. Plus, what's the point in recording anything if reality is coming to an end?" I narrowed my eyes at him, making the connection. "Oh, so if you can leave, too … Yeah. That makes sense. Does that mean wherever the souls go is going to be destroyed along with reality? Or is everything getting a complete reset? What exactly is going to happen when all of this is gone?"

"Do you ever stop asking questions? You could drive the most patient creature insane."

I scrunched up my nose. "Let me know when you come across someone who is patient, because it definitely isn't you."

He chuckled long and low, the sound surprisingly pleasant to me in that moment. "Touché."

I grinned. "I call 'em like I see 'em." *What are you doing?*

The smile slowly slid from my face. *Here you are joking with Alistar when the end is nigh ... literally.*

Notching my chin up, I stared into the shadows of his hood. "Let's get out of here already."

"Your wish is my command."

Swooping me up in my arms, darkness wrapped me in its sweet embrace.

Chapter 29

"Hey, Eighty-nine! This way!" Six called, dashing into a bar ahead of me.

Jazz music blared, the constant hum of chatter an annoying undertone. This was our seventh or maybe eighth bar on our night out. I'd lost track a while ago after Six had made me down some blue-colored shots. My vision was slightly fuzzy around the edges, but the happy glow that accompanied my buzz caused me to not care.

My attention was snagged by the band on stage, the music filling my head completely. Raising my arms in the air, I began to dance.

Six spun me around, laughing. "You're drunk," he slurred. "You're drunk because you're dancing."

I stuck my tongue out at him. "So what if I'm drunk? You're drunk, too."

His features pinched up. "No. I'm slightly buzzed, not drunk. You're the drunk one."

I rolled my eyes. We had this argument almost every time we went out together. It had become somewhat of a competition, the winner being whoever could drink more and stay awake longer. I was usually the winner, and clear champion, something Six denied vehemently. I'd even gone as far as to stick a Post-it to his forehead the last time he'd passed out before me, with "I win" written on it.

Poking him in the chest, I laughed. "When are you going to give this up? I'm older, wiser, and just the best at everything. You'll never win this game."

Grabbing my wrist, he tugged me to the bar. "We'll see." He waved at the bartender, who made eye contact with Six, letting him know he'd serve us soon.

I burped, covering the sound with my hand. Six tapped my nose with his index finger. "You're going down tonight. Down, down, down."

"Yeah, big talk for a man who got Post-it-ed last time."

He frowned. "That was a fluke."

"Please," I scoffed. "The fluke was the one time you beat me. I still feel like you cheated somehow."

He flung his arm around my shoulder. "It's not cheating if you don't get caught."

I guffawed. "You just admitted that I should have won that time, too."

"I admit nothing."

"You just did!"

He leaned heavily into me, his knees buckling. "Six always has your six, even when he cheats."

Alistar loomed over me, blotting out everything except

him from my vision. I blinked up at him lazily. "What happened?" I croaked, the random memory of Six still fresh in my mind. Or had it been a dream? "Where are we?"

"We're back at the hospital."

Sitting up, I took in the same empty room from our first visit. "The same year, too?"

"Yes, it's like we never left."

"How did you manage that?" Then I remembered the nurse I barely managed to escape. "There was a nurse who saw me—I mean, actually saw me—and she was convinced I needed medical assistance. How did she notice me like that?"

Alistar expressed his displeasure with a few swear words of particularly descriptive nature. "Your luna cover is beginning to slip. This makes things more complicated."

My eyes widened. I hadn't been aware that such a thing could happen. It explained the incident with the nurse for sure. "Okay, so why are we back here."

"To finish what we started."

I groaned. "You want me to follow Tina again? But why?"

"It's important."

My stomach fluttered, and an invisible thread attached to my sternum was yanked, drawing my undivided attention. The location of my pending job appeared in my mind's eye, along with every other detail I would need. Complete and utter shock washed over me.

It was the same job I just left.

But the pain had dissipated the moment I arrived on the scene, not having returned. I'd thought with everything else in the universe going on, I'd get a free pass.

I lifted my gaze to Alistar. "I'm being called to go to that same job again."

"Yes, I too am getting a repeat call for the same place."

"What will happen if we don't go at all this time?"

He sat down on the edge of the hospital bed, hunching over. "I honestly don't know."

"Should we try to resist, or go and then leave again?" Was showing up, even though the job wasn't completed, the loophole for the pain I experienced before? Or was the internal agony merely on a temporary timeout?

"If we want the scene to leave us alone, I'm guessing the best solution would be to simply do the job and put it behind us."

That was not the answer I wanted to hear. "There has to be a way to stop. To not do it. There just has to be." I didn't think I could handle it at the moment. It wasn't the deaths themselves, but the heightened awareness of what the deaths would mean for those left behind. *It shouldn't matter, not now anyways. Everything will be erased soon.*

But it did matter. It mattered more than I could express even to myself. *Is this what happened to Six?* About half a year before his death, maybe longer, I noticed a steady decline in his moods. He'd been more sensitive than me after his jobs from the beginning, but something had changed, making him worse than he'd ever been.

Six shifted, staring straight ahead as if he was suddenly somewhere else. "I've seen it. I've seen true love, and it changed me. It changed everything."

His words ricocheted in my mind, bouncing around and around, seeking to help me find clarity. Was what he witnessed what had altered him irrevocably? Had it gone from distasteful to unbearable having to do what lunas were born to do? Had it served to heighten his need to connect with someone like Tina, a human who knew nothing of our world? Or had all the events combined to form the perfect storm within him? A storm currently brewing within me.

I wanted to save humanity, not witness it die. Death was an avoidable part of life, to be sure, but the kind of events I had to record as a luna were something else entirely. There were no peaceful good-byes for me to witness, only violence and tragedies, pain, and regret.

Alistar reached for me, something I noticed he'd been doing frequently lately, but just as before, he let his arm drop before making contact. "We all have to do things we don't want to at times."

"Yeah, well, sue me for wanting to be a brat when the end of existence is looming. There will be no later for me, so I want to do what I want to do now."

"There's still a chance, a slim chance that we can stop this."

"But how? Things are already too far gone, aren't they?"

"It's never too late to turn around no matter how far down a path you've gone."

My nostrils flared. I was not in the mood for his vague-speak. "Unless you're Six, and you've created a paradox."

Alistar did touch me then, his long fingers sliding under my chin to tip it up. "Six will die. There's no way to save him. He made his choice. But you can decide if the world, this reality, is worth saving … without him in it."

I placed my hand over his, staring into his hood, wishing I could see his expression, or at least his eyes beyond a soft glow or glint. "Why me? If this reality is salvageable, then why is it up to me? How is it up to me?"

His hand slid out from under mine. "I can't tell you that."

Pressing my lips together, I barely kept myself from crying out in frustration. My emotions were fragile, ready to break. And hearing him tell me that there was one more detail I couldn't be privy to was nearly the last straw. "Fine. You keep your secrets. I just hope they don't bite you on the ass in the end."

"Me as well, little luna, me as well."

Wrapping my arms around my middle, I realized that I was right back to where I started. I didn't want to go to the submarine job, but I'd been left with little choice.

No. I have a choice, simply not the best one.

Tightening my self-hug, I regarded Alistar again. "I'm not doing that job. And if the pain starts up again, I'll go, but pop out again before it's done, just like before. I refuse to do it anymore. Out of principle."

"Then what will you do instead?"

I smirked. "Duh. Follow Tina. Isn't that why we came back here to begin with?"

He gave me one curt nod. "It's as solid a plan as any you've had before."

Ignoring the not-so-subtle dig, I tumbled out of the bed, and made my way for the door. "Guess I'll head on up to the third floor again."

A flash of light streaked down the wall beside me, and the scent of burnt ozone suffused the air. An oblong shape, rippling with rainbow colors, appeared, and I teetered back, already caught in its net.

Alistar bellowed, his words not reaching my ears as I was sucked into the RR.

Chapter 30

The moon hung above my head, full and bright, its luminous face beckoning. Wings unfurled from my back, reaching delicately for the night sky. Leaping into the air, I took flight, knowledge of my origins and duties awakening within my mind.

Weaving in and out between and through beams of moonlight, I climbed higher and higher, becoming aware that I was not alone. All around me other lunas filled the sky, doing their best to reach the same destination I had in mind.

Emptiness bloomed in my chest, sudden and acute, followed by a longing for something I couldn't quite put my finger on. I understood intellectually that my discomfort would be eased when I fulfilled my purpose, going on jobs to record and ensure fixed points in time and the souls who must die there. But since I had yet to experience it, I had no practical knowledge of such things. I was brand new to the world, a being created freshly today, along with all of my luna brothers and sisters.

I regarded them silently, having only mild curiosity about them, not caring enough to greet any of them. The silence was broken only by the animals in the nearby forest, and the sounds of us soaring through the air, letting me know that I wasn't the only one who felt that way.

My stomach fluttered, and an invisible thread attached to my sternum was yanked, drawing my undivided attention. The location of my first pending job appeared in my mind's eye, along with every other detail I would need. Excitement spiked through me, and I closed my eyes immediately, not wanting to wait a second longer to experience what I'd been born to do.

MY FIRST INTERACTION WITH HUMANS, if one could call it that, was exactly what I expected. They were loud and colorful, the warmth their souls exuded both terrifying and wonderful. I wanted to be like them, and yet I knew I never could. Sadness gnawed at my insides, highlighting the singular plight of lunas. We were forced to be near humanity, and yet never a part of it, always held separate.

This is what you deserve. This is all you ever deserve, a small voice in my mind whispered, not unlike mine, and yet not the same either. I didn't question it, and merely let it roll through my consciousness, circling around and around.

I watched with detachment as humans scurried around me, fire blazing bright. The entire village would be consumed in the flames, burnt to the ground, with many lives being lost in the blaze. I didn't care. What needed to happen would happen, I was merely there to enforce the laws of the universe.

A woman ran frantically down the path, screaming in horror outside of a hut that was already nothing but ashes. Dropping to her knees, her wail of agony pierced my heart, drawing me from my malaise. Her pain seemed familiar to me somehow, the nature of it unknown.

"Ilia was in there! Please! Ilia was in there!"

A man wrapped her in his arms, his comforting words too low for me to hear.

"Mama!" a little boy exclaimed, sprinting for her from around the corner.

"Ilia!" All her relief and love was wound up in his name as she repeated it over and over, smothering him with kisses. "Ilia. Ilia. My Ilia."

The three of them then embraced, and something undefinable ached within me.

Tilting my head, I regarded the family with curiosity. The love they seemed to have for each other was like nothing I'd seen before. Of course, I hadn't actually seen much with being new to this world, but a plethora of knowledge about human behaviors had been implanted within my brain. Love was a notion defined as something that could motivate humans to attempt to break the pattern set for them. It was something that drove most humans, and it was dangerous to one such as me.

A surge of energy danced along my skin, goose bumps erupting in its wake. *It's time.*

Although my first time, my actions were led by pure instinct.

My wings flared out behind me, and I threw my head back as I rose into the air. Hovering between worlds, the recently dead souls passed through me one after another in lightning-fast succession. I recorded their essences, making sure all that should be was.

As the numbers of dead added up, the warmth their souls offered seeped into my bones. My body hummed with delight, the energy of the deceased feeding me in ways I knew with surety would become an addictive force, for in those few moments I came to understand what it meant to feel satiated, content, full … like I actually belonged there … or anywhere. I was whole.

A moment of true peace.

And then it was over practically before it began.

The vast emptiness gaped in my chest once more, threatening to consume me. I blinked in confusion. *That's all there is? That's all I'll get? The only time I'll get to feel that way?*

My teeth chattered uncontrollably, and I stared at the reaper who had been by my side since I'd first appeared.

"Is that all there is?"

It turned toward me, remaining silent.

"Did I do something wrong?" I searched the database implanted within my mind, considering things from all the angles. As far as I could tell, I'd done everything just as I should.

This is what you deserve. This is all you ever deserve. The voice was back, circling round and round. It was odd, using language not of this time.

So cold. Need to get home.

You're not using language of this time either, I realized.

Clutching my head, I dug my nails into my scalp. Memories, memories I shouldn't have as one so new swirled just out of reach, nothing more than disjointed voices.

"Six will always have your six."

"Happy Birthday, Eighty-nine!"

"Lunas don't have birthdays. We're not born."

"That's why today can be your birthday, you get to choose."

"But I didn't choose today, you did."

"Because I knew you wouldn't."

"Six will always have your six."

A face in shadow, a smile out of focus. Things that shouldn't be in my mind pressed heavily inside of my brain, the weight of them unbearable.

"Eighty-nine." A reaper approached, arms outstretched. "You need to come with me."

"How do you know my name?" I ground out, my head pulsating in time with my heartbeat.

"Everything will be explained once you come with me."

He leaned over, sliding his arms behind my knees and back.

A part of me wanted to resist, to fight the way he lifted me in his arms like a ragdoll, but something else, my gut perhaps, remained passive, telling me to trust the reaper.

"Six will always have your six."

I bit the insides of my cheeks. "Wait. Stop. I must go to Archives."

"There's no need." The reaper shifted me in his arms, holding me tightly against his chest.

I shook my head. "Yes, I must go to Archives. It's protocol after a job. The whole point of my job, in fact."

"None of it matters anymore, Eighty-nine."

"That doesn't make any sense. Of course it matters—"

"Six will always have your six."

Tugging at my hair, I peered into the reaper's hood. "Do you know what's wrong with me? Did a flaw develop when I was created? Am I broken?"

"Close your eyes. It will all come back to you soon, I promise."

An oblong shape, a rainbow of colors undulating within, appeared behind the reaper's head. My ears popped, the scent of burnt ozone filling the air. The reaper's robe whipped around us, and I thought I heard him swear under his breath.

"Hold on to me, don't let go."

I nodded, unable to rip my gaze from the thing behind us. It was beautiful in a terrifying way. "What is it? That knowledge wasn't given to me." I suspected there was much knowledge not given to me, even though I was led to believe that everything I would need as a luna was in my brain. It was my first day alive, and already I was filled with confusion, and at a clear disadvantage if I was to perform my assigned task properly in this world.

"Archives. I need to get to Archives." My teeth began chattering anew, my fingers numb.

The reaper glided forward, but each inch gained in ground, we were pulled backward closer and closer to the thing hovering in the air.

Panic swelled in me, overriding the confusion. *This isn't supposed to happen.* A luna is tasked with recording and enforcing a fixed point in time. When completed, a luna must go to Archives to transfer the information it gathered into one of the books. Then and only then was the job complete. I'd done the first part, but I needed to do the rest.

Twisting within the reaper's arms, I hit my open palms against his shoulders. "I must go to Archives. You, being a reaper, don't understand. After I record, I must transfer the information, placing it in the Archives for the architects.

"You can't go to Archives, Eighty-nine."

"Yes, it's what I need to do."

"No. Your mind isn't working properly right now. You're lost in your past self, but there's a part of you deep down, somewhere, that knows this isn't your first job. Today is not your first day alive. Think hard. Separate from your past self."

Images of fires, car crashes, boats submerging, planes crashing, people falling from buildings, trains derailing… so many catastrophes, too many to count or catalogue, their pain, their suffering, all of if played across my mind's eye. Bits and pieces of a life I supposedly hadn't lived yet.

And Six. Of course, Six. Always Six. His face. His smile. His donkey-like laugh. The brother of my soul. My home.

The fog from my mind cleared, my brain fully coming back online. *This is my past. This was my first job. I was thrown back here when I got sucked into the RR at the hospital. Yes, I remember everything now.*

Digging my nails into Alistar's shoulders, my eyes widened as I took in the RR with understanding. "Why the hell was I thrown back into my past instead of Six's death scene, or even one of his timeline events?"

"Because you made the decision not to go to the submarine. The moment you actually decided with one-hundred percent certainty the tear appeared."

Shock ricocheted through my system. "I caused another RR? I'm the center of my own storm now?"

"Yes," Alistar grated as he managed to move us a few feet forward, just to be yanked back closer than we were before.

"What's going to happen if we get sucked into this one?" I didn't actually think it was going to be an *if* this time, it was most definitely going to be *when*. We were losing ground, and soon we'd both be tossed to some unknown spot in time.

Fuck. I knew reality falling apart wasn't going to be fun, especially for the few of us who realize what's happening, but I didn't think it was going to involve being lobbed about to random points in personal history. Maybe by the time my adventure comes to an end I'll be begging for the relief.

Having just relived my awakening and first job as a luna, the stark contrast in my personality was evident to me. I thought I'd been the same since the beginning, but I was wrong. I'd grown emotionally, opened up in a way that was eerily similar to a human. Perhaps Six had helped me more than I even had a concept of. If he'd never shown up—

Well, if he'd never shown up then a reality paradox wouldn't be ripping apart the fabric of time, but you'd be just as closed off and cold as all the other lunas. Six and I were truly different, and not because we were created that way. Or rather not because I was created that way. Six had been made with a different mold, one with more life than the any of the rest of us could perceive. Even me, with how much I'd changed, probably couldn't grasp what it was like in Six's head. The torment caused simply by being a luna.

No wonder he was the one who ended up causing a paradox. But then so have I now. Although the exact nature of mine remained a mystery to me. I'd simply not gone to a job, not created an unworkable event the way Six had. There were details I was obviously missing and didn't have time to figure out at the moment.

Leaning closer to Alistar, I yelled next to his hood, hoping he could hear me over the howling wind, "Now that there are two paradoxes, is it all over? Is that slight chance erased?" Sweet moon above, why didn't I just go to that job? There could possibly still be a chance at salvation for this reality if I hadn't been so stubborn. Personal sacrifice, especially of the mental kind, was nothing compared to what I'd caused with my carelessness.

Alistar pressed his face close to mine, his hood covering part of my head. His lips moved against my ear, eliciting a shudder from me. "It's not over yet."

Lifting up into the air, we were flung back, losing ourselves to the void.

Chapter 31

The sun hung high in the sky, its heat unrelenting. I swiped at the sweat dripping down my brow. Sand as far as the eye could see loomed in all directions around me. And I was alone.

Where the hell is Alistar? And where the hell I am for that matter?

I awakened with a jolt to the unfamiliar scene, no clue as to how I'd ended up in the sweltering desert in the middle of the afternoon.

Indecision was the only factor keeping me there, although it wouldn't for much longer. As a luna, and a nocturnal creature, the day, let alone the desert in the day, was pretty much my definition of hell on Earth.

Oh, crap. Am I actually in hell on Earth? Could reality have finished up and this is where I ended up because of my part in its destruction?

A glint and a flash in the distance to the left, lasting no

more than a second, caught my attention. Raising my hand to shield my eyes as best as I could, I trudged forward, hoping what I'd seen was a clue of some sort.

Each step was arduous, the sand not wanting to release my feet. I traveled no farther than a few hundred yards when light flashed in front of me, and a RR appeared.

Great.

Before I could react, I was sucked into it, my mind blanking once again.

IT WAS pitch black in all directions around me, and as I stretched out my arms, my fingers came into contact with something hard and slippery. Quite possibly a wall or rocks that were either wet or covered in mold or moss. My nostrils flared, picking up on notes of mildew, and I could hear trickling water of some kind close by. But the darkness that surrounded me was absolute and gave away none of its secrets.

Something snapped and popped behind me, and I whirled around, the tiniest hint of light emerging. I blinked and widened my eyes as far as they could go. *Now would be a good time for my eyes to glow. But like everything else lately, nothing was working quite right. Not even my own body.*

The light grew, forming into a small orb, floating about as high as my shoulders. I reached for it and the orb danced just beyond my grasp. Carefully moving forward, I reached for it again. This time my hands closed around it, and light exploded, causing me to yelp in surprise.

I was no longer in the cave, or wherever I'd been. Instead, I was in a sterile room containing several chairs, and a door. Everything inside was the whitest white I could imagine. It was unnatural somehow. Voices, low and melodious, hummed just beyond the door.

I'm not alone anymore!

Pressing my ear to the door, I attempted to hear what was being said. Even though I was elated to not be alone anymore, I didn't want to make my presence be known to creatures I was better off hiding from. I had no idea where or when I was either. It was plausible reality had been destroyed, and a new one was forming around me. Or that I had been lost in between realities. *Now that's a terrifying concept.*

"Do you understand your job, Alistar?" a woman spoke, her tone sharp.

"Yes," Alistar replied.

I stiffened, recognizing it to be *my* Alistar, or not my Alistar per say, but the reaper who'd become my near-constant companion lately. But of course, it was him, how many other Alistars were out there in the world that I kept crossing paths with?

"And what, pray tell, is it that you think your job is?" the woman snapped.

"I guide souls into the afterlife, and I comfort them if need be." Alistar sounded calm. Too calm.

"And are you supposed to care about a soul once it moves on?"

"No."

"Do you offer comfort to a soul once it has passed on?"

"No."

"Then why do you insist on doing such things when they aren't in your job description? Angels of death guide and comfort recently deceased souls. That's it."

"Her soul hasn't moved on."

"Loopholes. Is that what you're telling me? That you're using loopholes to help her?"

"I'm guiding her. Helping her to move on to where she's supposed to be."

"She's exactly where she's supposed to be. Simply because you don't agree doesn't mean you get to play God. You aren't any kind of god, you're an angel. I thought only the young ones got wild hairs such as this. I never expected something like this from you. You've gone rogue."

"I haven't gone rogue. Far from it. I'm simply attempting to finish my job. Her soul—"

"Made its choice. One you need to be at peace with."

A loud thump sounded, and I jumped.

"I cannot be at peace with it. She doesn't belong there. The others were taken to that place. What happened isn't like—"

"It doesn't matter if her soul isn't like the others there. She found her way there. Decided that's what she deserved. It's the downside of having choices. Or would you rather free will go the way of the dinosaurs?"

"Free will is a joke, and we all know it."

Nothing else was said, and I shifted, pressing my ear harder into the door.

"Fine. Finish this one out. But you don't get another chance at it. If you fail again, I won't be as lenient."

"Thank you," Alister said. "You won't regret this."

"I already do. Now get out of here. I don't want to hear about any of this mess again. Do you hear me? It will play out, and once it's reached the inevitable conclusion things will return to the way they should be. You will go back to being a law-abiding Angel of Death. One who doesn't cause trouble for me."

"Yes, I understand. This is my last chance. If I fail, I won't get another."

"Precisely."

My mind reeled. The paradox caused by Six, the bright soul, Alistar getting involved in my plight, the architects … I'd thought everything was linked somehow, but I hadn't been able to put the pieces together. I was sure everything had been about Six, him being the eye of the storm, but was it possible—could it be possible that there was someone else? It sounded to me like Alistar was attempting to help a human soul. But whose?

Realization dawned. *Tina. It has to be Tina. Everything from the beginning has been about her. Not Six. From the first moment I laid eyes on her, I felt trepidation. I'd somehow known she would spell trouble for the time-space continuum.*

Did Alistar want to ensure Tina's life? Had her soul originally ended up somewhere other than a peaceful afterlife before Six got involved? Was Alistar willing to use me to save Tina and reality, knowing Six would be cannon fodder?

A knot formed in my stomach, pushing bile up my esophagus. Had Alistar set this whole thing into motion, using me, using Six, both of us second rate lunas, easily disposable in comparison to a human soul? *Shit, we're both cannon fodder.*

Backing away from the door, I whipped my head around wildly. Somehow I'd ended up in Alistar's timeline, probably a past event. It didn't explain the desert and the cave, especially the glowing orb, but that all could have been a side effect of reality dissolving. The here and now was the past, before Alistar had started tinkering, subtly steering me to make sure things went exactly how he wanted them. How many times had he attempted it before? The woman in the room with him made it sound like it'd been many.

I wanted to know his end game, and now I do. I now know my future. I've heard it said that you can't change your future or destiny, whatever one chose to call it, but I'd also heard if you knew what it was, then you could alter it. Could I? Could I alter my future when I would be fighting against a determined Angel of Death?

What do I do now? I can't trust Alistar. But I can't let him know that I don't trust him anymore. Who knows how he would manipulate me if he found out. I have to play stupid and resist him at the same time. But how do I do that exactly?

The opposite. I do the opposite of what he wants me to do. Everything he advises, I merely feign ignorance and do the opposite. It's not the best plan, but it's all I've got.

Closing my eyes, I willed myself to the lunar realm.

Chapter 32

I'd never thought much about a god, or any higher power really. I believed there was something—man, woman, child, cat … something. There had to be. Knowing what I did about the universe, and the existence of creatures such as lunas, architects, reapers, it was all evidence of a being with a master plan. That being made rules, and we all had to follow them or suffer the consequences, some worse than others.

As I stared up at the moon in the luna realm, the urge to pray overcame me. I'd never done it before, nor had the urge, and besides what I read in books and seen in movies, I had no knowledge on the subject. I figured, in the end, it couldn't hurt.

Dropping to my knees, I bowed my head. *Please, whoever or whatever you are, please help me find a way to fix things. I want to save this reality. I want to save Six. If I can't save Six then at least let me save this reality for people like that little old couple in the hospital. Love like that is beautiful, and pure, and a host of other things I'm sure I'll never grasp as a luna, but it's too beautiful to never have existed. Don't let this reality fade away into nothing like it never was. Don't let love like that be lost forever.*

Opening my eyes, I stared up at the moon again. *Thank you, or Amen.*

Nibbling my thumbnail, I rose to my feet, uncertain of my next immediate step. I'd come back to the luna realm because Alistar insisted that I couldn't or shouldn't. I'd expected the architects to be lying in wait, or for me to run into the other me. But things were normal, for a lack of a better word. No one had even given me a sideways glance since I arrived.

No architects had come to find me, but I also hadn't dared step into Archives. They could be playing the long game, lulling me into a false sense of security, and then boom, I came to them.

"Hey." Six settled down beside me, his hand brushing mine. "You're looking a lot better. Wanna go to the human realm for some food?"

Oh, no! This is when I go to the diner for the first with him and see Tina. That also means my past self will be showing up any minute. Six found me before the other me came to the same spot. I need to get out of here fast!

I nodded. "Yep, mmm hmm. Let's go to the human realm. We can leave right now. Immediately." Shoving at Six, I kept glancing over my shoulder. If past me appeared, I was positive I would be sucked into her mind and would be doomed to repeat the day exactly as it had been before.

Six jumped into the air, his wings flapping hard, a huge grin adorning his face. "Great! Meet you out front after I change real quick." He zoomed into the air, calling over his shoulder, "You might want to change, too."

I glanced down at my attire. There was nothing wrong with it. I was wearing jeans and a plain black T-shirt. I even had shoes on this time. *Huh. This isn't a time loop, but even though I'm a different version of me, doing different things, Six is acting similar to the first time I experienced this day.*

Six's voice bellowed from inside, "Let's go, Eighty-nine! Chop, chop!"

Okay, Six is going to act the way he has a tendency to. It's just how things work. As long as I—

"Who are you? You can't be me."

Pivoting on my heel, I whirled around, coming face-to-face with myself. Her eyes widened with shock, and mine with horror.

"Wh-What's happening?" She backed away slowly, her hands raised in the air like she was surrendering. "You can't be me."

"Listen to me, Eighty-nine. I am you. Future you. I—"

"No. The time continuum doesn't work that way. There can't be two of us in one place so close together. And by you coming here then you change my future, your past, which should cause some kind of paradox."

"Yeah, I used to think that was all true. But I'm starting

to think paradoxes aren't what I think they are, and reality itself definitely isn't what I thought it was."

The world tilted, and I blinked a different perspective into view. Past me wasn't standing in front of me anymore. But my vantage point had changed. I peered down at my clothes, noting I was now wearing what she'd been in.

Shit. Guess what I believed about not being able to have two of me in the same place at the same time is true. I got absorbed into her just like I was afraid would happen. But I do seem to have control this time, unlike when I returned to Six's death scene.

Could it be because I wasn't at a fixed point in time? Or had reality dissolved to the point that the rules didn't apply to such things anymore? Either way, I supposed it didn't matter. I was going to go with Six, and figure out a new plan before it was too late. Spending time with him along the way, especially when it quite possibly could be some of the last, was simply an added bonus.

Pinching the bridge of my nose, I fought sudden dizziness, the ground coming up to meet me.

"YOU ALL RIGHT, EIGHTY-NINE?" Six squeezed my shoulder, chuckling under his breath.

Glowering, I squinted at him, the bright day practically blinding. "We need to stop to get me some sunglasses somewhere."

He shook his head slowly, fingering the pair on his face. "I'm not sure why you didn't think to bring any."

"I don't know, my mind was elsewhere, obviously." I swiped at the tears forming in the corners of my eyes. It wasn't like lunas had an aversion to daylight, not like vampires or other fictitious creatures of that ilk, we simply preferred the night, and to stalk in the shadows. Plus, being out in the day made me tired and cranky. But when moving around in the human world during times of leisure, I couldn't force them to function on my nocturnal schedule … unfortunately. It was only the promise of my favorite foods that kept me from going home.

"It's not that much farther, and you'll be fine once we get inside," Six said, fiddling with the zipper on his jacket. He'd chosen to wear clothes out of the norm for him. He swapped out his green, military-style jacket for a crisp leather one and his faded jeans for dark denim. Ratty sneakers no longer adorned his feet, but rather black leather motorcycle boots. If not for his neutral skin tone and hair, like all lunas, he'd almost stand out.

I narrowed my eyes while motioning to his suspicious attire. "What's up with the style change? Something you want to tell me?"

His shoulders wiggled as if he was rustling his wings that weren't there at the moment. "Just felt like something different."

"Uh-huh." If he didn't want to tell me, I wasn't in the mood to pry it out of him. "Can I borrow your sunglasses for a while? My eyes are watering, and my nose is itching.

I'm a few seconds away from a sneezing fit, I can feel it. You could have at least brought me somewhere overcast. You know, like Seattle or London, or I don't know, anywhere where I'm not like an ant under a magnifying glass."

Grabbing my forearm roughly, Six hauled me down the street, and into what appeared to be a small, bustling diner. "See, told you we were almost there. No need to be a drama queen about it."

"Fine. I'm sorry I'm being a brat. The copious amounts of junk food I'm about to inhale will surely put me in a better mood though. So, you won't have to tolerate it for much longer."

"Yeah, sure." Six was no longer paying attention to me, his gaze riveted to something or someone inside of the diner.

Peering around him, I attempted to trace his line of sight with my own. But it was too crowded for me to get a lock on what was drawing his undivided attention. "Maybe we should go somewhere else because it looks like we're in for a bit of a wait here."

"No. I want to eat here."

Nibbling my bottom lip, I surveyed the scene again. There were already a handful of humans waiting to be seated ahead of us. "You positive you don't want to go somewhere else?"

"Yup."

Crossing my arms over my chest, I leaned against the bit of wall space near me. "Fine." Although it wasn't completely fine since I was in a bad mood, and most certainly didn't want to wait to be fed.

A hostess waved Six over, taking down whatever human name he chose to give her. I scowled at the back of his head, not that it would make a difference. Even though lunas came into existence as adults, a creation of some higher power, we still all had very distinct personalities, and Six was someone who wouldn't budge once his mind was made up. It wasn't worth my time or energy to fight him on something unless it was extremely important. Now was not one of those times.

"It's only about a twenty-minute wait. The people ahead of us are all in the same party and are going to be seated at the big booth in the back." Six stood on his tiptoes, his gaze intent, and this time the recipient of his attention was crystal clear, and definitely a some*one*.

She was petite, somewhere between five foot and five foot one, I guessed, with a bright red, close-cropped pixie cut. Freckles dotted her tiny, upturned nose, as if underscoring her bright green almost cat-like eyes. There was a vibrancy about her, a certain *je ne sais quoi*. Whatever it was that made her stand out had definitely intrigued Six.

I cleared my throat. "This isn't your first time here."

Without taking his eyes off the redheaded waitress, Six said, "I've been here a few times."

"Is this what the style change is about? Do you like her?"

It wasn't abnormal for a luna to develop a crush or

infatuation on an especially dynamic human. After all, it was part of our nature to be drawn to bright souls, even if usually those souls only revealed their essence at the end of a life. But what concerned me was Six attempting to draw attention to himself. He could not have a relationship of any type with a human beyond casual sex.

I shook my head, and muttered to myself, "It doesn't matter." For a millisecond, a mere moment in time, I'd forgotten that it didn't make a difference how much Six tried to get a human's undivided attention, lunas were all just background noise in the end.

My stomach twisted, and nausea roiled through my gut. *So why is this whole thing making me want to puke with worry?*

I considered Six's behavior and my reaction. My stomach twisted again. *I think—I think I'm jealous.* But not of the girl in the way one might automatically assume. All lunas were like my brothers and sisters. Relationships beyond friendship never developed between any of us, and Six and I weren't to be the exception since my love for him was completely platonic.

No, it was something else entirely. There was some deep-seated fear that Six would abandon me, leaving me completely alone. Until he appeared, replacing the previous Six, I never realized how lonely I'd been. Six's friendship was a balm to my soul, and some days it was if it was the only thing that kept me from disappearing completely. I liked being the focus of his attention, even if I didn't desire any kind of romantic attention. Six made me feel important, like I mattered to someone. He knew things about me—details—that no one else did or cared to find out. Like what kind of books I enjoyed, and which tv shows I obsessed about. If I ever ceased to exist, I didn't want it to be as if I was never there, like my life had meant nothing. As selfish as it was, I wanted to be missed—to be mourned.

I bit the inside of my cheek, tasting a metallic tang. *Stop it. You* are *being a drama queen today. Since when do you fear death? If you ever burn up, then it doesn't matter what's left behind because you won't be here to know.*

Forcing a smile, I nudged Six with my shoulder. "You didn't answer. Do you like that waitress?"

Color bloomed across the tips of his ears. "Sure, I guess ... I mean, she seems nice."

"That's not the kind of like I meant." Snagging a menu off the hostess' podium, I scanned the food offerings.

What the hell? Clenching my jaw, I spoke between gritted teeth. "There aren't any chocolate items on this menu, Six. Why aren't there chocolate items on this menu?" I waved it in his face.

Six stabbed his finger on the back of the plastic. "Right there. Ice cream sundae."

I yanked the menu away, staring aghast at what he was attempting to placate me with. "It's vanilla ice cream with a little bit of chocolate sauce on top. Not what I had in mind, and you know it."

"Everything isn't all about you," Six grated. "How about compromising just a little—"

"Everything isn't all about me, but this little excursion was supposed to be. At least you led me to believe it was. Clearly, I misread the situation." I slapped the menu against his chest, pivoting on my heel. "I'll be at the closest Dairy Queen or Baskin Robbins or any place that actually has what I want to eat."

Don't leave. Don't leave again. Stay with him. Stay with Six this time. The voice was small, but it was different than my usual inner monologue, so it caught my attention. *Don't do what you did the last time you were here. Please.*

Closing my eyes, I rubbed the fleshy part of my palms into them. *Again? Last time? I've never been to this diner before. I've never—*

Yes, you have! You need to remember! Let me take control! This already happened, and you can't get caught up in it again or all hope is truly lost!

"Eighty-nine, you okay?" Six leaned close, studying me, worry etched into every line in his face.

"I … sure. I'm fine."

That's right. This is different. You already left by this point last time. Now let me take over. Please.

"I think—I think—" *Am I going insane?*

"Tell me, what's going on?" Six squeezed my shoulder, panic forming in his eyes. "Tell me what I can do."

Swaying on my feet, black starbursts danced across my vision, pain spiking through my brain. *Let me take control! Then you'll remember everything! I am you! I am you! Don't fight me anymore!*

Okay. Okay. Whatever you want. Just leave me alone. Stop

the pain.

I blinked once, twice, and just like that, I pushed past me out of the driver's seat.

Straightening up, I gave Six a tentative smile. "It's fine. Whatever it was is gone now." I refused to worry about past me taking over again. Compared to the me now, which oddly enough I was beginning to think of as a different person, I was strong, and she was weak. She couldn't fight me again. In fact, she gave up quite easily, much to my surprise. She hadn't wanted to deal with any of it. I'd come a long way since then, even though time wise it had been mere days since I'd been in her shoes.

Wait. Does this mean I might be able to overpower the past me at Six's fixed point in time death when I couldn't before? Hope, true hope buoyed in me for the first time since I discovered that I couldn't change my own actions in past selves. But all of that seemed different now. The fact that I had complete control of my past body was proof.

But it still might not work. There were too many unknown factors involved, reality already in a state of complete disrepair, so to speak. None of the normal rules seemed to apply anymore, unless they inexplicably did, without rhyme or reason. I was simply going to have to do my best to save … everything, and hope luck would be on my side for once.

"Do you still want to eat somewhere else?" Six gave Tina a wistful look over his shoulder.

I flicked him in the nose. "No, it's fine. I'll just ask for extra chocolate sauce on my sundae."

Rubbing his nose, he regarded me quizzically. "What's gotten into you? Mood swing much?"

Mood swing. Ha! Try two different people practically. Me from the past who was all about being grumpy, and the future me, who is now here presently, who is all about making the best from the cards I've been dealt.

I shrugged. "You know how it is."

The corners of his mouth twitched. "Yeah, I do."

He turned to resume his ocular stalking, and I considered the situation again. I was back at the beginning, so to speak, and I was in control. It put a whole new meaning to 'if I only knew then what I know now'. There was a chance I could alter the fixed point in time to save reality, but there was no guarantee. I would try though. There was no way I couldn't. But before I went hopping into the closest RR I could find, I needed to be prepared for the worst. I could still lose Six in the end, even if I saved reality and lived to tell the tale.

Letting my gaze run over him, my stomach clenched, a bubble of anxiety overriding my moment of ... not quite happiness ... but lack of despair. For me, with the way things had been going lately, it was the most I was going to get until everything played out completely.

I'm going to spend a little bit of time with Six. Tell him all the things I need to tell him, including good-bye. In case I don't get a chance later—in case there is no later.

"Come on, Eigh– Emma." Six waved at me, and I fell in line behind him as he followed the hostess to our table.

Please don't let this be our last meal together.

Chapter 33

Playing with the lid on the saltshaker, I fidgeted in my seat. "What would you do if it was the end of reality as you knew it? Any last wishes?" I attempted to keep my voice light, but I didn't think I quite managed.

Snatching the saltshaker from me, Six set it down in its spot beside the pepper. "I don't know. Guess I never thought much about it. Why do you ask?"

"Umm ... you know, just curious." I flicked my gaze up to meet his, then away.

"What about you? What would you do?"

Exactly what I'm doing right now. "Well, umm ... I don't know either. Good thing I don't have to worry about it, huh?"

His attention was back on Tina, who was flitting back and forth between the kitchen and her tables. We'd been lucky enough, or unlucky enough from Six's perspective, to not be in her section. I was relieved to have Six all to myself … mostly. I definitely didn't have his undivided attention, that was for sure.

"What about if I knew reality was crumbling, and you most likely were going to die, would you want me to tell you? Or would you want to continue in ignorant bliss until the bitter end?"

Six's brown eyes met mine, and his brows furrowed. "What are you babbling about? Do you think reality is ending or something?"

"No." I laughed, the sound hollow in my ears. "Just in one of those existential moods, I guess."

"Huh. Okay." He picked up the saltshaker and began spinning it on the table. "But yeah, I'd want to know the end was nigh." He grinned.

I stiffened. "You would?" What if I'd been going about all of this all wrong? What if I should have told Six about everything I knew as soon as I found out?

"I mean, yeah, unless there was nothing I could do to change anything."

"I assume if the end was coming then there would be nothing we could do about it, but wouldn't knowing give you the chance to be doing exactly what you want at the end, instead of, I don't know, maybe being on a job, or sleeping or something?"

Six dropped the saltshaker, spilling salt across the table. "Shit." He clamored to scoop it back in, grimacing. "The table's still clean."

"Sure." I took a pinch of salt and threw it over my left

shoulder. I paused, then took some more to throw over my right shoulder since I couldn't actually remember which one was supposed to bring good luck. I could use any and all I could get.

"If reality was crumbling and I knew, would you want me to tell you?" Six asked, spinning his fork on the table.

"Yeah, I'd want to know."

He tilted his head, regarding me thoughtfully. "Why?"

"What if I could change something?"

"What if you couldn't?"

"You never answered my other question: wouldn't you want to know so you could be doing what you chose to at the end instead of being blindsided?"

Six propped his chin up on his hands. "Sure, I guess."

"And what would that be? What would you want to do?"

He glanced over at Tina, a wistful expression passing over his features. "I could think of a few things."

My heart thudded dully in my chest. Of course he would want to spend the end with Tina, the girl he fancied himself in love with. I shouldn't have expected anything less. The elderly couple I saw in the hospital probably had best friends, too, and I was positive they'd choose their last moments to be with each other every single time.

I nibbled my bottom lip. "Why didn't you tell me about her before?" I wasn't sure how far along their relationship was yet at this point in time, but my question would cover his feelings no matter what.

Six's eyes widened. "How did you know?"

I gave him a tight-lipped smile. I hadn't known. It took being hurtled through time to random spots and witnessing him die for Tina to find out the truth. Ah, the truth—something I desperately wanted to give him so I could unburden myself, and yet he'd just said he wouldn't want to know if the end was coming.

I'd never felt so distant from Six since I'd first met him. He was my best friend, and a stranger rolled into one.

"I'm Eighty-nine, and you're Six. I know you." *At least I think I do. No. Stop. Don't begrudge your best friend his secrets. Everyone has them, even you now.*

I covered his hands with mine. "What is it about her? Tell me. I want to know because I've never experienced it."

I still wasn't sure if Six actually loved Tina, although I was fairly certain he'd convinced himself he did. One simply doesn't toss their life away for someone they kind of like. And yeah, I still hated Tina and blamed her for … everything, but I wanted to understand. I *needed* to understand.

Six's eyes glazed over, and a dopey smile stretched his lips. "She sees me, Eighty-nine. Like really sees me. It's like she looks into my soul, and instead of finding it lacking like I thought she would … she likes what she found there."

I blinked. "That's it. She sees you?"

He slipped his hands out from under mine and tapped his chest. "In here." Then he tapped his forehead. "And in here. She understands and she sees me."

"That's a basis for friendship, not whatever you think you have with her."

"No, it's different than what we have. I know you see me, too, but that's because it feels like we grew up together. We've lived together for longer than what a human's lifespan is." He shook his head. "Being seen by someone like her is just different. I don't think I can put it into words. But it … it's beyond—it's … I don't know. I'd give everything up for her without question."

You did. I swallowed around the lump in my throat. "Everything?"

He patted my hand. "Don't get your feelings hurt. You'll always be my best friend, and you know Six will always have your six." He paused to grin at me. "But I want to enjoy it—her while I can."

I knew in that instant, even if it was possible, I couldn't keep Six from Tina. I couldn't deny him the level of happiness he was eluding to.

But what if it's the only way?

A reaper appeared behind Six, and I almost choked on my own tongue.

"You okay?" Six leaned over the table to pat me on the back.

"Yeah, yeah. I'm fine. Just—" *Just was startled by Alistar popping in right behind you unannounced.* Clearing my throat, I repeated, "I'm fine." I wondered when my reaper stalker would show up again. I was honestly surprised it had taken him as long as it did.

"I'll be right back." I made my way to the bathroom,

knowing Alistar would follow. A niggling of a worry surfaced that Six would be gone when I got back. He'd gone on a job after he chased me from the diner the first round through this timeline, which meant that he should have already felt the pull. I'd gone on a job almost immediately after that myself. But with me having altered the past there was a possibility that those things had been altered as well. Of course, there was the—

I pinched the bridge of my nose. *Multiverses, multiple timelines, time loops, butterfly effects, paradoxes, reality tears, past selves, future selves ... aaaargh.* I couldn't let myself obsess about things I didn't actually understand. The best strategy was to deal with each event as they were presented to me, until the inevitable conclusion, whatever that turned out to be.

Alistar was already waiting for me in the ladies' room, his stance casual as he leaned against the door on one of the stalls.

Crossing my arms over my chest, I regarded him with what I hoped passed for indifference. "What do you want now?"

Mirroring me, he crossed his arms over his chest. "It took me a bit to track you down. Where did you end up?"

He was referring to my grand detour through the RR. I supposed there was no harm in telling him the truth, about my first two stops anyhow. "I made a pitstop in the desert, no people, and then I was in a cave or a cave-like place where this orb of light appeared." I shook the images from my mind. "It was all very strange."

"And then?"

Did he know I was in that room eavesdropping on him and that woman? Did he suspect that I now knew the truth?

I quirked an eyebrow. "And then I ended up here."

"Here at the diner?" He tilted his head, his gaze palpable. "You didn't go anywhere else first?"

"Oh, well, I mean I went to the luna realm first. Where I ran into my past self, by the way. And for a while there I thought I was trapped in my past timeline without any control. But then I broke through and took control."

He inched closer to me. "How did you get control exactly?"

I shrugged. "I don't know. I just did." Was he worried I'd be able to gain control of a situation where he secretly didn't want me to? "I'm guessing the only factor that changed from any of the other times is that reality has eroded more. The rules of—" I waved my arms around. "Everything no longer applies in most situations."

"Things haven't deteriorated as far as you think."

"Six didn't get called to the job he went to the last time we did this timeline, and neither did I. So, yeah, the fabric of reality is dissolving as we speak."

"It's not that simple."

"Nothing ever is," I scoffed. "Was there anything else that you wanted or can I go back to spending some time with Six?"

He slid his fingers under my chin, tilting my head up. "I thought you wanted to save reality—to save the kind of love that exists between people like the couple you saw in the hospital. Are you now back to wanting to only live out your last moments with Six?"

Jerking away from his touch, I glared up at him. "I don't know." I couldn't tell him that I wanted some time with Six to get answers and to prepare myself for good-bye if things went south. I also couldn't tell him that I was hoping the good-bye would be a moot point because Six and I would walk away from all of this in one piece. I couldn't tell him any of that because I now knew everything he'd done had been about Tina.

"You never told me why you wanted me to follow Tina at the hospital. Is that something you want me to do again? Follow Tina?"

"I had my reasons."

I ground my teeth together. "Of course you did. Reasons you're not going to share with me."

"You're acting strange. There's a certain level of hostility directed at me coming from you."

I snorted. "You think?" *Shut up, Eighty-nine. Don't say another word. Don't let him provoke you into revealing the exact thing you don't want to.*

"Was it because you were lost in time, and I didn't come for you?"

I resisted the urge to roll my eyes. "Sure. That's it. Now leave me alone." I pivoted on my heel, stalking to the door.

Alistar grabbed my arm. "Tell me what's going on in that infuriating head of yours."

"Me, infuriating? Me? I'm not the one who lied about

everything! I can't believe I trusted you again! Fool me once, shame on you. Fool me twice, shame on me!" I yanked my arm away. "It's not going to happen again. I know I'm the only one I can trust to fix any of this mess Six created." I narrowed my eyes at him. "Or did you create it?" I threw my arms up in the air. *So much for not blowing my cover.* I was shit at keeping my true feelings hidden. It was something I'd never had to practice at as a luna. It was a wonder I hadn't blabbed everything to Six yet.

"You think I created this mess?" He slashed his arm through the air. "Have you lost your mind?"

"I've lost a lot of things lately, so it's entirely possible that I have lost my mind, but not about this. I—" Pausing, I considered if I should say anything else. I'd told him pretty much everything, but not quite.

Ah, fuck it.

"I went to a third place before the luna realm. And I heard you talking to a woman."

Alistar stilled.

"Yeah, that's right I heard you talking to that woman ... about Tina. I know all of your meddling has been about her. What? Did she end up somewhere you don't think she should be after she died? Is that why you somehow forced Six to get involved with her?"

"You think I orchestrated the paradox because of Tina?" His voice was soft, barely audible.

"Yeah, I think you've been using us. Me and Six both. And we're collateral damage here. But you're going to fail because I've figured it all out. And just like that woman said, this is your last chance. End of story."

He threw his head back, his laughter jarring, and completely without humor. "She thinks this is all about Tina."

"Don't try to throw me off the trail now. It's pointless."

Flipping his head down, he glided toward me. "You ridiculous, stupid luna. This—none of it—had been about Tina. Except maybe for Six."

My back hit into the door, and I braced myself for whatever would come next. *Why couldn't I have kept my damn mouth shut? I'm such an idiot.*

Alistar's long fingers reached out from his robe, hovering over my face, and I flinched away. "I'm not going to hurt you, Eighty-nine."

"I don't believe you," I croaked, squeezing my eyes shut.

His hand slid down my cheek and lingered for a moment on my jaw before tucking my hair behind my ear. My heart took off at a gallop. The motion was agonizingly slow.

"Don't you see? Everything hasn't been about Tina," the hood of his robe abraded the side of my face as he pressed his lips against my ear, "because it's been all about you."

Goose bumps erupted in quick succession across my skin, and my eyes popped open with shock. "Me?" I squeaked

But I was alone, Alistar having disappeared the instant he finished speaking.

Running my hands up and down my arms, I shook off the incident. It was the only choice I had. Besides, clearly Alistar had lied again. It was his only recourse at this point in his game. I'd found out the truth and he was attempting to throw a fake revelation at me so I would end up on the wrong path again.

I'd fallen for his shady tactics before, but not again. Never again.

Chapter 34

The rubber band around my chest relented its constant strain the moment I laid eyes on Six. I'd been worried he wouldn't be there when I returned from the ladies' room. Unfortunately, there was also an unwanted guest at our table. *Tina.*

"Hey, what's going on?" I plastered a smile on my face, aching from the effort. I was positive the feigned pleasantness wasn't echoed in my eyes.

Six jumped to his feet, rushing over to my side. "Oh, Eigh– Emma, I thought you were leaving."

I raised my eyebrows, delivering a fake laugh. "And why would you think that when I merely went to the bathroom?"

He twisted his lips, shooting me a glare. I knew he made the excuse because he'd been under the impression I rushed to the privacy of the restroom to make my escape for a job. "I don't know, because you made me think that thing you had to do was important."

"Turns out it wasn't. Important, that is." I turned to Tina. "And you are?"

Her cheeks pinkened. "Oh, sorry, I'm Tina." She stood, offering me her hand awkwardly. "And you're Emma. Simon has told me so much about you."

Taking her hand within mine, I squeezed it tightly and moved it up and down for a moment before letting go. "Yes, of course, Tina. I know exactly who you are." *The evil bitch who kills my best friend, and who Alistar seems to think is so damn important that his death means nothing.*

Six elbowed me, hard. "Tina was just taking her break. But now we can all have a chance to talk." He smiled at me, his gaze pleading. Next to a puppy begging for food or attention, I was pretty sure Six had the market on manipulation by facial expressions cornered.

My shoulders sagged. I didn't want to spend time with Six and Tina together period, especially not now. But I also didn't want to disappoint my best friend on what could possibly be his last day alive. "Yeah, sure. We can all talk."

The three of us settled down at the table, uncomfortable silence blanketing us.

Six nudged me under the table with his foot. I kicked him. He then cleared his throat. "Soo … Tina was just telling me about applying to nursing school. She's been volunteering at a local hospital, which helped her decide that's what she wants to do. Be a nurse that is."

"Yeah, I know."

"How do you know?" Tina asked. "I just told Simon."

Oh, crap. There is absolutely no reason why I should know that. How exactly do I get myself out of this one? "Umm … I meant yeah, I know, volunteering often seems to be a catalyst for nurses. You get bitten by the wanting-to-help-people bug, and boom, you can't imagine doing anything else."

I eyed my half-eaten chocolate sundae. The one that had obviously been delivered when I was in the restroom. *Damn it.* Sliding it to me, I shoved the spoon in my mouth, smiling at Six. *Yep, can't talk with my mouth full.*

Tina pursed her lips, regarding me with some unknown emotion. "Yeah, I guess."

Six coughed into his fist. "Tina, I hate to ask, but can you grab me a glass of water." He coughed into his fist again, giving her his infamous sad eyes.

Her lips curled up slightly, and she shook her head. "Yeah, okay." Hurrying from the table, she went behind the counter to fetch Six some water for his poor throat.

As soon as she was out of earshot, Six hissed, "What's your problem? Why are you being a bitch to her?"

I wiped the corners of my mouth with a napkin, crumpling it up when I was done. "I'm not being a bitch. I'm being an annoyed best friend who didn't get told about the girl you apparently have a relationship with, and then boom she's just there when I come back to the table."

Six's expression softened. "I thought you went to a job."

"Obviously not."

"Can you please be nicer to her, for me?"

I ground my teeth together. "Why didn't you tell me about her, Six? I thought you told me everything."

The tips of his ears reddened. "I don't tell you absolutely everything."

That was true. We didn't talk like girlfriends about sexual exploits or such things like that. But entering a relationship with a human, something that shouldn't happen, was definitely something I would have thought warranted an honest conversation between the two of us.

I rubbed my temples, yet another headache blooming. If I wasn't a luna I'd swear I was getting a tumor or something. Sighing, my nose whistled with the force of my exhale. "No, of course not. I don't tell you absolutely everything either." I flicked my gaze to the reaper who was hanging out in the corner of the diner. Nope, definitely didn't tell Six everything, and the list of things I wasn't telling him was beginning to lengthen substantially. "But this seems like it would be one of the things you do tell me."

"I was going to. I just—"

Tina returned with a glass of water, placing it in front of him gently. "There you go, babe."

Ugh. Babe? Really. I plastered another fake smile on my face. "Tina, look. Si—" I swallowed his name, remembering he was going by something human in her presence. *What is it? Simon! That's it.* "As I was saying, Simon let me know that

I was coming off kind of bitchy, and I wanted to apologize to you. I've had a rough couple of days, and well, I'm in a bitchy kind of mood. Not the best time for me to meet new people. Please don't think it has anything to do with you." *Mostly anyway. You're only a small part of what's pissing me off. Six's death and the end of reality is the biggest piece.*

A hundred-watt smile brightened her entire countenance, and she nodded eagerly. "Oh, I totally understand. A bad day is a bad day. And Simon here," she shoved playfully at his shoulder, "sprung me on you, didn't he?"

"Yeah, actually, he did."

"I'm not surprised. He's always doing scatter-brained things like forgetting where he left things, or what time he's supposed to be somewhere."

Always, huh? Just how long has this little affair been going on exactly? The two acted with the type of familiarity that usually only developed over time.

"Yep," Six chuckled, his smile brittle, "that's me. Forgetful."

"Tina, break's over," a man called from the kitchen.

She leapt to her feet. "Welp, gotta run. It was so nice to meet you, Emma. We need to all get together soon." She leaned over and gave Six a quick peck on the lips, and a sweet smile. "I'll see you later." She practically danced off, her light attitude almost contagious. Almost.

I leaned over the table, growling under my breath, "How long have you been keeping her a secret?"

Six grimaced. "It's … well—" He palmed the nape of his neck and studied the table. "A while. It's been a while."

"No shit, Sherlock. But why? I don't get why you wouldn't tell me something as monumental as this. Do you love her?"

"I was going to tell you. I swear I was. But it felt like if I said it out loud, told the most important person in my life about it, then it would be real. And if it was real, then it could and probably would end. The longer I didn't tell you, the longer I felt like I could live in the dream."

I stared at him a moment, letting his words sink in. *Have I done it again? Did I take something that has absolutely nothing to do with me, and twist it around to take personal offense about it?*

Could Six have simply not told me because he was afraid to jinx the relationship that felt like a dream to him? He hadn't kept anything from me with a malicious intent. In fact, I didn't think I entered into the equation hardly at all. Something that was difficult for me to wrap my mind around because … *narcissistic much?* I often made things about me when they shouldn't be.

"Okay." I strummed my nails against the table. "I get it. You didn't want to jinx anything by telling me. But you do understand that you can't tell her about lunas? How do you expect to have any kind of long-term relationship with her when everything is based on lies? There's a reason human-luna relationships don't happen beyond the rules."

He sagged down in his chair. "Like I said, I'll enjoy it as long as I can."

Shit. I'd taken my anger from Alistar out on Six. All I'd wanted to do was understand the whole Tina infatuation, not drag Six's mood down.

Leaning across the table, I tapped his nose. "Look, you idiot. Don't be all mopey now. I'm not mad. Or I'm not anymore. I could never be mad at you for long because—"

"Six always watches your six, and you wouldn't know what to do without me?" His dark expression cleared, like the sun popping out from behind clouds.

I laughed. "Yeah, something like that."

I had a decision to make. One I thought I'd already made. To tell Six the truth or not? He said he wouldn't want to know about the end of reality if it was coming, but I know I would. Sure, we were completely different people, but hypothetical versus real-life often yielded different results. Although, once I let the cat out of the bag there was no going back.

I gnawed on the inside of my cheek, a metallic tang rolling over my tongue. I wanted Six to know how much I cared about him—how much he meant to me. Could the truth be the best way to do that? To make him truly listen to my words. For him to feel my love at the end, if it did indeed come for him alone? Or even if it came for us both?

Glancing at my stalker reaper again, I came to a final decision. I knew what I had to do, for the good of everyone.

Chapter 35

The best-made plans for humans, as well as lunas, usually go to shit. I found that out firsthand over the span of the last few days. My new plan was to throw everything out the window and to simply do my best to save the world, and Six. *So really ... I don't know what the hell I'm doing anymore.*

Night had settled over the human realm, the moon and stars hidden behind clouds. Six and I sat under a large oak tree in a city park, lightning bugs flitting around us.

I'd spend the better part of the last hour filling my best friend in on my recent adventures, leaving out a few bits and pieces. Like how he died. Or is supposed to die. *Thinking in tenses when time travel is involved is ... not as easy as the authors of some of my favorite books make it seem.*

"You know," I pulled at some grass, staring straight ahead, "you always said our lives were kind of boring. Even with what our jobs are. It was the same thing over and over, with little respite." I sighed heavily, leaning my head against the tree trunk. "Not anymore."

Six grunted. "Yeah, not anymore. I can't decide if it's irony or not that things are only getting interesting at the end. Probably just a last-ditch way to make us suffer."

I snorted. "Yeah."

"And even though it's gotten more interesting in theory," Six moved his arms in an arch, "still pretty tame right now. The end is coming for us, and here we sit." He took a swig of his beer. "Pretty anticlimactic if you ask me."

"It's not over yet." I lifted my own beer to my lips, taking a hefty swallow of the lager.

"Am I the rabbit?"

"Huh?" I crinkled my nose at him.

"Am I like the rabbit? You know, from Donnie Darko? I already died, but here I am. Like when the guy in the rabbit costume was dating Donnie's sister. He was still there, but already dead and communicating with Donnie. He had to have died in order to save himself. You know … the rabbit. Am I like him?"

"Yes, I know which rabbit you're referring to. It is one of my favorite movies." I pondered his question a moment. "It's not the same though. You're not the rabbit. Maybe I am."

"No." Six shook his head. "You haven't died."

"That I know of. Maybe I do die. I mean, you didn't know that you died until I told you. Which I'm still hoping to change, by the way."

Six crushed his beer can on his bent knee. "Like the rabbit. He died, but then didn't die."

"But then Donnie died in order for that to happen." I took another sip of beer, grimacing at how it was warm now. "So maybe I die, and you live."

"Could we both be the rabbit?"

I quirked an eyebrow. "We could both be Donnie, too."

"You seem different," Six said as he reached for the last can of unopened beer.

"I am different. I've been through a lot in the last few days."

"Not what I mean. Or I do, but it's more than that. You seem younger, more human somehow. Your emotions more open."

"Yeah, you know, I have felt more human lately, and less hollow. My mind isn't consumed with the emptiness here." I tapped my chest above my breastbone. "The pain never returned after the submarine job I skipped." Until that moment I'd forgotten. The first time I bailed on the submarine job I experienced excruciating pain which forced me to go back to the scene. Afterwards, the pain had never returned. Although a RR had been the result of my decision according to Alistar.

Speaking of the shady reaper. I peered around the tree, expecting him to be lurking. His absence was suspicious. He was bound to pop up eventually though. He always did, and at the most inconvenient moment.

"You're not going to tell me anything else about how I get snuffed out?"

Shifting, I faced Six again. "I want to tell you everything. You know I do. But if I stand any chance of altering what happens I can't." I hated how much I sounded like Alistar at the moment. He'd been using lines like that on me since I met him. *Sorry, I can only tell you so much. Oops, spoilers, can't risk those.*

"If I know then I can play an active role in preventing it."

An image of him burning up played across my mind, juxtaposed over the idyllic moment I was sharing with him in the here and now. I shuddered. Would he change his mind to save Tina if he knew about his sacrifice ahead of time? Probably not. In fact, if I told him he'd probably double down on the choice. Plus, he still died at a fixed point in time. That was the part I couldn't figure out a plan to get around. The paradox he created was unsolvable as far as I could tell. *But I'm not any kind of brainiac. There has to be a way.*

I took another swig of lukewarm beer, grimacing. "No. I'm pretty sure me telling you that part would have the opposite effect."

He grunted again, his gaze following the path of a lightning bug as it danced inches from his nose. "That doesn't seem right."

"It is what it is." I glowered, noting the parallels of my answer and some of Alistar's yet again. "I wish I would have told you about this sooner." I wasn't sure what it would have accomplished, but if anything, it would have taken the burden of hiding things from him sooner.

"Suppose it wasn't meant to be." He punctuated his words with a shrug.

"You're taking this all pretty well."

He shrugged again. "Sometimes death can be a gift. Maybe it's just my time."

My mouth fell open, a strangled sound lodging in my throat. "You can't mean that."

He shrugged a third time, and I smacked his shoulder. "Stop doing that."

"Doing what?" He rubbed his shoulder demonstratively, his eyes narrowed on me.

"Acting so nonchalant about all of this. Don't you care that you could be dead soon? It sounds like you might actually be welcoming it. You would leave me … and Tina behind without a second thought?"

"No, not without a second thought. But there's no point in worrying about it. If I'm meant to die, I'll die."

My nostrils flared, and my cheeks heated with barely contained anger. "How very … luna of you."

"It is what I am."

"What about Tina? You love her, don't you?" Tears welled in my eyes, turning my surroundings into a water-colored painting.

He upturned his beer, gulping down the last of it. "Yeah, I do. But that's bound to end eventually anyhow."

"And me?" A tear sprung free, tracking down my cheek. "You'd abandon me to this life? Leave me completely and utterly alone?"

"You were fine before me, and you would be fine after me."

"I wasn't fine!" I yelled, anger erupting. "I wasn't fine at all before you, and I won't be after you! Don't you get it? I was willing to let reality crumble because you weren't in it!"

"But that changed. Things are different. You just needed time. Something we have in abundance as lunas."

"No." I brought my knees up to my chest, wrapping my arms around them. "I won't be fine. I'll never be fine without you. Time won't fix that. Time could never fix that, even for a luna. Don't you get it? It's because of that old couple, because of that kind of love that I would save reality. Not because of me."

"I don't get it."

"You should. You're a luna. And us lunas deal with the worst kind of tragedies reality has to offer. It leaves us weak, and depressed … vulnerable after a job. I cry for humanity, and the suffering they have to endure. And yet we lunas crave what they have, every single day. We suffer, too, but in a different way. After you were gone, I questioned everything. Would it be such a bad thing for all of that to go away? To end the suffering of humans and lunas alike. My own personal suffering as well. But then I saw that elderly couple, and everything changed. I-I—"

Shaking my head, I turned away from Six's intense gaze. "I finally understood what makes their lives worth it. The chance for that kind of beauty. Chancing the rest of the pain is worth it when that could be the end result."

I ensnared his hand in mine, squeezing hard. "You have Tina. And even if that love is fleeting, it's something to live for." *Shit. Why did I say that? I pretty much reaffirmed his path to death.* "I mean … " *Fix it. Fix it now.* "What I mean is …" I swallowed, trying to bide some time while I thought of something to say to undo the damage I'd just done.

"It's okay, Eighty-nine. Lunas aren't meant to feel anything except maybe the pain of longing. And the two of us got to experience so much more, didn't we?"

I cracked a smile, despite still being disconcerted. "Yeah, we did have some crazy times."

His gaze turned inward. "I love Tina, but I'm not sure it's the same as what humans feel. And I know she can never love me. Not really, because she can never know the real me—the me you know. She loves a Simon who is a human artist, and he doesn't know the kinds of things Six does as a luna." Sadness seeped from every pore, oozing from him to me.

Sitting there with him, talking about life with such candor had transformed his death into something surreal for me. I knew he was going to die, or was already dead in some ways, but I was there with him, just like old times. And if I was destined to lose him once and for all, I was missing the opportunity to say and do the things I swore I would if I'd gotten one more chance with him. *Here it is … once more chance. Don't blow it.*

The next question was going to be a hard one to ask. It was the kind of thing someone only wanted to know the answer to if it wasn't going to be as bad as they thought.

After Six had thrown his life away, I'd wondered, I couldn't help it … what had I done to let him down? What could I have done differently to support him? To help him better than I had? To make him want to continue with his life instead of simply tossing it away on Tina's?

Pulling away from him, I cleared my throat. *Say it, just say it already. Spit the damn words out.* "Was I … or am I a bad friend?" The words hung there between us, thick and heavy.

"You can't seriously think that."

A lump had formed in my throat. "Yes, I can. What else am I supposed to think? You abandoned me before. And now, when I give you as much of a heads-up as I possibly can, you, in not so many words, tell me that you'd do it again."

"Eight—"

"No, let me finish." I had to get it all out at once or I wouldn't be able to at all. "I know our lives as lunas are not the best. But they're our lives. I thought … well, I thought—I made things better for you. Just like you make things better for me."

Six swung his arm around me, pulling me into his side. "You do make things better for me. And Tina does, too. But that doesn't mean I'm happy. Lunas can never be happy the way humans can be. You know that."

I nodded. It was true. We were created to yearn. To burn for something we could never truly touch. And that's exactly what Six had done. By loving Tina, by establishing a relationship with her, he'd dared to touch humanity, revel in it—develop love within it. He touched the flames and he paid the ultimate price for it. Maybe there was no coming back from that. Ultimately, he was not the same Six that had existed pre-Tina, and I didn't think he ever could be.

I pressed my face into his chest, needing to cling to him even if for just a moment. "It's not so bad, is it? Our existence?"

"You've only witnessed true romantic love, and look how's it's changed you. Imagine feeling that way toward someone."

I couldn't. My love for Six was almost too much to handle, and there were no romantic entanglements between us. He was only my best friend. But then, to me, he was family, my home. Now that he'd tasted love with Tina, what we had wasn't enough for him.

"I wish I could be enough for you. Like I used to be. Like when we were still young according to luna standards."

Six smiled ruefully, shoving me away from him. "You were never young."

I stared at him, and as I did his levity died. "I'm sorry, Eighty-nine. For hurting you the way I did."

I launched myself at him, ensnaring him within my arms, and squeezing with everything I had in me. "You could never hurt me. Not really. I was lucky to have had you in my life at all."

"I could live in the end, you know. Which it kind of feels like I might since you're being so sappy. And it would serve you right for acting so out of character. Then I would have the rest of eternity to mock you for these displays of very un-Eighty-nine like emotions."

"I welcome the chance to be mocked by you for all of eternity. Nothing would bring me more pleasure."

I sighed. There were endless things I wanted to say to him, but soon I'd jump into begging territory. And I knew Six wasn't one to change his mind when it was made up. It was definitely a battle worth fighting, but I knew I'd lose in the end. My only shot at saving his life would be to act on my own, without his help. Therefore, begging would only serve to sour our moment, and linger in my memory long after he was possibly gone. I didn't want to torture him any more than I already had when his death still loomed with near certainty.

We stayed like that, me squeezing Six as tight as I could, like I could force him to stay with me forever my sheer physical force, until exhaustion dragged me under.

Chapter 36

I jolted awake, soft light from pre-dawn filtering through the leaves on the trees. Yawning, I stretched, peeking around to ascertain where Six had gotten to. It wasn't like me to fall asleep at night since I was nocturnal by nature, but the emotional and physical drain of the last few days had finally caught up with me.

My gaze snagged on a piece of notebook paper, held down by a large rock. The paper was damp under my fingertips as I unfolded it. I recognized Six's sloppy handwriting right away.

Eighty-nine,
I have a feeling you really needed that sleep, so I didn't wake you. (You were drooling on me five minutes into your little snooze-fest.) I'm glad we got to spend some just us time together, even if the topics were all downners.

> *You're probably wondering where I am by this point. I thought about it while you were sleeping (a deluge of drool is seeping into my shirt right now, I swear) and I want to spend some time with Tina. If I'm going to die soon, I need to be with her at least one last time. And hey, if you end up figuring out a way to save me, then you can make fun of me for being all melodramatic over a girl. But don't blame yourself if you can't. You were a good friend—the best—my best friend. Please only remember the good times. And don't forget, whether I'm here or not ... Six will always watch your six, one way or another.*

Blinking away tears, I reread the note. When I first learned that Six had burnt up, before I'd even witnessed his actual death, I would have given anything to have found a letter, a note, any kind of clue to his mood at the end. I wanted to understand what had happened. I'd also needed to know how I'd failed him as a friend. Even with his reassurances from last night, I know I had somehow. I'd failed him. The only way I could forgive myself was to save him, and then spend the rest of eternity making it up to him. There was no other option.

Unless I fail at that, too. I was aware that the probability of me successfully saving reality and Six were slim to none. *But they aren't none. Not yet at least.*

"Eighty-nine." Alistar appeared in front of me, his arms crossed over his chest. "We need to talk."

I rolled my eyes. "I'm surprised it took you this long to show up." I was incredibly lucky my time with Six last night hadn't been interrupted by a RR, a job lure, Tina, or Alistar, to name a few things.

"I did my best to give you your space, but I can't afford to—"

"To what?" I swiped at my pants, the motion doing nothing to remove the moisture from them. *Sleeping outside at night isn't all it's cracked up to be.* Glaring at him, I said, "What can't you afford to do? Let me screw your plans up any more than I already have? Or to figure out any more of your carefully guarded secrets?"

He raised his arms in the air, palms up. "All of this is coming to an end soon, whether you want to spend time with your best friend or not. You need to decide how you're going to handle it."

Crumpling Six's note within my fist, I curled my lip up in a snarl. "I have decided how I'm going to handle it, but it's none of your business, reaper."

"Reaper now, is it?"

Turning away from him, I closed my eyes and counted to ten. I wouldn't go any further down this road. Alistar's tactics were fine-honed to the point that even though I knew exactly what they were, it was nearly impossible to not fall for them. He baited me and then used my anger to steer me in the direction he wanted. I had to resist.

Knocked onto my back, I sputtered in shock when I found myself sprawled in the grass, legs and arms akimbo.

"I'm so sorry!" A man stood over me, offering me his hand. "I can't believe I didn't see you there."

I stared at him, still trying to process what happened. *He didn't see me. Oh. Yes, of course, he didn't. Luna here.*

He glanced at his watch, panic flooding his brown eyes. "I hope you're okay. I'm really sorry, but I have to go. There's—" He shook his head. "There's going to be an accident, and I have to stop it."

Frowning, I played his words over again in my mind, even as he sprinted across the park. There's going to be an accident, not there has been an accident.

Springing to my feet, I pointed in the direction the man had just gone. "It was him, wasn't it? The bright soul."

In the grand scheme of things, I'd deemed the bright soul unimportant, filing it under things I wasn't going to have the answer to. But I also didn't believe in coincidences, and if the man who'd just rammed into me was, in fact, the bright soul ... well, I had to follow him. He'd been placed in my path for a reason, or rather me in his.

Unless he's meant to be a distraction of some sort. The universe attempting to keep me from focusing on what I needed to be doing ... but why?

Alistar. Duh. Of course.

Narrowing my eyes at the reaper, I poked him in the chest with my index finger. "You had something to do with this, didn't you? Do reapers have some kind of sway over living souls that I don't know about? Did you draw him here to be used as some kind of distraction to get what you want?"

"If you were human, you'd be a conspiracy theory whack-job."

"I don't know why I'm talking to you anyways," I huffed. My head swung back and forth between Alistar and the direction the man had dashed off in. Back and forth, back and forth. *Shit. Now is not the time for indecision, Eighty-nine.*

There was a pull in my gut, not like what I experienced when summoned to a job, but one that was of my own making. Something inside of me was letting me know what I needed to do.

Breaking into a run, I followed the same path across the park the man had just taken. I guessed his destination wasn't far since he'd been on foot, and I was right.

On the other side of the park, was a ramp to the highway, and at the top of it stood the man, his long, dark hair whipping around his face as he waved his arms from the side of the road at oncoming traffic. "Stop!" he yelled. "Stop! Don't get on the highway! If you get on you're going to be in an accident. You're going to die! Please, stop!"

Cars honked, some drivers even taking the time to roll down their windows just to flip off the man they perceived as crazy. It was early in the morning, the beginning of rush hour traffic, and people were merely trying to get to work on time. None of them paid any heed to someone throwing out portents of doom from the side of the road.

Goose bumps erupted across my skin in quick succession, a prickling in my senses alerted. It wasn't like a job when I knew exactly what would happen down to the number of dead to expect, but it was … something. Something beyond the ordinary. My luna awareness pressed outward scanning for more information, oddly coming up blank.

A reaper appeared at the top of the ramp. I peered over my shoulder, confirming Alistar was at the edge of the park watching me, and not inserting himself in yet another place he shouldn't be.

Where was the luna assigned this job? Lunas were the first on a scene, and the reaper or reapers second. It was just the way it was, the way it always was.

Unless reality has collapsed to the point where lunas weren't getting the call anymore. Neither Six nor I had been pulled to a job since I merged with my past self. I'd decided not to overthink that part, and enjoy our time together, but if things had indeed deteriorated to the level that lunas weren't going on any jobs … was saving reality even an option anymore? Had I procrastinated my way into an unfixable situation by letting things crumble past the point of return? All because I wanted some quality time with my best friend before he potentially was ripped from my life forever.

A loud pop rent the air, followed by the screech of tires and the grinding of metal on metal. It happened in an instant, leaving the aftermath of at least a dozen cars crumpled together near the on-ramp to the highway. Smoke wafted up from several of the cars, the scent of oil and gasoline causing me to gag.

The reaper near the highway turned toward me, somehow managing to radiate expectancy despite me not being able to see his face. *Must be a talent all reapers possess.*

When I remained frozen where I was, he appeared directly in front of me. "What are you waiting for, luna?" he snapped. "Do your job so I can do mine."

"Me?" I lifted my chin indignantly. "This isn't my job. I'm not the luna assigned to record these events. If I was then I would have been doing something about that guy, so he didn't screw up the tagged humans."

The man, the one who contained the bright soul, was nowhere to be seen. Dread twisted my stomach, and I dodged the reaper, sprinting up the ramp. I swallowed hard when I spotted him, bile fighting its way up my throat.

The man, what was left of him, lay on the side of the road, his bloody remains not even resembling a human body.

Dropping to my knees, I retched, spittle dripping from my lips. Why? Why did his soul, no matter the time or place, keep putting other people's lives ahead of his? He kept trying to save lives, but his only accomplishment, in the end, was throwing his own away. The bright soul knew things, things he shouldn't know. But why? And how was he connected to me?

A hand dug into my shoulder, dragging me to my feet. "Do your job, luna," the reaper growled.

"I told you. This isn't my job. I don't even know if I can when I haven't been called here."

"But you were lured here, otherwise you wouldn't be here at all."

That was true. I hadn't been assigned the incident in the traditional way, but I'd ended up there nonetheless. And I was the only luna present at the moment. "I'll try. I'll try to help."

It was all I could do really, even though I wasn't sure how I could actually help. It was instinct that took over, every catastrophe taking on the same exact feel as the last. The automatic process was something I'd never been required to think about. I showed up where I was needed, I waited, and then I recorded the souls and events of a fixed point in time. The sensations, feelings, hell, even my thoughts were identical at every single job. Not until I'd first encountered the bright soul had anything ever been different. Even then it hadn't required any effort to do my job. Completing what I was created to do never had been ... until reality began to slip.

Willing my wings to appear, they flared out behind me. This was the point where I usually rose up into the air, hovering between worlds. It was the beginning of the process of recording the scene. If I didn't reach the space that wasn't here or there, then I wouldn't be invisible, and I couldn't exactly hang around with my wings on display, and eyes glowing red, and expect not to get attention, luna or not.

Shit. Okay. You can do this. You need to do this.

The thing was … I didn't want to do it. Not deep down. The humans who'd been tagged were already dead, so I couldn't help that part, but I didn't want to benefit from their deaths in any way.

"Luna," the reaper said, his tone holding an edge of menace. Yeah, okay, what was he going to do? I might have been afraid in the past, but not anymore. Fear was something creatures who worried about death possessed. I no longer cared about that. Although I did still care about saving reality.

Wiggling my shoulders, I shook out my limbs. "Don't pressure me, it's not helping," I gritted out.

"Just do your job," the reaper repeated.

I bit my tongue, knowing a fight with him would be pointless. *Stupid reapers. Doesn't he know—*

Blinking, I turned to toward the reaper. "Don't you know about reality crumbling? Haven't you seen the RRs … I mean, reality rips? Don't you know that this world is falling apart right now even as I say this to you?"

The reaper's head tilted, and he clicked his tongue. "Oh, that. It will all work out in the end. Those types of things usually do. In the meantime, I'm not going to be the one to complicate things further, nor will I let you since I'm involved."

"I'm not assigned this job! I just happened to be nearby."

He clicked his tongue again. "I thought most immortals were past believing in coincidences."

Staring, my nostrils flared as I counted to ten in my head again. *Two reapers. Two is the number I've had conversations with over my entire existence. And both of them are arrogant, know-it-all, asshats.*

Fueled by anger instead of nerves, I said, "I'll do my best to assist."

"See that you do, luna."

Ignoring him, I flexed my wings, stretching them back and forth slowly. A prickling of energy danced along my skin, foreign and familiar at the same time. Leaping into the air, I threw my head back, willing the souls of the recently dead to come to me, to pass through me on their way to the reaper.

Heat suffused my veins, pumping through my body, creating an intense burning sensation. I was tossed in between worlds, the transition jarring instead of seamless. The dead souls crawled through our connection, their thoughts and emotions not simply perceived in a third-person kind of way, but in first-person. I was experiencing their pain and regret as they moved through me.

It was one thing to know, it was another to feel.

As the numbers of dead added up, the warmth their souls offered set my bones on fire, the pain an excruciating delight. Until I came to *the soul*—the bright soul. Where it had been hotter than any I'd come into contact with before, now it was a supernova and something too extreme for me to handle. Within the soul's essence were things I didn't want to see—things I couldn't handle seeing. I couldn't bear to look, and yet I couldn't force my attention elsewhere. My mind—my thoughts were melting in its presence.

Ice blasted through me, and I fell to the ground, landing in a heap. I lifted my head just in time to witness a RR appear above me, the colors astounding, like nothing I'd ever seen before.

I reached for it, unsure why.

Everything went dark.

Chapter 37

Headlights zoomed down the highway, cars kicking up water in their wake, drenching me to the bone. Standing the side of the road, teeth chattering, I hugged myself, my veins seemingly filled with ice. I was spat out of the RR into a patch of woods a few hundred feet away, and I'd ambled my way to my current location, hoping to figure out why I was there. Instead, I merely found an ordinary road, on an ordinary night.

Is this like the desert and the cave? Was I randomly deposited somewhere with no connection to me whatsoever? Does that mean I should wait for another RR to sweep me away, or should I—

A reaper appeared, his shoulders sagging when he spotted me. "It's me, Eighty-nine."

Alistar. Thank the moon above. "Oh, so you've finally figured out that all reapers look alike in those robes?"

"We don't have time for this anymore." His tone sounded defeated, which caused my stomach to flip with alarm.

Rubbing my hands up and down my arms, I audibly gulped. "Does that mean what I think it means?"

He nodded once. "Yes. This game we've been playing is about to be called. Either you make your final move, or everything will have been for nothing."

"I can't trust you, and I won't again. You know that."

"Then don't."

"What?"

"Don't trust me. But decide. What are you going to do, Eighty-nine? Decide now before the choice is taken from you."

I still had questions—an infinite amount of questions. And doubts. No matter how many times I'd claimed to have made up my mind about what needed to happen, I had no clue. I wanted to save Six, and to save reality, but I needed more information. I needed a better plan than "Yep, I totally got this". Unfortunately, whether I believed Alistar or not, I knew the hourglass had just about run out of sand. I felt it in my gut. The time for contemplation had come to an end. Action was needed.

The thing was … I was about to make the most important choice any luna had probably ever made, and lunas weren't the best at making complicated decisions. We didn't get to practice since choice wasn't something we often experienced in our lives.

Do or die, Eighty-nine, literally.

I have to do it. I have to face Six's death scene again.

Okay, okay. Focus. You need to focus.

I was able to mentally overtake past me in the luna realm, so I figured I had at least a slim chance of doing it with my past self to save Six. I'd been unable to do it before, but with reality as deteriorated as it now was ... things could actually work in my favor.

Perching my fisted hands on my hips, I notched my chin up to glare at Alistar. "I still don't trust you, but I need you."

He had the nerve to chuckle. "Of course." He bowed with a flourish. "Your wish is my command."

Raising my eyebrows, I regarded him with mild annoyance. Desperate times called for desperate measures. With him I could end up where I needed to be, without him I didn't have a prayer. Whether I trusted him or not was a moot point at this stage in the game.

"Take me to Six's death scene. Take me to where he created the paradox."

Grabbing me, Alistar threw me over his shoulder. "It's about time."

I didn't have time to process his words before we were gone.

SCREAMS SATURATED THE AIR, stealing my attention. I swung my head around, taking in chaos, buildings burning all around me. Confusion kept me rooted in place, my breath stuck in my throat.

And then my gaze zeroed in on him ... *Six*.

Lurking in the shadows, where lunas preferred to stay, my friend watched the disaster unfold before him, his expression much like I imagined mine was at every one of my jobs, twisted between anguish and anticipation. I'd never witnessed another luna at work, and seeing Six before me, I realized we were every bit the outsiders I'd come to think of us as.

How does no one ever notice us when we're so out of place? It should be clear to any and all who glance in our direction that we don't belong in the human realm.

His eyes sparked red as he moved a few paces closer to the building directly in front of him. I moved in tandem, shrinking the distance between us.

A hand clamped down onto my shoulder, pinching painfully. "Be careful what you do next, for you are complicating things more than you can possibly fathom as is." The reaper stared down at me, his gaze burning intently from the depths of his hood.

"Why did you bring me here? Why are you helping me?"

He tilted his head, a low chuckle rumbling in his chest. "Am I helping you? Are you so sure of that?"

He was right. I had no idea if he was actually helping me or not. In fact, being that his kind usually never got involved in anything beyond escorting souls to the next realm, I was guessing he had an ulterior motive, one that had absolutely nothing to do with me, or my end game.

I crossed my arms over my chest. "Different question then. Do your end goals align with mine?"

"Quite possibly. Hard to tell at this point."

"Whatever. I don't have time for your cryptic bullshit right now." Pivoting back in the direction of Six, I sprinted toward him.

"Six! Six, I have to talk to you!" I had no idea when or where we were, or how long ago in his timeline Six had done this particular job, but I knew I had to take him with me. I had to save him from whatever had stolen him from me.

He froze, every muscle in his body tensing, and just when I thought he was going to turn around, demanding how and why I was there, he ran across the street, and straight into the burning building.

What the fuck? How the hell didn't he hear me? It might be utter chaos around here, but I was just yelling his name less than two feet from him.

Dashing into the building after Six, the thick smoke ripped at my throat and welled up my eyes. I caught a flash of movement off to my left, and staggered that way, pulling my shirt up to cover my nose and mouth. Inhaling the smoke wouldn't kill one such as me, but it certainly could make things uncomfortable.

"Tina! Tina, where are you?" Six's familiar voice was strung tight with anxiety bordering on panic. "Tina! Please, answer me!"

I froze, fear spiking through my veins, and my heart thrashing painfully against my ribcage. *Why is Six searching for someone in here? It couldn't possibly mean what I think it does.*

A moment later, Six pushed past me with a girl his arms, completely oblivious to my presence. I trailed after them, my stomach twisting into knots. The girl was tagged, the bright orange aura of those marked for death visible even through the dense smoke.

No. He can't. It can't be what it looks like.

"Shh … Tina, I've got you. You're going to be fine." Six planted a tender kiss on her forehead before depositing her gently on the sidewalk.

Tina—the girl from the diner that Six had been so fixated on—squinted up at him, her bright green eyes brimming with tears. "Simon, I was so scared. How did you know? How did you get here?"

"It's going to be just fine, my tiny Tina." Six smiled, but the emotion didn't reach his eyes.

She doubled over as a coughing fit wracked her body, her lungs gasping for enough air to keep her breathing. Shuffling forward, I studied her, realizing that despite Six's efforts she would die without immediate medical attention. Not only had she inhaled too much smoke, but her shirt and hair were saturated in crimson, evidence of her severe injuries.

Tina will die this day as she's supposed to.

Six palmed Tina's face between his hands just as her

eyes slid shut. Her chest rattled out one last shaky breath before remaining still.

Dodging behind a car, I peered at Six over the hood, not wanting to interfere until he was ready for me to comfort him. I smiled to myself. *This is what happened. It has to be. He burned up from grief because I wasn't there in time to help him, but I am now. I can save him ... and change everything. It's all easier than I thought it would turn out to be.*

Six's wings flared out behind him, and his feet rose off the ground as he disappeared from sight. He was recording the calamity and the souls who died because of the disaster, invisible even to me until he was done.

My gaze dropped to Tina's body as I waited. Blood haloed her small form, the macabre scene oddly mesmerizing. When had Six met her, and why hadn't he given me any kind of clue about her? Sure, we both had occasional dalliances with humans, but it was clear that Tina was more to him than sex. There had been a moment when I'd actually thought Six was going to risk reality itself for her.

Six has a lot of explaining to do when we get home. But I couldn't even manage an ounce of anger with the jubilation rising up within me. I'd come so close to losing my best friend forever ... so close.

Six reappeared in front of me, dropping down to his knees beside Tina. A high-pitched keening sound filled the air, his glowing eyes casting shadows across her motionless features. He yanked her body into his chest, cradling her while swaying back and forth. A few minutes later he stilled, and then gently laid Tina back on the ground. His fingers danced along her hairline, smoothing a few wisps away from her forehead. Rocking back on his heels, he sucked in a sharp breath.

Move, move, move, this is the time. I have to talk to him now. Comfort him. Stop him from burning up. Stop hovering behind him like an idiot and save your best friend before it's too late ... again.

With lightning speed, Six exposed his wings and arched them forward. He bared his teeth in a grimace, ripping the delicate forms from his back. Blood spurted from the gaping holes in his flesh, his torn shirt billowing like a cape.

My mouth fell open, a scream bubbling up from my throat.

Six's head whipped around, our gazes clashing, his filled with determination, and mine with horror.

Golden energy blobs streaked out from Six's wings where they lay discarded on the ground. His attention shifted as he deftly plucked a blob out of the air, shoving it into Tina's chest before it raced away.

Tina jolted up, sputtering, her wounds fully healed.

My vision wavered. *What have you done?*

In a burst of flame, Six and his wings were gone.

Just like that, there one instant, gone the next.

"Simon?" Tina's hands passed through the empty space where Six had been. With a whimper, she fainted dead away.

Reeling back, I attempted to wrap my brain around

what I'd just witnessed. Six sacrificed his life to bring back Tina, and in the process, not only broke the rules, but released the other fixed-point souls before a reaper could collect them. I wasn't sure what would happen to those souls, but I did know that Tina was alive when she wasn't supposed to be. That was a threat to reality itself.

My instincts as a luna drove me forward, my intent to put to rights the fixed point in time.

I halted mid-stride, several humans rushing to Tina as if conjured from nowhere. A flurry of questions ensued, all directed at her:

"Are you all right?"

"How did you get out of the building?"

"Was anyone else with you inside?"

"Did anyone else make it out with you?"

A paramedic with an oxygen tank and mask scurried to her side. "Here, ma'am, put this on while I check your vitals."

Pain spiked through my skull, and I dropped to my knees, wailing. I made it, I came back to the point in time I never wanted to experience in any way again, but I'd lost myself. Utterly and completely. I failed. Everything happened just as it had the first time … everything. I hadn't taken over my past self's brain—I hadn't taken control of anything. I'd had better luck the other times of my return to the scene.

Yanking on my hair, I fell onto my back. *What was the point to any of it? Nothing's changed. Or is that what Alistar wanted the entire time? But no, that doesn't make sense either, because if he wanted to save Tina she'd be destroyed along with the rest of reality.* The simple answer was that I failed. I failed to make any kind of difference. I would die, with the rest of reality, as if I'd never existed at all.

"The baby. Is my baby okay?" It was Tina's groggy voice, faint behind the oxygen mask. Even with my heightened hearing, I barely picked up on it.

Alistar loomed over me. "You still have a choice to make, little luna. And now is that time."

Chapter 38

"Baby?" Shock held me captive, my pulse thundering in my ears. "But that's not possible. Lunas and humans can't reproduce. It—" Pushing myself up to my hands and knees, I stared at Tina's prone form, her slender hands covering her belly. There wasn't even a noticeable bump yet. "It has to be someone else's. She lied to Six. Betrayed him."

Alistar lifted me to my feet. "Or did Six sacrifice himself for something no luna has ever had before? A legacy?"

My eyes widened, stretching to their limit. "You knew, didn't you?"

Alistar nodded. "Six gave his life for Tina, but the paradox was actually created when he restored two souls, but only had one to give in return."

"One soul," I mumbled, my gaze returning to Tina.

"But human souls can't be changed out at fixed points in time. It's not how it works."

"True. But a luna can give their soul for a human's. They are the only ones who can."

"The only ones who can," I mumbled, my lips going numb.

I'd set out on my journey to save Six. But I'd refused to admit even to myself ... something that I knew in my heart of hearts, but wanted to deny with every breath in my body ...

Only Six could save himself.

He'd made his choices, and I needed to make mine.

I could still save reality, and not betray Six in the process by forcing my choices on him. As much as I wanted—needed to—the real paradox was me wanting to save my best friend when doing so would betray his autonomy, his choices. To be a true friend to him, I had to let him decide, and I needed to let him go if that's what he ultimately desired.

A flash went off in front of my eyes, images flickering through my mind.

The nearly transparent woman hovered above the vehicle, her face contorted with sorrow, and her flowered sundress drenched in blood. "It's my fault. It's all my fault," she wailed. "I didn't see the truck. I just didn't see it."

A reaper offered her his hand, just his fingertips poking out from the depths of his robe. "It's time for you to move on, Mia. Don't you want to join your loved ones? It's time for you to find peace—to move to the next plane of existence."

"No!" Her voice cracked. "I don't deserve peace of any kind. I don't deserve to be with my loved ones. I killed us. I killed my baby! I should be punished!"

The reaper reached this time, his palm coming to rest carefully on her shoulder. "You did nothing wrong—nothing punishable. Humans are not infallible, they make mistakes. None of this is your fault."

My arms dropped to my sides, limp, as realization dawned. Slowly, wasting time I didn't have, I turned toward Alistar. "You were the reaper who was supposed to collect Mia." It was how I stumbled onto the information in that room to begin with. It was connected to something, not random at all.

But what does it have to so with the here and now?

Flipping his hood back, Alistar's lavender eyes were lipid pools of emotion. "Yes. I was there." He captured my face within his large hands, pulling me closer. "And you were there, too."

Blinking rapidly, I covered his hands with mine, struggling to put some distance between us. "What? No. I wasn't there. I would remember."

I stopped breathing when his lips brushed tenderly against mine—once, twice, three times. "It was always all about you."

Abruptly releasing me, he pulled his hood back over his head, fading from view.

What the ... did he just ... how can I be—

My mind was fried. Alistar's mouth, both from his lips

touching mine and from his parting words, had effectively short-circuited my brain.

"Is my baby okay?" Tina demanded, her voice stronger than before, the steal of it drawing my focus.

Alistar's right. I need to make my choice now. I don't have time to figure out the rest.

Dizzy, I stumbled across the pavement, dropping down beside Tina. The paramedic registered me with alarm. "Ma'am, you need to step back to give me room to work."

Brushing the paramedic's hand aside, my eyes widened as heat suffused my skin, radiating in palpable waves from him. *It's him. The bright soul.* I'd never been able to detect him before, but I was painfully aware of who he was now from merely a touch. *That's new.* We ended up in the same place again, but then again, there were no such things as coincidences. He'd apparently been connected to both Six and me the entire time.

Taking Tina's hand within mine, I leaned in close to whisper in her ear. "When your baby asks about its father, make sure you tell him or her that Simon sacrificed himself for them. Make sure the baby knows Simon loved them enough to give his own life to protect theirs. And tell them his name was really Six. And I am Eighty-nine."

Reaching back, I tore my wings free from my body—the process easier than I ever could have imagined. I'd expected pain, but what I felt was relief.

In that instant, that singular moment in time, before I

burnt up, everything became crystal clear for the first time in my seemingly endless existence.

Reality isn't what humans or lunas think it is. Time isn't linear, or even circular. It's everything at once, a concept that I never would have been able to wrap my brain around before. But being close to death brought clarity, and some of the answers I'd unknowingly sought.

Time is also endless when you're in pain.

I was Mia. Or I had been. I lost my daughter in a car crash, and I blamed myself for not being able to protect her. I'd held that belief within myself so strongly that I decided I deserved to be punished.

Sometimes hell is of your own making, and I made mine well. When I joined the ranks of the lunas, I became a nocturnal creature, a beast who thrived in the dark. And yet I craved the warm embrace of the light ... the flames of humanity. Of what I used to be. The yearning never faded and was only heightened by the knowledge that I could look, but never truly touch. I thought it was what I deserved and would always deserve. A punishment suited to the crime.

I was caught in a loop of grief and I hadn't even known it. First with my daughter from my old life, and then with Six. My guilt, even though not conscious, forced me to stay a luna, my punishment potentially eternal. But I found redemption, and forgiveness within myself, when I was able to save Six's child, when I hadn't been able to save mine as Mia. Death would have never been a way out for me ... only forgiveness ... forgiveness of my own shortcomings and failings could release me from my self-made prison.

I didn't know how or why Six ended up sharing a hell with me and the other lunas, but he found his way out, just like I found mine. I hadn't been able to see past my own personal hell, nor would I ever have been able to, I suspected, without Six's help. I owed him more than he or I could fathom. He was the one who was different—special—not me. He'd simply taken me along on his ride, allowing me to question my lot in the luna life. I would never be able to save him, but in the end, he saved me in his own way.

Or perhaps it was just all things evolve ... eventually. And the seeming end of my story could actually be the beginning, because everything that dies is reborn in some manner. I'd been reborn once into my own personal hell, and now ... well, maybe a luna can become more, if it's willing to shed not only its wings, but its belief of what it truly is—to forgive itself for what it may have done in the past, and to let everything go. Maybe then it can rise from the burnt ashes like a phoenix, and claim what it's truly meant to be, whatever that is.

I was finally freed as the fires consumed me.

Chapter 39

It is said that the definition of insanity is doing the same thing over and over and expecting different results.

And that's exactly what Alistar had done.

Only now that things had finally come to a conclusion he was satisfied with, he couldn't help but wonder if what he'd done was something else entirely. After all, he had managed to wring a different result from the ludicrous situation in the end. Therefore, by definition alone, his actions hadn't been insanity.

A smug smile turned the corners of his mouth upward.

He went back in time, more than he could count, determined to break Mia's soul out of its hell. He'd broken rules, and dabbled in things he knew were forbidden, but he couldn't bring himself to regret any of it.

Brushing the pad of his index finger over his bottom lip, he tasted the lingering essence of his luna. *Yes, my luna.*

The most surprising part of any of the events was that Alistar had grown to care for her, despite what she'd become. He wasn't sure if it was love, an emotion he'd never felt before romantically, but he knew he would figure out a way to find her again, wherever she ended up.

A second reaper appeared, hovering off to the left of Alistar. "You did more than guide her," he said by way of greeting.

Alistar merely grunted, his gaze remaining fixated on the spot where his luna had last stood before burning up.

"But don't worry, I won't say a word." The reaper patted Alistar on the arm with a familiarity that wasn't warranted. "I'm one of the newer reapers. You know, one of the ones who have a tendency to go rogue."

Alistar didn't care what the new reaper thought, or even what he would do. What was done was done, and he would take his punishment if any sought to give it to him.

"I saw the kiss," the reaper prodded. "And with a luna of all creatures."

"She was different. Not like the rest."

The reaper clicked his tongue. "Maybe to you. But to everyone else, she was just another luna."

His anger simmering, Alistar didn't respond. Eighty-nine, Mia, whatever name she went by, her soul burned brighter to him than any. One might remember a beautiful face for a while, but a beautiful soul was unforgettable. And to him, her soul was the most beautiful he'd ever seen. She would be a part of him for the length of his immortal existence.

That's what his luna hadn't understood. The soul who tormented her at jobs had merely appeared different to her, it didn't burn bright for any other luna who catalogued it. And it was because on some level she recognized the soul of the truck driver from her life as Mia. The truck driver, carrying guilt of his own, was reborn life after life with a driving need to find and help her … but not just her. He wanted to save lives, as a kind of penance for what he perceived as his crimes. Ultimately, he sought atonement.

Eighty-nine had been right, there were no coincidences. And it wouldn't be one when he found her again.

"One more question, though, since I'm new to this whole thing. How did she end up a luna to begin with? Lunas have existed since the beginning of time, and she was one of the original one-hundred, and yet—"

"She merely believed herself to be one of the original. She found her way into the spot of Eighty-nine and her first job was near the beginning. Time passes differently for them than humans, and she lived as a luna longer than any of her human lives before. Reality is perception for most beings, and hers was no different. What she believed became her truth in all ways." He puffed out a breath, patience running thin. "None of it will make sense to one as young as you say you are. Knowledge and the concept of true reality will be gained … with experience. Not from a five-minute conversation, even with one as ancient as I am."

“I guess I need to do my job here then,” the second reaper stated, his tone bored.

“I will leave you with one invaluable piece of wisdom.” Alistar rose up in the air, hovering above the other reaper. “You’ll meet a lot of humans in your line of work. Their souls at least. Humans—” He cleared his throat, searching for the right words. “Humans are horrible creatures overall. Even the ones who are considered good by celestial standards have done morally questionable things. Love … love is the one thing they get right. True love, even as rare as it is, is enough to justify their existence.”

“Maybe love is the only thing any of us get right in the end,” the reaper replied, hood tilted to the side.

Alistar mirrored him, assessing him for a moment before grunting. He didn’t care about what the other reaper had to say, not really. He was already eager to begin tracking down the extraordinary soul which he couldn’t seem to be separated from for long. He needed to make sure she hadn’t entangled herself in some sort of new trouble. She seemed to have a knack for that. She would surely need him … even if she didn’t know it. Just like before.

Alistar willed himself away, effectively ending the conversation.

The young reaper chuckled at the ancient reaper’s hasty exit. He had one guess where he was off to—or who he was off to find.

Gliding forward, his gaze landed on Tina, and the baby he knew was within, then the spot where Eighty-nine had burnt into nothing. The loss of her presence was felt deeply within him.

But no matter, he would watch over all of them—Tina, the baby, and of course Eighty-nine. He would find her again … and soon.

After all, *Six will always watch her six.*

Acknowledgments

As an overthinker, acknowledgments are quite an arduous task for me. I wonder if I'm being lackluster or too intense with the thanks. Or did I forget someone? Possibly I gave too much credit to someone and therefore slighted someone else who actually did a ton. A part of me doesn't want to include these in my books at all because the people I appreciate should know it already … or do they??? No matter how I look at it these damn acknowledgments make me friggin' sweat.

But here there are anyways since if I don't include them then people will probably think I'm ungrateful and weird. I mean, I am weird, but I don't want people to think that. I am grateful though, so I'll just go-ahead and make this uncomfortable for everyone. Heh.

Okay, here I go. Right now. Actual acknowledgments to follow. Hopefully, they represent an appropriate level of gratitude to all the people in my life that deserve it.

(And yep … I have totally copy & pasted what comes next from my previous book acknowledgments, which I originally took from *Virtual Reality Bites* acknowledgments. I thought maybe after *Replayed* that I'd come up with something better. Or at least something new. Obviously not. So this is now copy & paste edition #4. Or maybe #5?. I've officially lost count. Mmm hmm … I'm thinking you should probably get used to it.)

My amazing Hubby! Words can't begin to explain how supportive and truly amazing he is. Hmmm … I think I already used the word amazing. But unlike in books, when honestly applied to someone, the word amazing means something, well, amazing. And my hubby is all of the things that word implies. Romance heroes are nothing compared to him.

Lindsay Tiry … what would I do without you? I hope I never have to find out. From cover design to interior graphics to logos, you do it all. Your talent is awe-inspiring, and I hope one day everyone else will be able to appreciate how you shine.

Melissa Ringsted … my illustrious editor. Without you, this book probably would have gone straight into the trash. Thank you for giving me the confidence to publish when I convinced myself that I was the worst writer in the history of writers, and for fixing all the words.

Ren, Kristin, Shona, Ruty … my O.G. chicas … I wouldn't be here without you. I'm beyond lucky to know all of you.

And last, but certainly not least, thank you to everyone who has taken the time to read this book. Hopefully, you enjoyed it, but even if you didn't, I still appreciate the fact that with so many options out there today, you even gave my book a fleeting chance.

About the Author

Ava Wixx escaped into books at a young age and decided to stay there. It was only a matter of time before she was driven to create her own fantasy worlds from fear of running out of places to explore.

Reader, writer, dreamer ... Ava only toils in reality when absolutely necessary. She lives in North Carolina with her husband, and spoiled mini-poodle.

www.ingramcontent.com/pod-product-compliance
Lightning Source LLC
LaVergne TN
LVHW041104080826
845145LV00007B/1687

* 9 7 8 1 9 5 5 9 5 0 1 5 2 *